The Miller's Son

By

Richard How

Copyright©2016 Richard How
All Rights Reserved
First published 2016
ISBN-13:978-1533322265
ISBN-10:1533322260

Front cover picture by Norman How

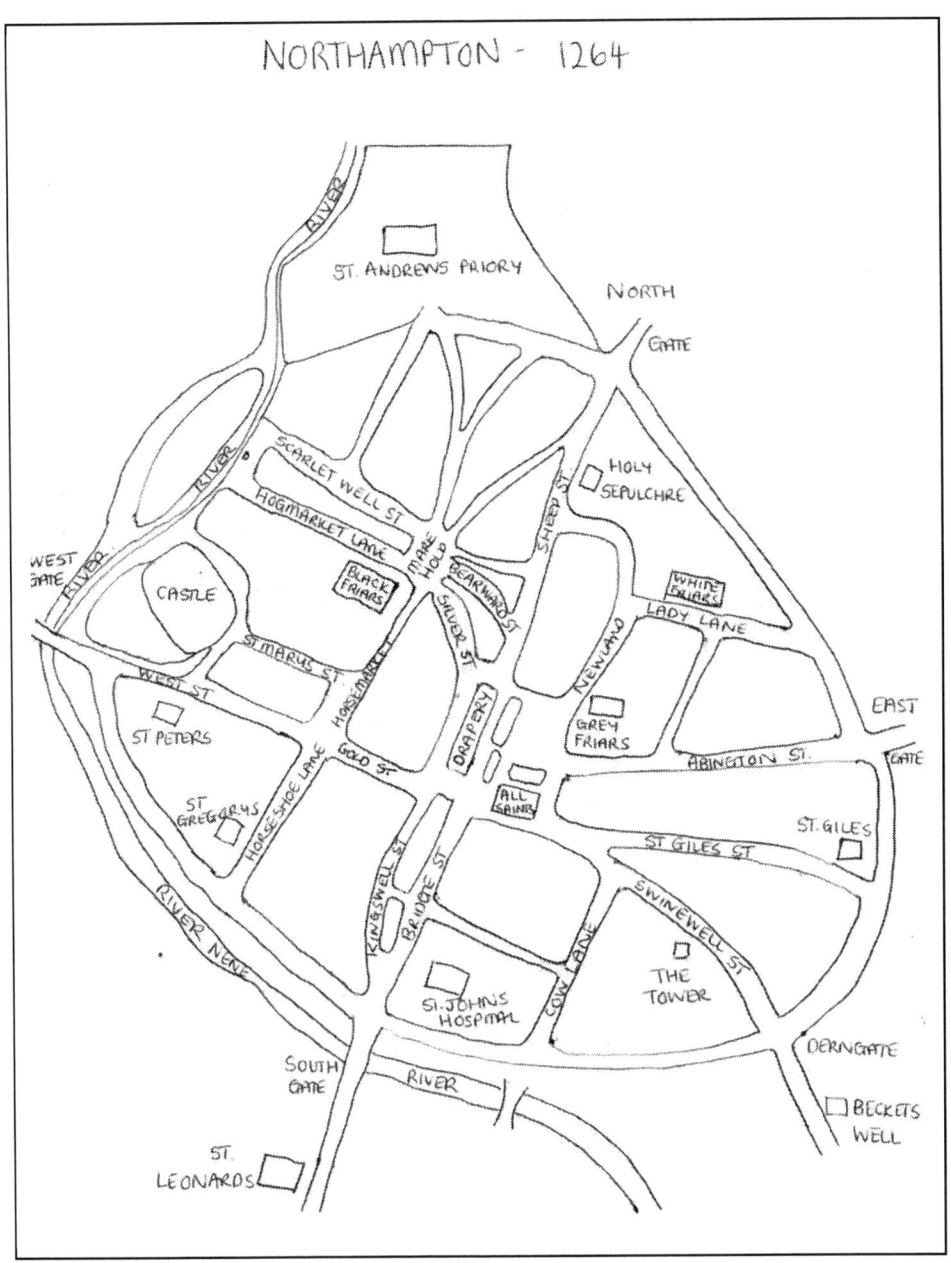

Chapter 1

Summer 1263

Thomas looked towards the altar. Past images of his mother wrapped in her shroud, lying there in the plain coffin, just a short time ago, flooded his thoughts. Feeling dizzy, he closed his eyes, oblivious to the Latin drone of the priest. Tears dripped from his chin. He felt his brother's hand grip his arm as he swayed; turning, he faced him. The cold proud face that looked at him seemed somehow distant. His eyes appeared already shut off to the scene that the two of them beheld.

Apart from the priest by the altar, the only other occupant of the church was an elderly man who knelt in front of them amongst the dirty straw-covered earth, between two trestles covered with black cloth. Thomas studied that stooped back, feeling the weight of years and trauma that now sat heavily upon it. He knew that back so well, even the creases and patches in the old dun-coloured tunic, each one a moment in time in the life before him.

The priest finished the mass and picked up a spade piled with earth. He moved toward the kneeling man, his face red. Thomas held his breath. Quickly the priest threw the soil across the old man's white and wizened bare feet, which protruded from his hose onto the brown earth. He rushed back to the safety of the altar; breathing in deeply, he turned to face his small audience.

Thomas heard the door creak. He looked over his shoulder, seeing a face, unrecognisable behind the piece of cloth held tightly across its mouth and nose. He knew it to be the face of the reeve, come to make sure the deed was carried out, so that he could report back to his lord.

Thomas grunted and spat over his shoulder towards the door. He felt the tug of his brother's hand. Turning back, he saw the priest standing before the altar, holding out a cross. Thomas noticed how the cross shook; he saw beads of sweat gathering on his forehead. In a dry croaking voice the priest began to speak, his words almost inaudible.

"Be thou dead to the world, but alive unto God." He took a few faltering steps forward and stood before the old man. His voice dropped to a quiet whisper. Thomas strained to hear; "… to enter churches, or go into a market, or a mill, or a bake house, or unto any assemblies of people. Also I forbid you ever to wash your hands or even your belongings in spring or stream of water of any kind; and if you are thirsty you must drink water from your cup or from some other vessel. Also I forbid you ever henceforth to go out without your leper's dress that you may be recognised by others; and you must not go outside your house unshod. Also I forbid you, wherever you may be, to touch anything which you wish to buy."

The priest took a breath and wiped the sweat from his brow; his hands shook. He wiped some spittle away from the corner of his mouth and then allowed himself a quick look at the face of the man before him. The eyes were sunken in and seemed empty, as though no human thought process controlled them. They frightened the priest; he quickly turned away; keen now to get the service over.

"You must swear never to eat or drink with clean persons nor even talk to them unless standing to the windward side; never to touch a child;" a sigh broke from the old mans cracked lips. "Always to stand clear of strangers when begging, and give warning of your approach with the bell of wooden clappers before you."

The priest waited, the church seemed inexplicably silent. It was too much for the priest. "You must swear Walter, please!" The voice was pleading. The old man looked up, holding the priest's gaze.

"I am dead, you have told me so. How can I answer Geoffrey; tell me that?" A slight sad smile broke from the corners of his thin lips. The priest's face creased in desperation. "Have no fear; I will do this thing that you ask, though I am desolate with the saying of it."

"Then swear, please." A door just off the chancel creaked open and the shadowy figure of another priest stepped out. Geoffrey's head turned slightly. He was becoming desperate.

"I swear."

Thomas stood up. "No!" he gasped. His brother jumped up quickly as the shadowy figure stepped forward. His slim face and stern green piercing eyes were lit by hazy sunlight breaking, falteringly through the window. Thomas had begun to move forward but stopped, gripped by his gaze. Another figure stepped out from the darkened recess appearing as if from the body of the green-eyed priest. He held a staff and light flashed from the sword at his side. The priest of the shadows said in a steady, icy voice.

"It is time to go Walter. My man will escort you."

Walter pulled himself up with the aid of a staff that had been lying in the straw beside him. Soil fell from his thin legs. He turned to face the two brothers. This time no gaze could hold Thomas; he ran forward and threw himself upon the old man before anyone else could move.

"Father!" he sobbed, burying his face into Walters shoulder, "Oh father!" He felt hands grab him from behind and begin to pull him away. "No!" he shouted with venom.

Thomas felt he was drowning, sinking deeper and deeper. He saw himself looking up through a tunnel of water, as he had done when, as a child, he had fallen into the millpond. He remembered seeing his father's face distorted through the water, his hand growing larger as he reached down and pulled him out. He once again saw that concerned face, a younger, smoother healthier version, studying him as he hung between his father's arms. It broke into a smile when he began to cry.

Now, as then, the tears streamed down his face as his father released his grip and turned towards the church door.

"Remember me."

"I'll come with you," Thomas sobbed towards the receding back. The grip on his arms tightened.

"No, this journey he makes alone. He is dead to us now," said the shadowy priest.

"How can you say that?" Thomas shouted, no longer afraid, of this outsider who had arrived and ordered his father away. "You never knew him; you come here and order him away and destroy our lives. Who gives you the right?"

"God," replied the priest, his calm expression turning to anger.

"God! God would not do this."

"Be careful boy!"

"Come Thomas," stuttered Geoffrey, "I will walk back with you and Nicholas." He gestured to Thomas's brother who had been standing silently watching the scene. Geoffrey turned to the other priest. "He is angry and suffering the loss. He does not know what he is saying."

"I will allow it to pass this time." The priest looked disdainfully at Thomas and Geoffrey and walked back through the dark recess in the nave of the church.

As the priest left, Nicholas stepped forward and took his brother's arm. Geoffrey grabbed his other hand and they guided him out through the open door of the church. Their father turned at the end of the lane, the wooden palisade walls of the manor behind him, and looked back at them as they emerged into the sunlight. He lifted his hand as if to wave. The priest's man behind him mouthed something at him and he lowered his hand and turned away, his shoulders slumping forward as he disappeared from view behind the dwelling on the bend of the road. Thomas stood and watched. Walter appeared again, for the last time, further up the Northampton road as it led upwards across the heath.

Thomas suddenly noticed the mass of villagers standing well back amongst the graves in the churchyard, silent and huddled together as if gaining support from their compatriots. Tightly did the mothers grip their children's hands. All of them had been drawn from their work and houses to see the spectacle that touched the core of their small community. They looked down as Thomas's gaze passed across each one of them, ashamed to be seen as spectators and relieved that it was not them. Thomas mumbled each of their names in turn, but they did not look up. Instead they turned and hurried away to their homes.

"Come on," said Geoffrey, feeling better now that he was out in the open and away from the other priest. The deed was done; he sighed deeply. Nicholas had still not spoken. He let go of Thomas's arm and with only the briefest of glances at the other two he turned and walked off in the opposite direction out to the hamlet where they lived on the edge of the village.

Thomas did not follow him but just stood vacantly in the middle of the dirt road, dry and dusty from the summer sun.

"Are you not ready to go back then?" Geoffrey wiped his sleeve across his sweating brow. Thomas did not answer him. "Let's go to Margery's. She has some good ale at the moment. Come on, it'll help." Geoffrey turned and began to walk up the slight incline to the centre of the village, which consisted of a patch of rough grass further up the hill, surrounded by a huddle of cottages. The dirt road that they trudged up was lined with the rest of the cottages that made up their small village of Buckbie. The sounds of pigs grunting and chickens pecking and clucking came from the gardens that surrounded each building. Voices drifted from their interiors, through the thin wattle and daub walls.

"Well at least it gives them all something to gossip about," Thomas mumbled, in response to the voices that seemed to follow them as they headed up onto the green. It was in fact an area of trampled earth, upon which a few snorting pigs and thin dogs roamed and villagers constantly crisscrossed whilst going about their daily business.

"Aye, for some time to come I should imagine," replied Geoffrey, puffing.

They walked by a group of village boys so intent on their wrestling match that they did not notice their passing. Ahead of them the road led out of the village past the manor, surrounded by its ditch and hazel fence. Thomas spat on the ground as he eyed the reeve, who was watching them from the gateway, and then followed Geoffrey into the large cottage on the corner.

Thomas waited at the entrance for his eyes to adjust to the darker interior. A dog sniffed at his leg; he kicked it away; it gave an anguished yelp.

"That's right; just take your anger out on the poor beast then." He looked at the woman sitting on a small wooden stool by the fire in the centre of the room.

"Can I have some ale, woman?" ventured Geoffrey.

"The name's Margery, priest. I suppose you can if your money's good. Got ya pitcher?" she asked.

"No, I hoped we might borrow one. We will return it directly." She eyed him suspiciously.

"I'm sure you would. Can't go upsetting the villagers now can we?" she looked at Thomas. "Alright, just this once, on account of the circumstances, but don't make a habit of it." She stood up, picked up a grimy pottery jug and began to fill it from a large barrel in the corner. Thomas studied Margery's dirty face as she concentrated on her task. Wiry grey hair projected from the sides of her rag of a wimple. Her nose and cheeks were of manly proportions and hair sprouted from her chin and upper lip, but her eyes were young and bright. When she turned and looked at him, he felt as though they reached in and read his inner thoughts. He looked away, unable to hold her gaze and she gave a squawking laugh.

"Priest paying is he?" she said to Thomas. "Must be feeling guilty;" She turned to Geoffrey as he handed over the money. "Why so guilty, priest? Is it 'cause you sent poor Walter away or because you intend to take the lads' second best?"

Thomas gave him a sharp questioning look. Geoffrey could not hold his gaze and looked at the ground.

"Here's your pitcher. It's good ale so get some down yer, it'll help take the pain away." Margery handed Thomas the jug. He walked out onto the green, slumped himself up against the rough wattle and daub wall of the cottage, and drank deeply. He half listened to the voices inside as they rose in anger. A pig came grunting up to him. He pushed it away with his foot and continued to drink. Finally Geoffrey appeared before him.

"I would not take your second best animal, Thomas; you know that."

"You have it, Geoffrey. Father would have wanted it that way. Besides," Thomas gave a barking laugh, "the beast isn't mine. The farm is now in the hands of my noble brother Nicholas!" He poured some ale for Geoffrey and then filled his own cup. "Here, let's drink to my father." The priest sat down heavily on a pile of firewood. After they had both drunk deeply, he asked,

"What are you going to do now then, Thomas?"

"I don't know. I hadn't thought that far ahead. I'll keep on as husbandman I suppose. Somebody'll have to do it; Might even work the mill. Nicholas'll be up at the manor most of the time, I'm sure!"

"Will he want that? You still being around, I mean?"

"I don't know. We don't get on too well, do we?"

"You're very different."

"You're right there!" They sat for a moment contemplating and drinking their ale. "I'll stay till the fair and make a decision then. I just need time to think. Everything is changing so quickly." He put his cup down and held his head in his hands. "What's it like at St Leonard's, Geoffrey? Will they treat my father well?" Thomas turned and fixed Geoffrey with his wide grey eyes. Geoffrey studied the proud face surrounded by thick black hair, which reminded him of Thomas's mother. It was the face of a man born free, not wealthy but with rights above most in the village. Now, the tanned forehead bore furrowed lines of worry. Thomas's world was changing, as was his position in the village. His face had already begun to show the painful signs of that change.

Hearing footsteps, they turned to see the reeve accompanying the other priest across to the manor entrance. He held up the edges of his robe, keeping it from the dirt and dust.

"I see he dresses a mite better than your average village priest. Tell me about him, Geoffrey. I want to know more about the man who has sent my father away."

"If the rumours are right, he's one of De Montfort's lackeys."

"He didn't come all this way just to declare my father a leper, of that I'm sure!"

"No, that, from what I can gather, he did as a favour. I believe he has brought messages for Sir John from De Montfort, who is keen to keep the barons and knights on his side."

"As a favour!" Thomas jumped up. "What do you mean?"

"It is all I heard him say." Geoffrey looked away, not wanting to confront Thomas's growing anger, or commit himself further.

"Damn them! What are they plotting? Why was it so important to get my father out of the way?" He tipped his head back and finished the rest of his ale. "Why didn't you stop them Geoffrey?"

"Curses will not help you Thomas," said the priest trying to divert him.

"Come on Geoffrey. You owe me an explanation."

"The signs were all there, you know that; your father's illness, his losing his fingers." Geoffrey shrugged "How could I stop them? They have power. I'm just a lowly village priest. If I stand in their way, I too will be thrown out of the village." He drank from his cup then clambered to his feet and patted the silent Thomas on the arm. "Whatever they are up to, I'm sure they must be planning something, anyway whatever it is, you'll find out soon enough. Here, drink some more. Mourn today, fret tomorrow." Thomas angrily pushed his arm away.

"I cannot mourn!" he shouted, throwing the cup to the ground, His emotions finally taking control. "He's not dead Geoffrey!" Thomas turned and walked away, tears rolling down his cheeks. The wrestling boys jumped out of his way as he crossed the green and headed out of the village.

Margery emerged from her cottage and tutted at Geoffrey who sighed. "You'll have to pay for that too, priest," she said, picking up the shards of broken pottery.

"Yes, of course. Here." He threw a clipped farthing on the ground in front of her and walked off towards the church, pitcher in hand. He was troubled. What was happening, he mused, could not be good for the village or the church. Change was never good he decided, and change must surely be coming. He needed to drink, and drink deeply, to escape his agitated thoughts. He hurried on to the church.

Thomas continued along the dusty lane out of the village. He noticed that the villagers had soon returned to work after the service. Haymaking was in full swing and there was little time to rest during midsummer when the weather was good. He found it difficult to think about work, keeping his head down as he passed the wain, half loaded with hay. The workers paused as he passed but he did not catch their gaze, intent only in getting away from them and the village. Soon he was running up the hill and over the rise, sweat pouring down his face. He did not stop until the village had disappeared behind the hill.

Puffing hard, he sat down and breathed deeply. He pulled off his woollen tunic and used it to wipe the sweat and tears of anger from his face. He thought of the priest's menacing man-at-arms leading his father slowly towards Northampton and St Leonard's; he prayed he would come to no harm. They said there was no cure, but he felt sure there must be. He would find out, he thought; the scholars at the University at Northampton would surely know. He wiped his face again, his tongue now feeling leathery with thirst.

Thomas's thoughts moved on to his brother Nicholas. He was always in Sir John's company. What was he up to? He knew his brother disliked him and was jealous of the love father had given him. It would be difficult to work for Nicholas. Father had told him not to do anything rash. He had wanted him to make sure the harvest was gathered and that the mill was running well, smoothly and fairly when he was gone. "The villagers cannot do without a mill and a fair miller, son." he had said. It had been the previous night, their last night together. Father had sat outside their cottage and talked with him. With the memory his eyes once again welled up with tears.

Thomas reached into his tunic and pulled out the small bronze medallion that his father had given him. He pulled the leather thong over his neck and held it in his hands, studying the image of Thomas the martyr, his namesake.

"I picked it up on my pilgrimage to Canterbury. A great man he was. Your great-grandfather saw him when he was in Northampton for his trial. He walked there to see him. A proud man tall and strong full of God, he said. Your grandfather was called Thomas after him; wanted me to name my son after him too." His father had said, smiling. "Keep it, for it was meant for you I'm sure. May he protect you;" He hung the medallion over Thomas's neck.

Chapter 2

As the weeks passed, Thomas had little time to worry about his father, though he missed his presence keenly. The weather was warm and the hay and harvest good. He and the other villagers worked from dawn till dusk harvesting and haymaking.

News arrived in the village that Simon De Montfort, the Earl of Leicester, was now calling himself the Steward of England and that the rebel Barons had achieved their goal of renewing the Oaths to the Provisions of Oxford, a governmental reform, which restricted the powers of the king. But as the summer wore on the travelling traders began to report unrest at the parliamentary council; that the barons' cause was becoming soured by violence, injustice and greed amongst its members.

Thomas continued to live at the mill with his brother, though they saw each other very little. At the occasional meal they would sit and eat in silence. He rarely saw Nicholas in the fields or at the mill. He seemed content, for the present to let Thomas keep everything going and yet Thomas was aware that his every move was being watched. Nicholas was quick to comment if there was an opportunity to attack Thomas's ability or actions. He knew that soon they would argue past the point of no return and that he would have to leave. He feared that moment.

As the September fair of St Gregory's approached Nicholas put up the mill prices.

"You can't do that!" Thomas replied sharply on hearing the news. Nicholas had entered the mill dressed in a new tunic and climbed the ladder to the first floor, where Thomas was filling the hopper with grain. The large millstones below ground noisily beside them, hungry for the corn. In the background the overshot wheel turned slowly with the sound of a waterfall. Its slow progress turned the great kingpin connected to the millstones. The floor shook with the power, lost corn jumping up and down. Dust filled the air.

"The villagers can't afford that!" He threw down the sack and advanced towards his brother.

"Rubbish of course they can!" said Nicholas backing away.

"They'll starve." Thomas felt his anger rising. He was now shouting at his brother.

"They'll just get leaner. They waste too much at Margery's anyway. Sir John says…"

"Oh Sir John, I might have known he'd be involved." Nicholas seeing the menace in Thomas's eyes quickly slid down the ladder. Thomas leaned over and kicked flour dust down upon his brother angrily. "What do you get out of being his lackey? That's what I want to know!" he shouted down at the upturned face. Nicholas gave a sly smile and tried to brush the dust from his shoulders. He felt safe now.

"Wouldn't you just," he said and with a barking laugh, turned abruptly away. "Lackey indeed," he mumbled.

"Get out of the way!" He shouted at Alfred the mill worker bringing in sacks of corn, and pushed past him, knocking the man to the ground; then he was gone.

Thomas watched him ride off on his new horse up towards the manor. Angrily he wondered at the beast. A gift from Sir John, Nicholas had said. No wonder he needed more money.

As the days of August clicked by Thomas saw less and less of his brother, who hardly left the manor and Sir John's side. He worked steadily harvesting the family's land, looking after the cow, calf and the sheep plus milling the villager's corn. In fact he saw little of anyone unless they visited the mill. He put all his effort into his work, thinking of little else and hiding from the changes that the year had so far brought, knowing that they were not over.

Alfred the illegitimate son of one of the manor servants helped him. He was a simple hard working young man grateful for the job and happy not to be beaten, which had been his sorry burden in the manor. He kept Thomas company, but never questioned him and happily accepted his every decision. He hated Nicholas and just about every inhabitant of the manor.

As Thomas and Alfred worked early one morning shifting sacks of grain from the yard into the mill, he heard the sound of an approaching horse. He stopped and watched the horse turn into the yard. He recognised the rider as Lucy, Sir John's ward. He had often played with her and Sir John's own daughter before she had been sent off to another household. Alfred grunted unhappily at her approach.

"It's alright Alfred, you carry on."

The horse came to a halt in front of him. Lucy reached up and quickly pulled away her veil revealing a face displaying an expression full of distress.

"Hello Lucy, I've seen little of you recently. What is wrong? I can see you have not come on a social call." He finished somewhat sarcastically, as she had not been to the mill for many years. He helped her from the horse and led her through the low door of the family house, which was one large room. The floor was littered with straw, a dying fire in the hearth at its centre. She sighed deeply and collapsed onto the bench by a table at one end of the room. "Ever the drama queen," thought Thomas, remembering their childhood games.

"Would you like a drink? You look thirsty and flushed." He studied her round, red face and noted that the once high cheekbones and a strong jaw line had disappeared under layers of good living and a lack of exercise. Beads of sweat hung on her forehead. Her pupils, wide in the dark room, flicked constantly about, never still.

"Yes," she croaked in reply patting her chest. Thomas grabbed some cups from a shelf and poured out some ale from a jug on the table. She drank thirstily and he followed suit, having worked hard during the early hours. Thomas watched a drop of sweat run down from her wimple between wisps of mouse brown hair. Fascinated he followed its path as it slid sedately between her eyebrows and slowly down the bridge of her nose. Becoming suddenly aware of this distraction she brushed it away. Thomas smiled.

"Sorry Lucy, what were you saying? What's brought you to this neck of the woods? You haven't been out here since we were children."

"It's Sir John." She stopped, wanting to prolong the suspense.

"Well, come on then. What's the old fox up to now? I'll wager my brother is involved." She looked up in surprise.

"How did you know?"

"Just a guess," he smiled. "Well go on then, fill me in."

"I am to be married, so Sir John told me last night. My father has agreed to the match."

"Is this good news or bad news?" said Thomas looking bemused. He poured out some more ale.

"I don't know. I can't see how it can be good though." She paused, waiting for him to respond, enjoying her moment of drama.

"Why?"

"Well for it to be good the match has to be advantageous."

"And this isn't?" She shook her head. "I'm surprised your father agreed then. Who is it? Do I know the man?"

"You certainly do!" She jumped up and paced across the room. Looking out of the door she studied the yard remembering the hours of fun they had had as children. A heron flapped heavily up from the millpond and flew slowly across the yard and cottage. She turned facing Thomas who sat on the bench smiling at her, waiting; his grey eyes twinkling in the beam of light that came in from the door. It agitated her, that expression. It always had, she remembered.

"It's your brother!" she shouted at him. Then turned and stalked out but not before seeing him jump up in astonishment and spill his ale down his leg. She heard him swear and smiled to herself. He ran out and grabbed her, spinning her round to face him.

"My brother!" he stuttered, repeating her. "You mean Nicholas!"

"Why have you got any more brothers?" she replied, enjoying his confusion and temporarily forgetting her own. "Of course it's Nicholas."

"Why? It doesn't make sense. Sir John told you this, did he?" she nodded. "You're right, the match doesn't seem advantageous." He turned away and walked to the water's edge. She followed just behind. They stood watching the water bubble out from the wheel, which turned slowly. Some ducks dabbled at the water in front of him. On the far side a moorhen snapped at the many summer flies. Swallows flashed past picking them off on the wing. "It doesn't make sense," he mumbled. She moved closer. "Your father wouldn't agree unless there was some benefit. So what's the pay off?" He looked at her; she just shrugged. "He didn't say anything else?"

"Only that I would understand later; after he has spoken at the opening of the St. Gregory fair. He told me not to worry. He said I would see the benefits and be very happy with the match after that!"

"I don't know; I can't make head nor tail of it. I think I'll go up Margery's tonight. See if I can find anything out." He watched a fish swimming in the shallows effortlessly holding its position in the swirling current with slight movements of its tail fin. "I could do with a drop of decent ale anyhow. Our brew just doesn't seem to come out so good."

He began to wander along the bank of the stream, picking up and throwing the occasional stone into the water. Lucy followed. He turned suddenly causing her to pull up short just inches from him.

"How do you feel about this Lucy? Not the official line about how advantageous it is to you but how do you feel inside?" She backed away from the intensity of his gaze, reddening, feeling his searching reach inside to the places she kept hidden, often even from herself. She took a deep breath, for a moment wishing it were Thomas and not his brother that she was marrying. He was the more handsome, she sighed, but he did not exude the strength and power that his brother seemed to. He was earthier. She saw an image of Nicholas dressed in his finest tunic and hose standing in her guardian's hall. She remembered the powerful affect he had on the servants and the way Sir John looked to him.

"If he is my husband I will make it work."

He realised she had thought little of the future.

"But can you love him?"

"I don't have to love him!" she said looking sharply at him. "Respect is more important."

"Ah I see you've been well indoctrinated in the courtly Norman ways of Sir John and his circle. I remember it was different when we were children living out our fantasies for the future down on this very bank. You and Eleanor were always full of romance and love."

"More Eleanor than I, I think."

He smiled sadly at her. She would suit his brother well he thought as they both believed that ambition and advantage were the reason for marriage. If their union had that then she would be happy, although where the advantage in marrying his brother was he did not know. He looked at her red round face and caught a glint of the toughness within. She would give his brother a run for his money anyway, he thought.

"Come on." He took her by the arm and led her back toward the mill. "By the way, have you seen or heard anything from Eleanor? I wonder what she would think to all this."

"I have written to her but since Sir John sent her off to be a ward with the Menhill's I have seen little and heard little, though I'm sure we'll see her at the wedding." She looked quizzically at him and smiled at his flushed face. "Your brother may be good enough for me, Sir John's ward, but I don't think he will ever perceive you good enough for his only daughter!"

He turned away from her as she laughed. He had always known it to be a hopeless fantasy but he could not rid her from his thoughts.

"Let's get back, I have a lot to do if I'm to get up there tonight." He nodded towards the village, hiding his confusion by marching off towards the mill and Lucy's tethered horse, which blew through its nostrils at the sight of their approach. He helped her up on her horse and bade her farewell, saying he would visit if he found any news.

"Mind, it's not long to the third and the fair, by which time we'll all know anyhow," he said as she rode off. He turned back to his work but found it hard to continue with these new thoughts in his head. He gave Alfred some instructions as to what to do in the afternoon and headed up into the village to the church. He needed to pray and think.

Saint Gregory's was a rectangular stone building on the corner of a dirt street. The road curved up from the mill along the southern edge of the stream and then, after slowly climbing the rise up to the church, turned sharply up the hill and went up to the manor. It then wound around it to the east, where it joined with the roads to Northampton and Daventry in the market square. The Northampton road went on up to the hamlet of Coten, where a huddle of hovels clung to the edge of the heath.

The village of Buckbie was a large one. Wattle and daub cottages were clustered around the market square, the manor and down the street to the church. The manor sat on the remains of an old castle and was surrounded by the embankments of the old inner and outer bailey walls, which were now topped with a wooden palisade.

The church was relatively new, built by Sir John's father, through an increase in tax. Thomas walked through the gate in the hurdle fence. The woven hazel protected the small graveyard and kept the priest's livestock in, where they grazed amongst the burial mounds. Walking round to the side of the church he entered the small side door, not wanting to be seen on the street at the church's main entrance, where invariably villagers gathered in the porch to gossip and do business.

He crossed himself as he entered, noting that the church interior was empty and quiet apart from one of the priest's hens, which pecked contentedly at the earth floor. Thomas smiled to himself, remembering the priest's efforts to get Sir John to aid in the laying of a stone floor. A job not completed due to the early demise of John's father.

He moved to the altar and knelt down. Since the loss of his father Thomas had kept away from the church, attending only on Sundays. Previously he had been an almost daily visitor. He realised he had missed the cool interior where occasional quiet calm could be found. He turned his mind to God and quietly recited the Lord's Prayer.

Life had been so simple back then, helping his father at the mill and in the fields, his mother in the house, the familiar routines. Even the hard times, when the harvest had been poor, seemed somehow preferable to his present emptiness. He now felt lost and alone. He felt that nothing now was as it seemed.

"God!" he shouted half in anger, half in yearning, holding his arms towards the altar. Tears for his father, mother and his own loneliness trickled down his cheeks. He lay down on the earth floor, prostrate.

Lost in prayer he did not hear the creek of the door as it opened, allowing in the heavy, robed shape of the priest. He crept forward and knelt down behind the figure of Thomas, silent but for the rasping of his breath. Thomas heard the sound and turned.

"Hello Thomas," the priest said continuing to look at the altar so as not to embarrass the younger man, who quickly sat up and wiped his face with his sleeve. "It's been a long time since you've ventured in here."

"I attend on Sundays," muttered Thomas understanding the priest fully and feeling guilty at his neglect.

"There was a time, not so long ago when I would see you most days."

"It's been harvest, besides that was before..." He tailed off "I couldn't ..." He stopped again.

"I miss those sessions," said the priest pretending not to notice Thomas's confusion.

"You have many visitors, I was just one."

"They respect the church and fear it but they resent its priests for taking the tithes." Thomas sensed his loneliness and felt a surge of emotion for this old priest who had watched him grow. "You have taught me a lot Geoffrey."

"Just about all I know, I guess. Your Latin and script is as good as mine, though your knowledge of the bible and holy works could do with a bit more attention. Still, it's difficult without the texts, but you could have done more with the bible that we do have." He turned and smiled sadly to Thomas.

"You would have me as the next village priest!"

"That was my intention originally, but now I fear you would quickly fall out with Sir John and his Norman ways."

Thomas stood up and helped Geoffrey to his feet.

"Come on; let's go to the Chancery for some refreshment." He smiled and led Thomas across to a curtain entrance. Passing through, they entered a small room, which served as the priest's home. Thomas sat down on a small bench and leant up against the white washed wall.

"I've always wondered how you ended up here," he said.

"It's a long story; suffice to say I met Sir John's father who asked me to come and set up his new church. I could not refuse him. Things were good until he died." Geoffrey sighed and crossed himself. "God rest his soul. He wanted me to stay on, so I have."

"You're wasted here."

"No, I did God's work. This was where he wanted me, besides if I had not come, you would not have had such an education now, would you. How do you intend to use this gift I have given you?"

"I don't know but I'm certain I cannot stay here much longer, besides I need to visit my father."

"Yes, time away would be good but after that you must still decide." Thomas walked to the wicket door. Pushing it open he looked out across the fields to the mill.

"I would like to study more," he said distantly, thinking of a possible cure to the leprosy.

"You do not have the wealth to be a scholar," said Geoffrey handing him a pot of ale.

"Yes, you are right although father did leave me some money."

"Don't tell Nicholas."

"Don't worry it is well hidden. If I worked in Northampton maybe I could study there as well." He drank his ale. It tasted sour and it made him shiver.

"My own brew, I'm afraid," said Geoffrey. They lapsed into silence, standing at the door looking across the small valley created by the stream that ran along not far below the church and on to the mill. "I have a friend at St. John's Hospital in Northampton. I haven't seen him for years. Still if he's still alive I'm sure he'll help you. I'll write a letter of introduction for you if you intend to go there."

"Yes, that would be good. Thank you," said Thomas, walking back into the room. "I guess I'll go after the fair."

"That's not long away now."

"Sir John has an announcement. I would like to hear it before I go." The priest eyebrows rose with interest.

"Oh! Spill the beans then! What's this gossip that you know before I do?" As the village's confessor there was little that he did not know and he wondered if what Thomas had to say would actually be new news to him. He poured Thomas another ale and sat down on the edge of his palliasse. Thomas sat on a bench opposite and filled the priest in on all of Lucy's news.

"Well that is interesting." He sat back on the cot and rubbed his chin, thoughtfully, scratching at the bristles growing there. "I wondered what he would do." Thomas looked up surprised at the priest's mumblings and at the fact that all that he had said was obviously not new to the priest.

"What do you mean?"

"What?" said Geoffrey looking up, startled.

"What do you mean by 'I wondered what he would do'? What do you know Geoffrey?"

"Oh," Geoffrey studied Thomas's face. "I'm sorry, I shouldn't have said that. That's the trouble with being on your own a lot. You tend to talk to yourself."

"Yes but you know something. You can't just leave it like that. What do you know?" Thomas got up and moved across to the palliasse.

"What I know I cannot tell you."

"Why?" said Thomas raising his voice in irritation.

"It comes from the confessional." Thomas began to pace the room. Geoffrey looked on concerned.

"Well the 'he' is obviously Sir John." He stopped abruptly and faced Geoffrey. "Is it the confession that we will hear on September the third?"

"Ah, as to that I cannot say, though I think the two are related but it was not Sir John's confession that I heard."

"Who's then?" said Thomas, turning and kneeling before the priest; "surely you can tell me that?" he pleaded.

"I don't know." Geoffrey felt unsure, not wanting to break the religious confidence of the confessional but feeling that Thomas needed some warning of what was to come. He got up, went to the table and poured himself a drink, feeling Thomas's eyes follow him across the room. He turned, offering the jug to Thomas who declined, his eyes not leaving his face while he nervously gulped the ale. He came to a decision.

"It was your mother." He blurted out. Thomas jumped up but Geoffrey held up his hand stopping him. "I can say no more, she may be dead, God rest her soul, but I will not break the sanctity of her last confession." Thomas slumped back onto the bench, leaning his back on the cool wall. 'What did it all mean?' He wondered to himself. This time he did not refuse the ale handed to him. He pleaded with Geoffrey to tell him more. A man usually all too willing to discuss the village's gossip but on this count he would not budge.

"If you want to know more talk to the reeve. He will not make it easy for you but he has been here many years. He worked for Sir John's father before Sir John made him reeve. He knows most of the villagers' secrets although much of it is lost in gossip speculation and rumour, so it can be hard to find the truths. Whatever he tells you, it will hurt, he will make sure of that. You will have to use your own judgement to decide whether or not it is true." Thomas nodded and got up but Geoffrey continued, "Not now; wait until he is at Margery's. He will say nothing inside the bailey walls. Come sit at the table. I have some stew. It just needs warming."

Thomas followed Geoffrey outside to the small lean-to shed, where he cooked his food. A small fire burned in the hearth. The priest picked up his iron cooking pot and brought it over to Thomas who studied the mess of vegetables.

"How do you get so fat on that?" Thomas remarked. Geoffrey smiled back.

"I have the dubious pleasure of being a regular visitor to Sir John's table." He hung the pot above the fire. "Will you eat?" Thomas nodded, not too keen on the prospect of the cabbage and oatmeal stew that was obviously more than a few days old, but not yet wanting to leave the security of the large priest, who always seemed to have the answer. While the pottage warmed Geoffrey cut some trenchers from an old dark coloured loaf and put them on the trestle table. Then from a fresher loaf he cut some more hunks of bread.

He soon placed some semi-warm broth on the trenchers and they ate silently, occasionally slurping down some more ale. When they had finished Thomas made ready to leave.

"I'll come with you," said Geoffrey, "I could do with some better ale!" Thomas noticed the concern hidden in his smile and knew that it was more than that, but he accepted his company, pleased that he would not have to face the reeve alone.

Dusk was approaching as they walked up the street to the gates of the manor. The road turned and followed the outer bailey wall into the market square. Once a week local traders would bring in their wares, set up small stalls and sell anything from pots to vegetables to animals. It was market day but the few traders had all but cleared up and a small gathering stood and sat around Margery's front porch. As they approached, they were greeted by the group and nodded in return. Thomas was soon quizzed about his lack of presence at the market and explained to those that did not already know the problems at the mill.

Geoffrey fetched a couple of pots of ale. They found themselves seats and listened to the conversation, which tottered between talk of harvest by most of the villagers, to trade from the peddlers, finally to the growing tension between the Earl of Leicester, Simon De Montfort and the king.

"Whose side is Sir John on then?" asked a trader from another village.

"Oh, not sure," came the mumbled replies as the villagers looked round furtively, not wanting to commit themselves or their lord.

"What say you priest?" persisted the trader enjoying the tension he was causing.

"Sir John holds the land from the Earl of Winchester, Roger De Quincy," said the priest, puffing out his chest and leaning back, enjoying the attention and also not afraid to speak. "Now his father sided with the barons back in seventeen against Henry. What was his name? Let me see." He scratched his chin. He now had the full attention of all those gathered below the broom, which hung above the alehouse door. "Ah yes, Saier De Quincy that was it. He died on pilgrimage not long after. Now Earl Roger may be more cautious but he certainly has more to gain siding with De Montfort. My guess is that he will stay in Scotland, where most of his lands are, sitting on the fence. He seems happy for his tenants to side with De Montfort. Many are already obviously in the De Montfort camp. Now Sir John…"

"And what do you know?" came a loud voice full of sarcasm from the edge of the group, which cut the priest off in mid-sentence. They turned as one, many of the villagers edging back into the shadows. Geoffrey looked up and smiled. Thomas on the other hand eyed up the reeve and not hiding the contempt he felt for the lord's lackey, he took a mouthful of ale, swilled it round his mouth and spat it on the floor between his legs.

"Ah the fountain of knowledge and our oracle the reeve has arrived. Perhaps you will share your opinions with us?" replied Geoffrey. The Reeve eyed the priest nervously, knowing that he was not equipped with the skill to outwit him in a verbal contest.

"You think I would break my lord's confidence so easily." He smiled smugly pleased with his reply. Keen to change the subject before the priest could get in another jibe, he turned his attention to Thomas. "How's your father?" He sneered, drinking deeply from his pot of ale.

Thomas jumped up but Geoffrey pulled him back, whispering, "That was just a cheap shot to change the subject. You want information; he'll supply it. Just let him have a few more ales." They both sat down.

"What size is the fair to be this year? Sir John has not yet spoken to me regarding any ceremony to mark St. Gregory's feast day," said the priest to the reeve.

"Oh, I'm sure he will," replied the reeve wiping beer from his grey beard with a dirty hand. "He wants it to be an occasion to remember. Got a special announcement he has," he said in a loud voice, for all to hear. He leered at Thomas. Leaning forward he spilled his beer on Thomas's foot. Thomas pulled back unable to escape his foul breath. "You best get your bags packed. I'm not sure you'll be wanted round here for too much longer."

"My brother would never throw me out. Father made him promise."

"Father.... Ha, that's a good one," he roared, drinking deeply. "Don't you listen to the gossip? Mind it was time ago you and he were just sprats not worth spit. Now look at him, lording it over every one at the manor with Sir John. Sits at the top table he does." Thomas turned to Geoffrey who nodded confirmation. "Why do you think he's so pally with our master? Ever wondered why Sir John would bother with him?" The reeve leaned back his face creasing in a cruel smile.

"The mill..." started Thomas.

"Oh ah, yes there is that I guess. Still you'll know all on September the third!" He jumped up and slapped Thomas on the head, then walked away once again. Thomas jumped up and Geoffrey pulled him back once more.

"You'll not want to end up beaten and in the stocks. It's not worth it Thomas! He's not worth it. You'll just be playing into his hands." Thomas pulled away from the priest's grasp and stormed into Margery's.

"Ah, I see you're ready for another pot," she said sitting on a stool by her barrel. She put down her wool and distaff, took his pot and filled it, all the time watching him in his confusion.

"Why?" He looked at her intently. "Why would he bother with him Margery?"

"Your brother has the mill. He wants control of it." She shrugged at him.

"That may be so, but he is not marrying Eleanor." He looked beseechingly at her. "There's more Margery isn't there?"

"There were rumours," she said looking away not wanting to commit herself, but when she turned back he was still watching her expectantly. "Years ago, still there's always rumours around here. Folks didn't take much account of them though."

"What rumours? Come on Margery. Nobody wants to tell me but I need to know!"

"Can't you figure it out boy!" she said agitated by him persistence.

"I'm sorry," he said in a conciliatory tone. She suddenly felt pity for him. She saw his anguish and loneliness. She thought little of people, seeing only their greed and selfishness, but she remembered the miller. He was a good man, always fair and honest. The miller's wife had been a good woman too. She had often protected Margery from the teasing of the boys and other girls when they were young. She had not forgotten their callous comments. She was not pretty and had always had an odd twisted appearance. The teasing had made her hard and turned her against most folks, still they needed her now, she thought. Her mother had shown her how to brew and she had perfected that skill. Hers was the best ale around.

"Margery?" She looked up, brought from her musings by Thomas' enquiry. His grey eyes were moist with emotion. They were his mother's eyes, she thought. Yes, his mother had been a fine woman. How was she going to tell him?

"Well," she sat down, picking up her distaff and setting the spindle into motion, her deft fingers working quickly. "These rumours, they were about your mother and…"

"What were?" He broke in.

"The rumours stupid. Just listen!" At that moment a white faced white haired boy came dashing in followed by the sound of laughter from the crowd of drinkers outside. Thomas recognised Alfred's younger brother. "Cor' you look just like a ghost," Margery laughed. "You're white all over!" The boy rubbed his hands through his hair showering the floor in flour.

"What's up Elias?" Thomas asked, agitated at the disruption but concerned.

"It's Alfred sir, there's been an accident Mister Thomas." He looked about him, his eyes wide.

"Okay…mm." It took a moment for Thomas's thoughts to focus away from his original direction on to that of the present dilemma. "Is Alfred okay?" Elias nodded. "Right, let's head down there. You can tell me on the way." He took a quick look at Margery who smiled at him relieved she did not have to finish her story. Gulping down his ale, he shot out of the door followed by Elias. Geoffrey stood just outside, a look of concern on his face.

A sea of red laughing faces, their attention focused on the white Elias, surrounded him. He looked at the ground and kicked the dirt while he waited for Thomas.

"There's a problem at the mill Geoffrey, I'll see you tomorrow." He set off at a run down the hill with Elias who was relieved to be free from the mocking crowd. He knew he would be in for some serious ribbing from his friends for this one. Thomas broke him from his thoughts. "What's happened Elias?" The boy trotted beside him shedding white dust with every pace.

"The water shoot collapsed. It hit the wheel and jammed it. The pit wheel lost a few cogs. The millstones stopped as the axles jammed." Elias recited the words exactly as his brother Alfred had told him, puffing with each word.

"How come you're so covered?"

"Alfred fell off the ladder, dropped a sack of grain. The jolt of the jammed wheel shook the whole building. Some sacks of flour fell over. The whole place is full of dust and scattered grain." They had left the houses and the church behind them and jogged down the lane to the mill.

"Thank the Lord it's all downhill," muttered Thomas, "How's Alfred?"

"Shaken; he banged his head but it's pretty solid." In spite of the situation Thomas grinned at the youth. It relieved their tension.

They arrived at the mill sweating. Thomas felt dizzy and stopped short of entering the mill. He stood, watching the dust billowing out of the doorway.

"Where's your brother, Elias?"

"Alfred!" called Elias. A ghostly figure appeared, even whiter than Elias. His head was crowned by a red sticky mass of hair, blood and flour. Thomas ran over to him.

"Alfred! Are you okay?" he said without thinking.

"Yes Master Thomas," he mumbled

"Let's have a look at that wound." Thomas grabbed his arm. "Come and sit by the house." They moved across the yard and sat on the plank bench, which ran along the front wall. "Elias get some water; we'll clean this up and bandage it," said Thomas, wiping the sticky mess away from Alfred's head with his sleeve.

"What about the mill?" said Alfred wincing.

"Oh that can wait. It's not going anywhere!" Once they had washed the wound, Thomas went into the house to make up a herbal poultice of sage and yarrow to place on the wound. His interest in curing people had not just appeared with the loss of his father. His mother had taught him many remedies and he kept a good stock of herbs, which he grew behind the cottage. The power of plants had fascinated him since childhood and he felt sure there was a cure for every ailment locked up in them. It was just a matter of discovering the right herbs. He was certain that God would not have made the illness if there were not a cure for it somewhere.

Soon Alfred was fixed up and drinking heartily from a pot of ale.

"Well, before it gets too dark we must divert the water from the overshot wheel. It's crashing all over it at the moment. We don't want it turning and chopping off more cogs from the pit wheel or for that matter damaging the kingpin. Come on Elias. Alfred do you think you can help?"

"Oh yes." He guzzled down the rest of his ale and slowly followed them. With Alfred sitting on the bank muttering advice, Elias and Thomas managed to divert the water around the wheel using planks and staves to dam the stream and alter the course.

With the sound of a screeching owl, they finally tramped off to their respective homes, just before dawn. Thomas immediately fell upon his bed and dropped into a deep sleep.

He awoke with his head thumping from dehydration and his body aching from over exertion. Struggling from his straw mattress he pulled on his hose and picked up his tunic; grabbed a bucket and walked down to the stream. Filling it up, he dashed the water over his head.

"That'll be the death of you," said a voice from behind. He recognised the voice and turned, water dripping from his hair and short beard.

"Hello Geoffrey, nice of you to pop down."

I've told you before, too much water's not good for you."

"Better than smelling like an old sow!" he replied shaking off the water and rubbing himself down with his tunic.

"Oh, a bit touchy this morning, are we?"

"It was a tough night," replied Thomas, walking back to the cottage.

"Yes, I looked in on Alfred and told him to stay in bed; hope you don't mind. He looked very pale." Thomas shook his head. "Thought I'd better come and survey the damage. Doesn't look too good does it." They had reached the yard and stood in front of the mill studying the collapsed shoot.

"I told him about that ages ago. He said not to worry it would be fine for a while yet. Well he isn't going to be happy when he sees this lot." Thomas smiled and went into the cottage coming out with bread ale and cheese. They breakfasted on the bench in front of the cottage, and studied the damaged mill.

"Well you don't seem too concerned for your dear brother," said Geoffrey between mouthfuls. He looked up at the sun. "It's going to be another hot one, in more ways than one I think."

"I can't wait to tell him, just to see the expression on his face, besides," Thomas became serious and looked Geoffrey in the eyes. "How much of a brother is he?"

"Ah…mm, I see," mumbled Geoffrey turning away.

"You make no comment?" Thomas turned his face to the sun and felt its hot rays eating into his skin.

"You know I cannot." Now they both fell silent. When they had eaten their fill, Thomas got up and carried the plates back into the house.

"I'd best be up to the manor to see his lordship then and report the damage," he said as he came out. Geoffrey grunted and raised himself up.

"All I ask, Thomas, is don't forget the villagers. They need this mill if they are to get through the winter."

"It'll be fixed before the fair, have no fear, priest." Geoffrey nodded.

"I'll walk with you part of the way." They parted company at the church and Thomas continued up to the manor. He passed through the open gate of the outer bailey and stopped. He did not often enter the confines of Buckbie's manorial seat. The outer walls consisted mainly of an embankment; much of the wooden wall that had topped it had fallen down or been reused in house repairs. The outer bailey area was full of the manor farm buildings; to his left were stables for horses, winter quarters for animals and housing for staff. On his right, he passed two large barns.

He listened to the sounds of activity and watched as people bustled around. The outer bailey was always busy, the manor staff and villeins nodded to him as they passed about their business. He walked across the hard-baked earthen yard littered with the flotsam of a busy farm, careful to not tread in any of the waste that was scattered across his route. It was filthier than it need be, he decided, watching a rat run from the barn door. The smell of animal dung was soon intermingled with that of cooking and wood smoke as he passed the kitchen block.

In front of him stood the gateway to the inner bailey. It still had gates, which had long since disappeared from the outer bailey, but they had not been closed for many years. Ferns and grass sprang from their many seams. A neat hazel wicket fence topped the raised banks of the inner enclosure. The wooden defensive walls had all been removed.

As he made to enter, a call came from behind, which stopped him in his tracks. He went cold. He had not come to do battle with the reeve. Turning he smiled sourly. The reeve sat on a stool outside the kitchens.

"To what do we owe the honour of your presence?" he called, sneering at Thomas. "It's been some time since you ventured in here!" Thomas just nodded, holding back a retort. When the reeve said nothing more, obviously waiting for Thomas he finally replied.

"My brother," and pointed through the gateway.

"What do you want to see him for?" From the sound of his voice Thomas decided that he disliked Nicholas as much as he did himself. The reeve had got up and swaggered slowly across towards Thomas.

"You two don't have much in common nowadays, apart from the same mother I suppose."

He sniggered and slurped some ale down. It dribbled through his greying beard.

"Mill business." Thomas turned away biting his tongue and feeling himself redden with rising anger.

"Wait." He stopped. The word was spat out, full of menace. "I decide who enters through there, Thomas the Miller's son. Thomas turned his mouth open. "They're all busy. You'll have to come back later!" The reeve laughed at his confusion. Before he could reply a sudden movement from the top of the inner bailey wall caught his eye and made him stop and look up. The reeve also followed his gaze.

"Do you have no work, reeve?" came a shrill voice from the parapet. Thomas saw Lucy looking down at them over the wicket fence. He turned and smiled at the reeve.

"I was just seeing to the Miller's son my lady."

"Ah Thomas," she said as if just noting him for the first time, "Do come in I would like a word with you." Thomas nodded and his smile broadened as he saw the reeves darkening face, "Be about your business reeve."

"Yes my lady." He turned angrily and stomped off back to the kitchen.

Thomas jogged quickly up the short flight of wooden steps just inside the gateway and joined Lucy on the small track that ran round the top of the embankment, which circled the manor. She gave him a quick smile then gazed out across the valley to the hamlet of Murcotte on the far side, a small group of about six cottages.

"You can see a long way from here, I never realised."

"Yes in all directions."

"Now I see why the De Quincy's built it here. A good spot for a Norman to watch and control his Saxon underlings." She gave him a sharp look.

"I am a Norman and proud of it too!"

"Never fear Lady Lucy," he smiled. "I have no anger towards the Norman people, not like my forebears. I have met as many horrible Saxons as Normans; though I am young and my opinions are still formulating, as Geoffrey would say."

"You have an unhealthy relationship with that priest," she said gruffly, studying him closely. Slowly her frown softened as she recognised the teasing twinkle in his eyes. "Come on, let's walk." She turned away slowly and began to walk along the embankment. "Have you any news?"

They had walked half way round before he answered.

"Some." They stopped to look down onto the Green, which abutted onto the junction of roads that converged on Buckbie. It was surrounded by a smattering of cottages owned mainly by those who had wares or services to sell during market days, such as Margery. Thomas noticed her busying herself in the strip of land behind her house.

"Well?" He turned, to see Lucy watching him.

"I've spoken to Geoffrey, your reeve back there and Margery." He turned once more to absently observe the bent figure of the old lady below. "I gleaned information of sorts. You have gained no more here?"

"None," she replied. "Come on I'm on tender hooks."

"Well you'll be pleased to know I think your intended has Norman blood in him." He saw her smile.

"I thought as much from the way he carried himself." She seemed satisfied and was about to turn away when a quizzical look came over her.

"But you don't?"

"Same mother, different father."

"Oh!" This time he noted surprise. They had begun to walk again and as they neared full circle they heard the soft pad of feet on the steps. A head appeared above the parapet.

"Ah, my dear Lucy. Brother! What are you doing here?" He had reached the top step and was momentarily confused by the appearance of Thomas.

"Hello Nicholas, we were just talking about your engagement; congratulations!" Now his brother was totally off his guard and Thomas enjoyed the moment. "Don't worry she hasn't been telling me any sordid secrets! She has just mentioned your engagement. Being your brother, she thought I ought to know." He felt Lucy nudge him and turned to see her now annoyed features. He smiled at her and then, turning back to his brother, he said, "Actually Nicholas, I came to see you." Nicholas was once again on his guard.

"Why?" He muttered sharply

"May we talk?" He looked meaningfully at Lucy, but she did not want to move, keen to be involved in whatever it was they were to discuss.

"Excuse us my dear," said Nicholas bowing to her. He grabbed Thomas' arm and led him back to the rear of the castle embankment. Lucy huffed and stomped off.

"What are you up to Thomas?" said Nicholas looking out at the Daventry lane. Thomas watched a small boy using a stick to move a cow slowly along the lane out of the village in search of grazing. He looked across to his left. The ground rose slowly into the heathland through which the Northampton road came. A wagon trundled along it with as much slowness as the cow.

"Actually brother, I was wondering what you and your new pal Sir John were up to. I hope you're not in over your head." He wondered absently what the wagon was carrying as it crept ever closer to the green.

"What do you mean?"

"Well this engagement, bit out of your league isn't she? Or are you now above us lowly freemen in social standing. Guess I must be a bit of an embarrassment now, hey?"

"I thought you were moving on Thomas. Is that going to be soon?" Thomas recoiled from the barbed comment stepping back and facing his brother who would not look him in the face but continued to stare out across the countryside.

"So you do want rid of me then?" He turned back to watch the wagon arrive on the green, where it headed across to Margery's "I guess I don't fit into these new plans of yours then." He sighed. He had known it all along but to see it in the eyes of his brother made complete the feeling of alienation that had been slowly growing. "I will leave after the fair." He faced Nicholas, "I need to see my father." He accentuated the 'my' and turned to watch the surprise on Nicholas's face.

"You know?"

"Enough I think, the rest I can guess, but how long have you known Nicholas? How long have you been scheming?"

"How dare you say such a thing! I could have you thrown into the stocks!" Nicholas stepped forward angrily. Thomas just watched his reddening face, though full of sadness, he could not help but smile at his brother's pompous anger, which filled his newly fattened jowls. He now knew that Nicholas had known for some time.

"No, I don't think you have sunk that low." He replied quietly. "Besides, who would fix the mill?"

"The mill? What is this? Thomas what are you up to?" The vein on his forehead began to pulsate vigorously. Thomas studied it, fascinated and at the same time annoyed that Nicholas believed that he was out to injure him in some way.

"I have promised the priest, Geoffrey, that I would fix the mill before I left. I came to tell you that there has been an accident. I thought you might be interested. I'm surprised you haven't heard about it already. Mind, I guess you don't communicate with many of the serfs round here now do you; except to order them about, that is?"

Thomas turned away from his brother and stared up the Northampton road, which disappeared through the heath. He yearned to get going now and escape the village, which seemed to be rotting at its heart. He wanted to see his father again. He felt hate creep into his soul and knew he must escape before it gained a dangerous hold. Distantly he heard his brother shouting at him as he walked slowly away.

"Come and see for yourself!" He called back without turning. "Perhaps you would lend a hand fixing it!" He walked down the steps and out of the gate feeling weary with the emotional exertion, he turned towards Margery's.

"I thought I'd find you here," said Geoffrey puffing as he walked across the green. "How did it go?"

"Well enough, I suppose," said Thomas noncommittally, as he supped his beer.

"Margery!" called Geoffrey collapsing by Thomas's side.

"Ah! Priest, how pleasant to see you!" she said appearing from the dark interior of her cottage.

"Ale and some of that broth Thomas is picking at please." She shuffled away. "Well talk to me boy, I won't leave you alone you know." As they sat and ate Thomas told him how the morning had gone.

"Well you've only a week to the fair. You can travel with the traders to Northampton afterwards. It'll be safer than going it alone." They ate on in silence for a while then Geoffrey continued, "Did you know the wedding is to be the day after the fair? Sir John wishes to entertain his guests with the fair then have the wedding feast and ceremony the next day."

"But the engagement is hardly common knowledge. You haven't said anything in church yet. Don't you have to?" said Thomas looking up.

"I will be this Sunday and for the following three days after that, not that anyone will be there after Sunday, but he's the lord of the manor, so I can't argue if he changes the rules slightly. Besides those distinguished guests who are to be attending already know."

"And who are these distinguished guests then?"

"Apparently one of the Earl of Leicester's sons is to attend and many other tenants and land holders connected to De Quincy. I think the Earl is using the occasion to make a play for their support. Thomas Menhill is coming apparently.

"Menhill," Thomas repeated the name. "He will surely bring Eleanor?"

"I'm sure he will." Geoffrey smiled. "Sir John will want her here, to parade her before all these influential friends he seems to have, in the hope that she may be able to hook one of them." He watched Thomas's brow furrow and thought he better quickly change the subject. "Still I think there will be little talk of marriage between the lords at the top table at this wedding. Lucy's family are also bringing a few friends and acquaintances who I believe are connected to the 'Barons Party'."

"Quite a gathering for a millers wedding!" said Thomas sarcastically.

"I think the fact that your honourable brother grew up on a mill was not mentioned in the invitations and will not be discussed in any of the proceedings."

"I was going to leave before the wedding but I think I'll stick around."

"I had better warn you then Thomas, I will not be doing the service. De Montfort's son is bringing the well-dressed Norman priest who presided over your father's council hearing."

"Henry of Leicester!" Thomas spat out the words with loathing. He drank deeply. "So that's why he was here, to set up this barons meeting." Thomas stood up. "Nicholas is going to let him bless the marriage!"

"Remember he does not feel the way you do about your father. Never did either from what I can remember." Geoffrey stared across the trodden earth of the market green at the few cottages opposite; homes of Buckbie's few traders, the smith, the potter – of dubious quality and a peddler who seemed capable of laying his hands on almost anything at a price.

He turned and looked up the road at the sound of horses' hooves and wagon wheels. Thomas, who was still standing, had also turned his gaze towards the visitors that rode slowly towards him kicking up dust, which fluttered up towards the afternoon sun in hazy clouds.

"Eleanor," muttered Thomas making out a female figure leading the group.

"It appears so. We had just mentioned her and here she is riding out of the sunset," replied Geoffrey, raising himself up and coming to stand by Thomas, a wry smile on his face.

"Lucy said she was coming." Thomas continued his eyes fixed firmly on the approaching figure swaying gently in the saddle of the lead pony.

"Control yourself lad. She's not for you. I'm sure she's no longer the girl you remember. Besides Sir John expects her to wed a duke and certainly nothing less than a knight and even then only if he is a Norman! You may be a freeman but that's little different from a villein to our John." Thomas turned away angry at the comments and at his own transparency.

He stepped away from the priest and out from the lean-to shelter that protruded from the front of Margery's alehouse. Standing still in the afternoon heat, the sky a perfect blue, he watched the approaching horses.

He had missed Eleanor; their secret chats and games as children had left their mark. He had not experienced such feelings with anyone else and found himself very alone when she had left. He had been fifteen, she was just thirteen but he had been heartbroken. Her mother had kept her at home, because she had been ill and had not wanted to be parted from her only child. When she had finally died her father had quickly packed her off to the Menhill household at Hemmington, as she was betrothed to their son.

That was four years ago. Lucy had said that the Menhill's son had recently died which left Eleanor without a future husband. Sir John would not be happy with that state of affairs thought Thomas. Since leaving Buckbie, she had not been back. He wondered if she would recognise him. The horses grew nearer as did the sound of their harness's jangling. A fly buzzed in front of his eyes. He brushed it away without a thought, his heart pounding.

As she grew closer, she seemed not to have noticed him. Her gaze was fixed on the inner bailey wall that climbed up from behind the cottages. He studied her face. She looked strained and pale. Her deep hazel eyes were lost in thought behind her flickering eyelashes. Her thin lips were drawn inwards, pensive; wisps of jet-black hair glistened in the sunlight.

She glanced down at him as the horses trotted slowly passed. She nodded absently, as she would any peasant who stood to greet her. His gaze followed them as they headed on and he let out a deep sigh, the held in air rushing from his lungs. As he turned back towards the alehouse he sensed a sudden change in the clatter of the passing wagon.

"Thomas!" He looked up as the lead horse now stopped, swivelled sharply round and cantered back. "Thomas! It is you; I know it is you!" The horse came to a stop in a great cloud of dust. He laughed loudly, releasing the pent up emotion at the same time attempting to brush away the small particles that threatened to envelope him. The laugh grew, releasing the bound up energy of the past months. She too had begun to laugh. A tear ran from his eye into his cropped beard. He reached up and held the bridle of her horse. Her hand automatically touched his and held it briefly. Her face had changed; it seemed full of the sun's reflection, almost giving off light.

"I thought you did not know me!" he said, as she looked down upon him. The thin gawky girl had blossomed. He looked up at the sky to gather his scattered emotions together on a wisp of Cirrus that hung lazily in the air. It reminded him of the lock of unruly hair that gently brushed her high cheekbone, now almost white in the bright sunlight. He turned to see her brushing it back. She laughed again.

"How could I forget you Thomas"

"My lady?" The other rider pulled up and gave Thomas a disdainful look. Eleanor quickly released his hand.

"My guardian's steward, Thomas," she said in introduction. "He has kindly escorted me here. Master Paston, this is Thomas the Miller's son, an old friend from my childhood." Master Paston nodded, his expression not changing.

"We must move on my lady. Your father is expecting us. I am sure we have been spotted approaching."

"Yes, yes," she said absently, still staring at Thomas. Only when Master Paston coughed to get her attention again, did she say, "I must go, but it's good to see you Thomas, you have improved my mood and reduced my trepidation. You have changed though," she said ignoring the steward, "There is a sadness in your eyes." She had not forgotten those grey eyes that always seemed connected to his heart. Often when they were young they had glistened with excitement and mischief. Now they appeared dulled.

"Much can happen in four years."

"Yes, indeed," she said to herself, now also looking back and inward. She let out a sigh and her face became pinched and pensive as when she had first ridden past him.

"My lady!"

"Yes, we must go on. Goodbye Thomas." She turned and quickly rode away. Geoffrey came out from the hidden shade of the lean-to and put his arm on Thomas's shoulder. He had not moved and was watching the horses as they headed round to the outer bailey gateway.

"Well, she certainly has blossomed. A real beauty now, just like her mother was."

"I wish that she had been ugly then…"

"Oh well lad, come finish your drink and then get down to that mill. A bit of physical exercise'll keep your mind from thinking about what cannot be."

"I guess so." Thomas allowed himself to be led back to the tables and downed the last of his ale. He was quickly on his way down towards the mill only faltering as he passed the entrance to the manor compound.

Chapter 3

Thomas rose from his cot and wandered out of his cottage. He plunged into the cool waters of the stream. Holding onto a stake driven in near the bank, he let the crystal clear water rush over him as he watched the rising dawn. Slowly his aching muscles softened and his eyes cleared of the mists of deep physical sleep. Climbing out he sat on the bank and allowed the cool morning breeze to dry him. The dawn chorus sang around him.

He wondered what the day held and felt his heart beat with excitement. It was St Gregory's day. To Thomas it had always been the best day in the year. The fair would be open after the morning service and for the next three days there would be games, competitions feasting and drinking. The whole village would burst into celebration. He was determined to try and enjoy these last few days in the village where he had spent his entire life.

Thomas had worked hard the whole week with Alfred and some of the village villeins sent down by Nicholas and they had finally finished at dusk the previous day. He had not ventured into the village for some time. He knew that now it would be alive with visitors, traders and artisans. The road past the mill had been busy for the last few days with riders, pedestrians and wagons. He had seen Eleanor only once, when she had walked past with Lucy. He had been standing in the millrace with water up to his waist. They had said 'hello,' but would not let him stop. After five minutes they had walked on upstream.

A warbler chattered to him loudly from a nearby reed. The first swallow swooped down across the water, insects began to scratch and kick the chorus percussion. The day was going to be warm, he decided, standing up and wandering back to the cottage to dress and break his morning fast.

He was soon on his way to the church. As he got closer the lane began to fill up. This was the busiest service in the church's year. He entered the already crowded building, dipped his fingers into the stoup of holy water and crossed himself. The smells of incense, candles, sweat and body heat wafted over him. The inside of the church filled him with delight. Morning beams splashed through the windows across the painted walls, flowers were everywhere, banners hung from the rafters. The congregation were excited and expectant. They chattered, joked and jostled each other as they looked for friends. Thomas noticed that the benches placed at the front were already full. He recognised Sir John, Eleanor, Lucy and his brother sitting together. There seemed to be more than the usual number of important looking guests.

A gathering of monks from the priory at Daventry began to chant. Thomas loved to hear them on their annual visit to this ceremony. Their song echoed eerily through the building. Thomas felt his heart race and body shudder. He was sure God's spirit had entered the building; many people sank to their knees, eyes closed in prayer.

When the monks fell silent, Geoffrey appeared in his robes. Thomas recognised the nervous look he gave the seated guests. He told the story of St Gregory and lit a large candle by his statue. He then continued the service in Latin. Thomas knew that he was one of only a few in the church that understood the words. He felt the packed crowd begin to get restless, bodies around him started to jostle and push. Thomas tried hard to cut out the noise and listen to Geoffrey's words. He found the very foreignness of the words moving. He knew that many believed they must have come from God for this very reason alone.

The monks began to chant again and once more the people stopped in awe. When they ceased, a silence had once again settled over the audience. Thomas felt beads of sweat forming on his forehead in the now oppressive heat. He saw Geoffrey had now sat down and another priest had moved to the altar and knelt to pray. His robes were the finest that Thomas had seen. When he stood and turned, Thomas staggered, his face going pale. He felt faint. A man next to him grabbed his arm and studied him with concern.

"You all right?" he whispered. Thomas nodded vaguely. Memory of Geoffrey's warning returned. He looked once again at the face of Henry of Leicester and felt suddenly filled with the horror of their last meeting three months previously. He turned and pushed his way through the crowd and out into the morning air. Breathing deeply he collapsed by the church door. Behind him the muttering of the service continued.

How could God speak through that man? He hit the ground in anger, beating his fists until they began to bleed, his eyes full of tears. What if it really was God's will, that his father should be sent away, to be dead to his family, ejected from the life he had lived for forty of more years. Doubt churned up his emotions. He shivered uncontrollably. His breakfast rising in his stomach, the acid burned his throat and he tasted bile, while his heart raced with unstoppable speed. Surely it could not be so. He vomited by the doorpost, retching out his emotional turmoil. The white emaciated body of his mother, his pale stooped father, staggering as if already a corpse. He wiped his mouth with his sleeve and brushed the vomit from his shirt.

Chanting filled his ears; the cowled monks appeared. He staggered to his feet, tears still in his eyes. He saw Geoffrey, carrying a cross, walk through the doorway and give him a concerned glance. Behind him came the wooden statue of St Gregory. Thomas crossed himself, reached out and touched it as it passed on its journey to the green where Sir John would open the fair. Henry of Winchester passed him without a glance, then John, Lucy and Nicholas who looked at him with disgust. Only Eleanor gave him a glance of pity and concern. Her eyes seemed to reach into his, calling for understanding. Her step faltered, and then she was gone, pulled on by her father.

Soon the whole congregation was weaving along the street towards the green and he stood by the deserted church. He felt his fingers hot from the touch of St Gregory. He studied his fingertip, noticing a small piece of gold paint. He felt sure it was a sign. His heart raced to this call from God. He knew that he must not give up hope. He hurried inside and genuflected before the altar.

He left the church feeling dazed and slowly made his way along the street, around the edge of the outer bailey wall and on to the green. He found it flooded with the canvas of the stalls. A stage stood in the centre surrounded by an expectant crowd. He stopped; his breath tight in his chest with expectation. Sir John stood before St Gregory, who was still held by his bearers, peeling paintwork clearly visible in the dazzling beams of morning light. Sir John took Nicholas's hand.

"This day, the feast day of Saint Gregory, I do declare that this man," he held Nicholas's hand in the air, "be my son by blood." Some gasps rippled through the crowd, "I do adopt him fully and legally as my heir...." The rest faded in the sound of cheering. So thought Thomas, Nicholas is to be the heir to the manor. He spat angrily on the ground. His body began to shake with hate and anger. He kicked out violently at a mangy mongrel that got to close. The terrible thud of contact and the following yelp calmed him slightly. He walked towards Margery's, deciding that alcohol might just dull his battered emotions. The lean-to was surrounded by trestle tables and benches. It was already quite busy. He sat on the end of a bench. Margery had some of the village girls helping and he soon had a pot of ale, which he drank down thirstily.

The fair was soon open and Saint Gregory on his way back to the church. People began milling excitedly around the stalls as acrobats performed on the stage to a large crowd. Thomas marvelled at the transformation of the green from the previous week. The quiet dusty patch of ground with the odd bit of withered brown grass, inhabited by grunting pigs, scratching chickens and the occasional group of scruffy village children had become a massed group of stalls and tented areas, containing the calling, shouting and excited population of the whole region within a day's walking distance. The place heaved with bodies, dogs barked, horses neighed; a thriving animal market had begun at the far end, where cows, pigs and sheep could be heard.

As the ale coursed through him, for a moment the old excitement filled him; the buzz he got each year from seeing the village come alive. First as a child running from stall to stall, watching the shows, then as a young adult in the tournaments, wrestling, the quarterstaff, and the grand football match. A vision of his mother's hugs and father's gentle pat of pride floated before him as he remembered his last year's success in the quarterstaff competition. He felt the tears welling up again and quickly wiped his moist eyes as he called for more ale.

The sun was now high and beating down on the busy scene. Thomas slowly drank the morning away, afraid to step into the throng. From a distance he watched the performers. The acrobats had gone, to be followed by a religious play put on by the parishioners. Thomas smiled at their amateur theatrical antics; glad to have escaped Geoffrey's net this year. A storyteller now sat upon a stool surrounded by children ensnared in the wonders of his bloodthirsty tale of heroism, battle and love. He looked across the stalls fascinated by the foreign wares that were on display mixed in with the mundane and necessary items that were the real reason the community needed the fair.

A shadow appeared before him and he looked up to see Eleanor. She looked upon him with her wide hazel eyes.

"It is midday. Would you join me for some food? There are some interesting delights at some of these stalls and I would enjoy a chance for us to talk. I have seen nothing of you this past week!"

"I am not welcome at the manor," he said, looking at the ground, not wanting to meet her eyes.

"My father did not wish me to walk by the river." Thomas smiled and looked up at her.

"But you wished to?" she nodded. After a moment's hesitation he continued, "in that case I will join you for some food." He finished his ale and stood up, his head swam slightly; she laughed and took his arm.

"Come, I can see you need some food to soak up that ale. There are some nice roasted chickens at a stall over this way." She pointed and began to pull him along, "And I've seen some lovely Custard Lumbarde too, and a stall with tasty looking sweetmeats." Thomas walked with her, enjoying her company as they moved through the stalls, past the central stage, where mummers now danced in masks and fancy dress costumes. People threw coins onto the stage, which were quickly scooped up.

"At the food stall they sat and Thomas greedily attacked his chicken. Eleanor watched him, picking slowly at her food, more interested in Thomas.

He had grown broader and more muscular but he was still the way she remembered him. She realised how much she had missed his company. Her guardians had tried their best but they were busy at court and with the loss of their only son they had found it harder to have her presence regularly in their midst. She had had little chance to find companionship with any one. Her main companion was Menhill's wife, Jeanette. All the women she had come across on her visits to court seemed only interested in successful marriage and the latest top single men at court. The young men all appeared to be arrogant fools.

"I have managed to catch up on all the news," she said. "I didn't know about your father." He looked up at her, his grey eyes intent. She saw them flash angrily. "He was a good man," she continued, not wanting to upset him.

"He is not dead!" Thomas had raised his voice. She put her hand on his arm.

"I know that Thomas, I have prayed for him and for his recovery. I prayed to St Giles two days ago on his feast day. The priest says he has worked many miracles."

"Thank you," he said softening. "I have been too busy, I should have prayed also." He lowered his head.

"You needed to have the mill working. He would understand that. Your father loved the mill."

"How would he feel now that it is back with your Sir John?" Once again his grey eyes reached into her mournfully. She felt her heart beat faster.

"He is my father! Besides, Nicholas will continue to allow you to run it as the miller."

"I am leaving." He put down the chicken carcass and wiped his hands. "I cannot stay here anymore. I will not work for my brother. He watched her face crease in confusion. "He wanted my father out of the way. He cared nothing for him and wishes me out of the way also."

"Your father was ill, Thomas. He had to be sent away for the protection of the other villagers. You cannot blame your brother."

"There is nothing for me here."

"Where will you go?" Her face was now full of concern.

"Northampton; after the wedding." He paused, taking a drink. "I intend to leave after the wedding. I can see father and find work in the town. I would like to try to study there."

"At the University?" he nodded. "Can you afford it?"

He shrugged.

"I have some money." After a moment Thomas continued, keen to change the subject, as he was as yet unsure of his plans, just knowing that he must leave. "Where is your guardian? I didn't see him this morning and he didn't arrive with you."

"I came without him. He is to arrive the day before the wedding. So is Simon de Montfort."

"What, the Earl himself?"

"No, silly, his son! They have the same name." They smiled and both visibly relaxed the previous tension broken.

"What's he like?"

"Who?"

"Menhill, your guardian."

"Oh, old, proud, believes he is always right, loves power; although he does care for his villeins. He has been good to me too."

"Are you happy there?" Her hazel eyes looked into the distance. He studied her long jet hair flecked with silvery flashes, like shooting stars in the night, caused by her minute movements in the dazzling sunlight. He became conscious of the heat on his face and moved uncomfortably.

"I am a companion for his wife," she said vaguely. "Hopefully, I can better myself through a marriage contract." Her voice seemed distant and mechanical.

"You don't mean that!" he blurted out. He saw a tear in her eye. "It's your father I hear."

"It is what I must do. What else is there for me?" Their eyes met and united in understanding and sadness.

"Life is full of burdens. Can an adult ever touch the pure happiness that a child can pick up naturally as they race and play in the meadow?" She touched his hand.

"They are memories we must cherish." She stood up her mood suddenly changing. "Come let's get to that sweet meat stall before the best are gone and before I'm discovered by Clarice my maid and scolded for being with a man at the fair!" she laughed grabbed his hand and pulled him along.

They ate sweetmeats and chatted merrily until their capture by the maid whilst they watched entranced as a group of singers sang a sad ballad full of love and bravery on the stage.

"We must meet again before we go our separate ways," she whispered. Then she was gone, leaving him before the stage. He sat alone amidst the crowd on the earth until the ballad came to an end then reached into his small leather purse on his belt and threw a battered and clipped coin onto the stage.

"I recommend a pilgrimage." He turned to see Geoffrey still dressed in his best robes. "Yes," he continued holding his ample chin in his large dirty fist. "A pilgrimage would certainly help to cure all your woes. I suggest that you do this soon; the quicker the treatment the sooner the cure; come." He reached down a hand towards Thomas, "I have my best robes on; I cannot sit down there in the dirt. Let's find a more comfortable spot with some fluid refreshment." Thomas took his arm and got to his feet, swaying as he stood.

They were soon settled back at one of Margery's tables under the awning.

"A pilgrimage you think," mumbled Thomas into his ale.

"Yes, not only do you have a father to pray for but also that beautiful young lady that you have spent part of your day with." Thomas looked across at him, reddening. "Yes, you need to get her out of your system and pray that she can do the same." Thomas nodded glumly. "Now," said Geoffrey, rubbing his hands and smiling. "We don't want you running off into the wild lands of England. I suggest something closer." He had Thomas's full attention and was enjoying it. "How about the Church of Saint Peter of Burch?"

"I have heard of this place from my father." Thomas's eyes sparkled. "He said it contains a beautiful reliquary in which are the remains, or part of them anyway, of Thomas Becket." Thomas crossed himself at the thought of such holy treasure.

"Your father was a great fan of Saint Thomas."

"He went on pilgrimage to Canterbury."

"Yes and named you after him! It would be fitting for you to visit the holy relics at Saint Peters Burch. If they cannot help you then it is left only to God." This time Geoffrey crossed himself and slipped into silence.

"Do you know more about these relics?"

"Yes, the blood soaked robe and a stone flag plus two phials with some of his blood."

"You have seen these wonders?" Geoffrey had a distant look in his watery faded eyes, which were almost lost in his rounded red cheeks.

"I went with Sir John's father. The reliquary is of great beauty, like nothing I have ever seen. It was made in France apparently at a place called Limoges, but I'm sure God had a hand in it."

There is more there though. The church itself is a place of wonder. Inside there is a chapel containing the arm of Saint Oswald. Surely over such holy relics you can find the cures you need." As the priest went on to describe the wonders of the Abbey at Peterborough, Thomas's eyes grew wide with excitement and promise. His hand began to fiddle with the small bronze medallion he wore around his neck. He touched the six prongs of the star shaped badge that his father had brought back from Canterbury.

They sank the rest of their ale as Thomas listened to Geoffrey.

"It's a good idea, Geoffrey." He stood up to get some more ale, as the girls were all busy. As he turned away he stopped and looked back at the priest. "You will still give me a letter of introduction for your friend in Northampton." For a moment Geoffrey looked puzzled, and then he remembered.

"Are yes, my friend at St John's Hospital. Are you still set on leaving after the wedding?"

"The following day, yes."

Chapter 4

Lucy stood flushed and excited in the doorway of Saint Gregory's Church. She saw this as her greatest moment, marrying the heir to the local lord. Only bringing a son into the world could better it. She looked across at her future husband who was studying her with a stern and serious face. She studied his finery. She too felt grand in her new dress, made especially for the occasion. The powerful guests that surrounded her made her now certain that her match was suitable.

Henry of Leicester began the service, calling for quiet from the gathered guests and villagers that filled the churchyard and adjoining road. Thomas watched from a bank on the side of the road looking over the heads of the gathered crowd. Silence had fallen.

"Hast thou will to have this woman to be thee wedded wife?"

"Yes sir," replied Nicholas looking into Henry's face.

"Thou will find at thou best to love her and hold her and to no other to thou lives end"

"Yes sir." He replied again now studying the ground.

"Then take her by your hand and say after me, I Nicholas take thee Lucy in form of holy church to my wedded wife." Nicholas's reply was lost to Thomas in the shuffling of feet and slight wind, "forsaking all others, holding her wholly to thee, in sickness and in health," once again came a slight pause as Nicholas mumbled his reply. "In riches and in poverty, in well and in woe till death us depart and there to I plight you my troth." Cheering broke out as Nicholas mumbled his last line. They turned to face the crowd and it slowly fell silent. Thomas studied the villagers around him as they looked upon their future lord and lady.

He crossed himself and quietly turned and walked up through the village. He wandered up to the manor, passing through the empty village and outer bailey. The only sounds were those coming from the kitchen block.

He entered through the large doorway and found himself in the main hall. Smoke billowed up through the centre of the building from a small central hearth. It had been hot outside but it was stifling in the dark gloomy interior. As his eyes became accustomed, he noticed the tables ready set for the banquet. The raised dais to his right contained the main table. Running down the hall each side of the hearth were the long tables for the lesser guests.

He sat on the last seat as far from the top table as he could and called for some ale. A young boy who had been nervously watching him ran off and soon returned with a pot. He drank it quickly. It was good strong ale; Sir John had obviously brought in some special bride ale for the occasion.

He could hear the sound of music growing closer as the wedding procession came up through the village. Soon the hall would be bedlam. He enjoyed the quiet contrast that the present moment held.

Within a minute a group of gaudily dressed minstrels had burst through the door followed by a merry chattering crowd led by the newlywed couple. Behind them came Sir John and Eleanor who were closely followed by two men who Thomas assumed, from their attire to be Ralph Bassett and Simon De Montfort the younger, who were in deep discussion. They were followed by a group of other knights. Thomas recognised

Thomas Menhill with his wife. The others he assumed were Arnold Du Bois, Peter le Porter and Saer De Harcourt who were all tenants of Roger De Quincy and who Thomas had heard were attending the festivities. Thomas studied their serious faces. He felt sure that they had not met here for the celebration of a wedding. Their secretive plotting intrigued Thomas. He remembered the stories of the previous De Quincy's involvement in the 1217 rebellion and his subsequent banishment on a pilgrimage to Jerusalem from which he never returned. The young De Montfort's father was the most powerful baron and, at present, was even more powerful than the king. De Quincy was playing a careful game allowing his barons and knights to become a part of the new ruling party without actually setting out his own stall for the new De Montfort regime. That suggested to Thomas that perhaps the present situation was less stable than many believed.

The feeling that someone was watching him distracted his thoughts. He turned to meet Eleanor's gaze. She sat next to the young De Montfort. A ploy by her father he mused, although so far they hardly seemed to have acknowledged each other, so intent was the conversation he was having with Ralph Bassett.

She smiled at him amongst the merry crowd. She looked alone, on an island. Her gaze held them like a rope. He felt adrift, being swept further away by the rising wind. Finally with a snap, the rope had broken; she turned away as De Montfort spoke to her.

Thomas turned his attention to the food, studying the fine array of dishes placed along the top table. There was capon, pheasant, heron, sturgeon in a sauce, and that was just the first course. In front of him arrived a large platter of mutton in spiced gravy. He tucked in. Filling up his ale pot, he noted the laughter and shouting that now filled the hall, drowning out the minstrels who were still playing, now all stationed around the hearth. He piled more food onto his trencher, feeling the ale go to his head. He ate till he was bursting, talking little to his neighbour. Often he felt Eleanor's eyes reaching out to him but he could not look at her.

Finally sounds of clapping and cheering forced him to study the top table where the Soltety had just been placed. It was a giant elaborate erection of pastry and sugar intricately decorated. It was soon being carried around, and admired by the guests to the clapping and banging of feet and hands.

As the top table played with their final course, a plate of Doucette was brought and placed before Thomas. A sad smile spread across his face and he turned and met her gaze. The memory of the sweetmeats at the fair flooded back. He felt the emotion rise in his chest and quickly raised his pot of ale. She raised her goblet and they drank together.

He staggered through the night back towards the mill. He was one of the first to leave; many would not raise themselves before the morning. The bright midnight moon guided him through the quiet village. He collapsed upon his straw mattress fully clothed.

Thomas woke late to the sound of someone entering. He jumped up, his head thumping and eyes unfocused. In the gloom he slowly recognised a female shape as his pupils constricted. She stood watching him, smiling.

"Eleanor!" He tried in vain to tidy himself up as he scrambled from his bed. "What are you doing here?" He pulled his clothes into shape, then his unruly hair. Then groaned to the thumping in his head and fuzziness he felt.

"I came to see you before you left." They sat down at the table and Thomas poured himself some boiled water from a jug on the table and drank deeply. He then poured some on his hand and splashed it across his face. "Though, you don't look as though you're in a fit state to go anywhere." She laughed at him.

"I talked to a group of traders from Northampton. They leave at noon. I'll be fine by then. I've packed up what little I'm taking."

"Here." She passed a small leather pouch the table. Thomas touched it then let it fall.

"I don't need charity!"

"I cannot see or help your father who was a good man to me but I can through this. The priest Geoffrey said you wanted to study. This would help you besides it's not much. Do not look upon it as charity; it is a gift for you and your father."

He grunted and walked out of the house. She followed, leaving the money on the table.

"I am afraid I will not see you again, Thomas." He looked at her and his anger evaporated. She had a great sadness in her eyes. They glistened with the precursors to tears. He turned away.

"Do not dwell on me, my lady. Take care of yourself; live; search out happiness. You are one of the favoured few. Opportunity is yours for the taking." He turned and forced a smile.

"I am a woman, Thomas." He lost his smile and looked seriously at her.

"If you ever need me, Geoffrey will know where to look." He took her hand and held it. A tear finally broke away and trickled slowly down her cheek. "It is time you returned. Your maid over there is beginning to look agitated."

"I left when all slept at the manor." On an impulse he reached up and pulled the star shaped medallion over his head and passed it to her.

"It was my father's. It's not much but it may protect you and perhaps remind you occasionally of me when you are at Court." She took the small medallion of rough bronze. And after a moment's hesitation placed it round her neck. She then quickly kissed him on the lips and before he could respond she ran off up the stream to her maid. He felt the moisture of her tears on his face and slumped down on the bench outside the cottage, his head whirling.

That was where Geoffrey found him.

"It's all happening Geoffrey. I don't know that I have the courage to leave."

"Yes there are many memories here." He sat down beside him, "but you have to go; you know it in your heart Thomas." He handed Thomas a letter. "Give this to my colleague at St John's when you get there. His name is Robert. I don't know what help he can be but I am certain he won't turn you away." He patted him on the shoulder. "Saint Peter's Burch first?"

"I don't know. First my father then," he shrugged. "I have a box. Will you look after it for me? It holds my parents and my own possessions. There is little there but I would rather it did not go to my brother."

"Yes, not a problem." He rubbed his hands together and laughed. "That'll annoy him." Thomas nodded smiling. "Come on then, gather your stuff. We will go via the church and drop it off. Then we can have one last drink before you leave up at Margery's."

Thomas went inside and picked up his bag, pushed his dagger into his belt and tied his gypciere to it, a small leather pouch, in which after a moment's hesitation he added Eleanor's money purse from the table.

"Is this the box?" Thomas nodded at Geoffrey, who grabbed one end. Thomas picked up the other and they carried it out.

"Just one more look around then I'll be with you." Thomas walked back in. He knew every corner of the room. Memories flooded in, his mother shouting at him and laughing; his father sitting by the fire; Nicholas. He sighed and with a last glance tuned picked up his quarterstaff and left.

Walking round the yard he went into the mill and had a last word with Alfred whose face was creased with worry. He patted Elias on the head and told him to look after Alfred, then re-joined Geoffrey.

They spoke little as they trudged up to the church carrying the box. Quickly and quietly they continued on to Margery's.

"Here this one is on me," she said, handing Thomas a large pot of ale. Geoffrey looked on amazed. He had never seen her give away her ale before. She handed Geoffrey a pot. "That doesn't apply to you priest!" she said looking at him gruffly. He handed her a coin. She turned and winked at Thomas as she went inside, a smile on her face.

They sat and watched the last few traders pack away their stalls and tents. Eventually at just before noon the trader, with whom he was to travel, wandered over, leading some donkeys.

"You ready!" He called as he approached.

"Come, break some bread with us sir and have some ale to set you on your way," replied Geoffrey. The trader hesitated for a moment then shrugged and nodded. He was soon settled and they all lunched on Margery's pottage.

A crowd of villagers began to gather. Thomas walked round saying his goodbyes to the people he had known all his life. After a short while the trader, becoming concerned about the time, took his arm and led him away. With much handshaking and backslapping he walked out onto the green.

He felt as though he was dreaming, faces came into view then faded to be replaced by others; finally Geoffrey came and hugged him.

"Go with God," he said. Eventually, following the trader's mules he headed up the Northampton road. He stopped to look back and wave. As he stood there, hand in the air he noticed two figures slightly apart on the inner bailey wall. He saw Eleanor lift her hand. The other figure did not move. Thomas recognised his brother. He turned back and looked up at the road, a dusty trail that led up through the heath. He did not look back again.

Chapter 5

Autumn 1263

The journey to Northampton had been slow and arduous in the oppressive heat. The dust rose up from the baked rutted track. It was not a main highway and was little cared for. As they approached the small village of Duston, Thomas made out Northampton a few miles off. He felt sticky with sweat. The evening air was heavy, the sky slowly filling with towering cumulus clouds, God's anvils. The weather was going to break; the dry spell had lasted much longer than usual. In some ways the rain would be a welcome relief but it also signalled the onset of autumn and winter. He reminded himself that the harvests had been good so no one would go hungry this year. He remembered the tight empty cold feeling of winters past when harvests had been poor.

Good harvests mean more time for politicking and on that front, Thomas was sure the storm clouds were gathering. The king and his brother-in-law Simon de Montfort were at loggerheads. Thomas was sure that soon not only the rich would be involved in this dispute.

"Come on, let's get into the town before they close the gates," said his travelling companion. The cloth merchant stood up and got his two donkeys on the move. He was keen to get back home. "It's going to rain soon too." Thomas nodded and picked up his quarterstaff and bags, then took up his position behind the donkeys as they slowly trudged the last mile.

As they grew closer Thomas's gaze became fixed on the growing panorama of the castle, a russet coloured building of enormous proportions, the like of which he had never seen before. It stood upon a hill surrounded by great battlements, the outer bailey walls running down to the marshes and stream that flowed into a great river off to their right. The trader had said it was called the River Nene. A series of bridges took them up to the West Gate.

Their passage through the gate was watched lazily by some men-at-arms who leaned on their pikes resigned to waiting for sundown before they could close up and head back to the castle. As they entered the town the first spot of rain splattered the dry earthen road.

"My home is at the Drapery. It's in the centre. You'll find cheap lodging there for the night. Come on."

Thomas nodded as he pulled on his liliripe and cloak to keep out the rain, now heavy. They walked up through the streets, the like of which kept Thomas amazed; rows of stone and wooden dwellings lined each side, people ran purposefully about trying to dodge the rain and growing puddles and rivulets. The smell of waste filled his nostrils.

"The street'll soon be a quagmire," mumbled the trader as they walked side by side up its centre. "Mind, at least it'll wash away the refuse." The trader increased his pace. The streets seemed to go on and on. Thomas wondered at the number of people that must live there; the houses seemed to crowd in on every side.

The street suddenly opened into a square in front of the largest church Thomas had ever seen.

"All Saints," mumbled the trader. "Drapery's this way. You should find some cheap lodgings down Bridge Street, over there. It leads down to Saint John's." Thomas's ears pricked up at the name. The trader pointed down a road that ran off to their right. A river of water and refuse was running through its centre.

"Thank you." Thomas shook hands and the trader turned and led his donkeys away. Thomas wondered at his ability to sell anything as he had hardly spoken a word the whole trip. After a moment's hesitation and in the closing light he carefully picked his way down the street trying hard to keep out of the centre. A rat ran in front of him and he watched it squeeze through a crack in a building wall.

He spotted a rundown looking inn and pushed open the door. The room was full of smoke and noise. It seemed to be crowded with tonsured young men in groups talking loudly, all with pots of ale or wine, some eating noisily. His entrance went unnoticed, for which he was glad. He approached a woman, serving ale, who said she was the innkeeper along with her husband. She showed him upstairs to a long room where the walls were lined with raised wooden flooring on which lay straw mattresses. They agreed a price and then they returned downstairs so that he could get some food.

He squeezed himself onto the end of a table next to a group of the scholars he had noted earlier and waited for his ale and pottage. His neighbour turned and nodded to him in greeting.

"Here to study are you?" he asked. Thomas studied the young man, who was wearing a dirty threadbare tunic. His face and tonsure were covered in stubble, his eyes red rimmed and skin tight and tallow coloured. Thomas decided he looked ill and was suffering from malnutrition. He looked at the young man's eyes, which struggled to stay away from the bowl that the inn keeper had just placed before Thomas. He looked around at the other clerics and noticed how they mostly seemed roughly dressed.

"Maybe, I'm not sure yet. You're all students?" Thomas asked; the scholar nodded.

"We have only just returned after harvest to start our studies again."

"Would you like some?" Thomas once again noticed the boy's watery eyes on his food. He called for a trencher and dolloped some of his pottage onto it. "I'm Thomas."

"Thank you, I'm Edward" The scholar said between mouthfuls, "Named after the Prince." He continued apologetically. "Most people call me Heycock. It's where I'm from." He then fell to eating and had soon eaten pottage and trencher leaving not a crumb on the trestle table.

"Why did you come if not to study?"

"Oh, I probably will study but I don't know if I want to start straight away." Thomas explained that he had lost his job, that was why he had decided to come, and that he had an ill relative to see, who lived nearby. It was enough to quell any further enquires.

"What are your interests then?" said the boy, smacking his lips noisily. "When you do decide to study that is. Now's the time, you know, to try out the different lecturers. Mind you we mostly all do the same. Good old Dividium and Trivium."

"I'm interested in Medicine," said Thomas hesitantly.

"You want to be a physician?"

"Maybe," replied Thomas, wondering at his surprise. "Is it possible to study that here?"

"Let me see." He turned and began to chat to others down the table. Turning back he continued. "Kyftyll down there says Peter the Franciscan often lectures on it. They have a copy of one of Galen's texts apparently."

"Galen?"

"The famous doctor."

Oh," said Thomas bemused but not wanting to show his ignorance. "How do I get to attend these lectures?"

"First you need to go to the Town Hall and report that you're here to study and get your papers. That'll cost you by the way. Then you go along to the lectures you want to and if you like them you keep going and pay the lecturer his tuition fee. Mind you'll probably need to study Dividium and Trivium, as well as any medical lectures, if you want to obtain a degree."

"Mm," Thomas drank. Geoffrey had told him about these. He enjoyed some of them especially the maths, astronomy and logic but he could not see how they would help him. He did know that the study of the stars was an important aspect of medicine. Some of the other subjects he was sure he did not want to study such as music and rhetoric. Still he did not have to decide just yet. He suddenly felt very tired. It had been a long day. He excused himself and retired.

The next morning as was his usual custom he rose early and breakfasted alone.

"Students stay up late and rise late," The landlady had said, shrugging. "As long as they pay up I don't care." She directed him towards Saint Leonard's with a quizzical look.

Stepping out of the inn he continued down Bridge Street, stopping momentarily in front of Saint John's Hospital. He thought of the note of introduction he carried.

He felt very unsure of what he should do and as he continued he hoped that his father would give him some idea of which direction he should go.

Walking out of the South Gate he followed the large muddy road through the suburbs finally coming to a bridge, which crossed a large slow flowing river. He surmised that this must be the Nene that the merchant had mentioned the previous day. From there he was directed off to his right where he could see a gathering of buildings surrounded by fields with a small church at it centre. A wicker fence surrounded the whole community. Coming to a large wooden gate he pulled a rope attached to a small bell and heard a shuffling of feet. A hatch in the gate opened.

"Yes," came a gruff voice.

"I would like to talk to the priest in charge." The gate swung open and he was soon sitting inside the cool church waiting for the gatekeeper to fetch the priest. The man had been well covered but Thomas stomach had still not settled at the glimpse he had caught of his distorted face. What if his father now looked so! He found it hard to sit still. At the sound of footsteps he turned to be greeted by a young priest tonsured with a thin grey face.

"Hello how can I help?" he smiled. "We don't get too many visitors willing to enter the compound!"

"I would like to see my father," Thomas replied hesitantly, standing up he continued. "His name is Walter the Miller. He came from a village called Buckbie."

"Ah, Walter yes. You do understand though, that it is the church's recognised policy that family should remember those with leprosy as they remember those loved ones that they have lost in death." He said it as though recounting a speech in which he did not totally believe.

"I know this but if we had the opportunity to see the loved ones that we have lost would we not give thanks to God for the chance." The priest smiled.

"The people who live behind these walls are very much alive."

"How is my father?" Thomas' stomach churned as he waited for the reply.

"There has been no change in his condition since he arrived. He says it's the water." The priest smiled at Thomas who looked at him bemused. "He drinks daily from the waters of Saint Thomas' well," he said in explanation. Now Thomas smiled back. The priest continued. "He spends most of his time down at our small mill by the river." Thomas made to leave but the priest raised a hand. "If you will wait here I will fetch him for you. Our residents are not used to visitors walking round. I hope you understand." He nodded and as the priest left he sat down and studied the wall paintings, deeds of saints, depictions of hell. The usual, thought Thomas. Then his eye caught a depiction on the wall behind the altar, a crudely drawn representation of a leper over which were some Latin words. He translated them as he read out loud. "Christ's special sufferers."

"We don't usually feel that special." Thomas turned quickly recognising his father's voice. He ran over to him and held his arms. "Hello Thomas, I wondered how long it would take. You should not have come but I am very glad to see you!"

Thomas studied his father who still looked gaunt and pale, untouched by the summer sun.

"The priest says you are no worse."

"No, still just the hand." Walter held up his hand showing the stubs of his missing fingers, pink in the hazy window light. "Let's sit, I want to hear all your news. How is Nicholas?" Thomas frowned his eyebrows came closer together. He sat and told his story from the moment Walter had left three months earlier.

"His Norman blood is strong. I am not surprised Thomas. I always thought his true father would have plans for him, especially when he did not have a legitimate son. Sir John was always angry that his father had given me the milling rights." Thomas stood up.

"Why? Why did he father?"

"It was part of your mother's dowry. You see she was already pregnant. Sir John's father wanted her married and with a good income." Thomas nodded surmising as much. They sat silently for a while. Then Walter continued. "I am certainly interested in your news of De Montfort, our Constable, Ralph Bassett and the others gathered together at the wedding. I reckon the Earl of Leicester is desperately trying to hold his co-conspirators together. If King Henry gets the chance he will certainly try to oust him. Do we have revolution and civil war in the offing? Take care Thomas. I am safe in here." He smiled sadly. "But Northampton is a hot bed." He stopped and took a deep breath.

"What do you think father; who should we be supporting?"

"De Montfort is right in many ways I suppose, but Henry is our king. I am not one to back treason Thomas. If you have to choose be careful. There will be no quarter for the losers." They sat reflecting on their discussion. "Enough of that though. What are your intentions? Do you intend to stay for a while in Northampton?"

"I don't know. I thought I might go to Saint Peters Burch first. I do want to study though, so I would come back afterwards."

"That sounds pretty good but beware of the students Thomas. They are all for De Montfort at the University and they're pretty hot-headed."

After a moment Walter stood up and walked towards the door. "Come, I will walk with you to the gate. Return again after your pilgrimage. I would love to hear of Saint Peters Burch and Saint Thomas's relics." They walked in silence to the gate, both in companionable contemplation. On an impulse Thomas grabbed his father in an embrace. As his father pulled away he remembered their last embrace in the Buckbie church.

"Take some of Saint Thomas's water. It has worked well for me so far. But some blessed over the sacred relics..." He paused and gave Thomas a wistful look "Well, you never know." Smiling at his son he pushed him through the gate. "On your way then, don't you worry about me. You can see that I am fine. You take care; I hear the roads are unsafe at present with all this political uncertainty."

Thomas returned to the inn, had some pottage and ale, then he walked into the centre of the town and purchased a small flask for his father's water, at a stall by the pillory in the huge market square by the All Saints Church.

He decided not to enter, feeling an urge to go straight to Beckets Well. The stall owner had pointed him in the right direction and he walked off down Swine Well Street and headed out through the Dern Gate and for the second time that day passed out of the town.

Off to his right a large meadow of windblown grass swept down to the river. Animals grazed contentedly in the afternoon, flicking their tails against the many flies that buzzed in swarms across the swards. An occasional bright flicker marked the passing of a butterfly flitting between the last of the seasons flowers, which littered the ground. Summer was breathing its last breath. Thomas shivered as the new coolness of the air touched him

Ahead he spotted a sandstone building. There were a few people about, entering or leaving the building. A man was coming in and out with a bucket and filling barrels strapped to the side of a donkey. Thomas noticed that a lot of the people going in and out of the building were invalids or looked unhealthy, thin or coughing badly, pale or sweaty with fever. He tried to stay clear of them as he entered.

Inside he found before him a pool of crystal clear water rippling out from its centre as it rose from the earth. He knelt at its edge, dipping his finger in and genuflected. Using a small copper cup on a chain he drank, feeling the cool water trickle down into his throat. He shuddered with emotion, sure of God's presence. Closing his eyes he had a vision of the Bishop approaching the small spring in the dead of night with his companions, rain pouring down and thunder cracking in the heavens above, climbing wearily from his horse and drinking from the spring before heading off towards the coast and sanctuary in France.

Carefully he filled the flask that he had brought with him.

Chapter 6

The next morning Thomas was up early and on the road to Peterborough. The previous night he had met up with Heycock and told him of his plans. The sky was overcast with a prospect of more rain on the way but Thomas walked with a spring in his step feeling fresh and alive; rejuvenated by the visit to his father and the thought of Peterborough. His only concern was that he was now alone but he knew that he did not look like much of a target for any thieves that wandered this road. Even so he gripped his staff tightly and studied the terrain ahead carefully. Strip fields bordered the rough road with only the occasional oak along its route.

He stopped for some food at a small village by the name of Ecton where he enjoyed the hospitalities of an inn by the side of the road. Having enjoyed an extra pot of ale, it was late afternoon when he finally set off again. He walked fast, head down. It was not long before he felt the road slope downwards; he began to feel nervous at the sudden appearance of undergrowth on both sides of the road. In his determination to get on he had walked right into a wood. Either side of him were birch, willow and oak trees. The more steps he took the denser it seemed to become. It began to rain gently; the sky had darkened. He held his staff tightly with two hands ready for the rush of an assailant. Slowly he made his way down, deeper into the wood. The road dropped gently and he could hear water rushing ahead. Soon he was able to make out a small stone bridge.

Hearing a faint noise he stopped and listened. It was the sound of approaching horses and a wagon. A movement caught his eye. He saw a man come out from beside the bridge. His heart began to race. He dared not move. Suddenly there were four of them; two each side, hidden behind the stonework of the bridge. They were looking intently up the road and had not noticed him behind them. He recognised their ill intent. The horses were getting closer as was the slow trundle of the wagons wheels.

Quietly Thomas slipped into the woods and dropped his bags amongst the roots of a willow. Holding his quarterstaff, he silently made his way down through the trees to a point ten yards from the bridge. During his approach he had not dared look ahead. He rested for a moment; his back up against a tree, forcing himself to breathe deeply and relax he slowly regained control of his racing heart. Then he looked cautiously around the edge of the tree.

The wagon was in fact a carriage. They had picked their victims well, he decided. In front of the carriage was a horseman and another rode behind. They came slowly onto the bridge. He held his breathe. What should he do? His indecision lasted a moment too long.

Suddenly the man nearest him stepped out onto the road and let fly a well-aimed arrow. The horseman was hit squarely in the chest and fell backwards from his horse. Thomas felt frozen to the spot. He tried to call out but no sound came. The horseman at the rear had also fallen. Both lay motionless and he was certain they were dead. He was used to death from malnutrition and disease but this was different, so instant. He felt stunned, unable to move as he watched the drama unfold.

He heard a scream and saw the bowman pull the carriage driver from his seat and beat him with a club; another man joined him. The dull thuds echoed in the woods. A woman was wrenched from the back of the carriage. She wailed shrilly, birds in the trees above Thomas took flight with a beating of wings, then silence. The man holding her had punched her in the face knocking her momentarily senseless. He then dragged her off the road into the woods.

The fourth man climbed into the carriage. It seemed to rock crazily on its axles then to Thomas's surprise the man fell out of the carriage. He watched as a woman leaped out and over the edge of the small bridge. A deep pool below the bridge broke her fall. He heard the men laughing at their companion, as he picked himself up and jumped off the bridge after her. She had pulled herself along the stream to the shallows and now waded along it, her wet dress clinging to her body and hair sticking across her face. He listened to the jeers and laughter as the men stood along the parapet urging on their companion as if it were a sport. Thomas began to feel anger rise within him at the sound of the laughter, which seemed to go on and on echoing through the trees. His hand felt sticky on his staff. The girl rounded a corner followed closely by her assailant and he lost sight of them.

This time he did not stop to think but jumped up and ran quickly through the trees, dodging outstretched branches and jumping roots, his hands clutching his quarterstaff. Suddenly she was in view thrashing in the water as her attacker pushed her under. Then laughing callously he pulled her to the bank and began wrenching at her clothes. Thomas broke into a run and leapt the stream, landing, staff in hand, by the writhing pair. The brigand looked up startled; the girl's screams stopped abruptly. For a moment they were held as if bound by an invisible web; but Thomas, who had the upper hand, moved first. Years of training with the quarterstaff now meant that his body began to move with fluid automation. He spun the staff and brought it round in a wide arc. The haft crashed into the bridge of the man's nose. He saw his head fly back and blood spurt, fountain-like, into the air, droplets crashing into the grassy bank and staining the stream for one small instant. Even as the man staggered to his knees in the water, Thomas brought the staff down once more upon his head, this time to the sound of a bone-crunching crack. The staff shook, numbing his hands. The brigand dropped like a dead weight into the water face down and floated slowly down the stream in a growing pool of blood.

Thomas watched fascinated, unable to tear his eyes away, not able to comprehend what he had just done. There was a sound of shouting from behind, upstream. The girl had got to her feet. She was soaked through. Her dress clung tightly to her young body. He tore his gaze away from her shapely curves and studied her face. Her green eyes were wide, her pupils deep with fear, her skin pale. Her long copper-brown hair was matted and wild. He thought she looked like a frightened woodland fairy. She was shivering uncontrollably. The shouting was growing louder. She turned her head and looked upstream towards the bridge so suddenly that her wet hair caught him across the cheek. It was enough to snap him out of his own shock.

"Come on!" He turned towards her and grabbed her hand. They ran up into the woods, scrambling quickly into a thicket of bracken, where they dropped down low and lay still, side-by-side. Thomas felt around them and pulled some loose ferns and leaves across their prostrate bodies. They lay silent but for the rushing of air into their starved lungs and the beating of their hearts, which they tried to quell, thinking that surely it was loud enough to hear a mile away.

They listened to the shouts from the stream below and the crashing of feet through the woodland, coming closer. Their fear grew. Thomas felt sweat running down his nose and buried his face into the earth, smelling the rich woodland soil. They heard the sound of a stick being swung at the bracken. Thomas gripped the girl's hand tightly and in his other he held his staff. He stiffened his body ready to jump and attack or run.

Suddenly the heavens opened. Rain began to crash down through the trees. They heard a man close by curse and turn away, heading back down to the river. He felt her body shake with silent sobs and quietly placed his arm around her, pulling her closer.

It was an hour before they dared to move. The woods had fallen silent apart from the patter of the large raindrops falling from the trees. Both of them were now soaked through by the steady rain and beginning to shiver from the cold. Thomas carefully stood and looked around. In silence hand in hand they crept to the bridge. Through the trees they could see no sign of the carriage, horses or the bodies.

Thomas decided that the road was still not safe, so they made their way through the trees back up the hill, the way he had come an hour before. The girl followed obediently, not saying a word.

Thomas retrieved his bag and cloak, wrapping it carefully around the girl's shoulders. Then led her out of the wood and cautiously down onto the muddy road. It was raining hard now but they could not stop to find shelter, both preferring to walk on as fast as they could towards the small village of Ecton, where Thomas, only a few hours before had stopped to eat. They still had not spoken, neither wanting to break the protection of their quiet companionship. Words would mean thinking of what had happened and before they could face that they needed security.

Finally they arrived at the small gathering of cottages and entered the little inn, where the landlady looked up in surprise. Muttering like a mother hen she quickly took the girl's arm and led her to the fire. She did not ask any questions but bustled off to get some warmed wine and bread and cheese.

"I have no money." The girl said looking miserably up at him through her tangled hair. He smiled at her comment, so unrelated to the terrible things that had happened.

"Don't worry. I'll take care of it." Thomas took a sip of wine. It was warm and spiced. He savoured the feeling as it coursed through his body. "I'm Thomas by the way." He bowed his head toward her. She looked up; the hint of a smile touched her lips.

"I have a lot to thank you for Thomas. I know my fate if you had not happened by." She paused. "My name is Matilda." She rested her head in her hands. "What are we going to do now?"

"It is five miles to Northampton. We could continue there but the weather is awful and it is getting late." He stopped then as an afterthought. "That was where you were heading?" she nodded.

"I live there, yes, with my husband." The words did not come with longing. "I am exhausted Thomas."

"You could stay here. The accommodation is spartan but it is clean. What has happened needs reporting to the sheriff at the castle. I could walk on." He did not want to, but he knew he must. If the incident was not reported he could be in trouble, and somebody must contact the girl's family."

"You are a good man. No one should go out in that." She looked towards the door; the rain was drumming against the building. "My father-in-law will be concerned," and as an afterthought, "so will my husband, I suppose." After a moment's hesitation Thomas spoke.

"I will go then my lady. Will you be all right here though? For I would think you must stay on your own for tonight." He looked at her young round pale face. She appeared frightened but determined.

"Yes, I should be safe here. Thank you." She looked around as if taking her surroundings in for the first time.

"I will talk to the landlady." Thomas went through a door to the rear of the building where in another room he found the woman busy by a fire. A man stood by the rear entrance. They fell silent as he entered.

"I am going to return to the town. Can you put up the lady and care for her. She has powerful connections in the town." He watched them fidget nervously. "I'm sure you will be well rewarded." The man shifted from the doorpost where he had been leaning and kicked at the floor.

"What if those villains should return this way? You saw them didn't you?" He looked up accusingly but Thomas saw the fear hidden behind his hard worn features. "They might come back."

"I think not. Anyway there are enough of you here to protect her. My lady's friends are sure to reward you for your help; but if you are not prepared to do so…" he looked menacingly at the disgruntled Tavernier. "Well let's just say you might prefer taking on the villains." The man would not hold eye contact and looked at the ground, shuffling his feet. "I take it you'll look after her then." He said sarcastically. "Here is the payment for our food and a little extra for your good will! I will leave now." Returning to the front room he tried to calm the anger that had risen within him. The landlady followed him and took his arm.

"Pardon my husband, he does not mean to anger you." She looked fearfully up at him. "We have a small solar." She pointed to a stairway. "She can use that room. I will take her up. The villagers will soon be arriving." She bustled past him to where Matilda lay with her head on her arms. He too felt tired but he dared not sit down now that he knew he must return to Northampton. He gently touched her shoulder. She lifted her head and stared at him vaguely through bleary eyes. The heavy spiced wine was taking affect.

"I am going to leave now." She nodded back at him. "Where must I go in Northampton, lady?" he said realising he had no clue what he should do.

"My husband is Master Gobion's son." Thomas heard the innkeeper's wife's sharp intake of breath. Her fussing around Matilda became more intense. Thomas realised that his hunch about the power of her family was truer than he had thought.

"Where will I find him?"

"You are obviously not from Northampton;" said the innkeeper's wife looking up. He shook his head. Matilda looked at him searchingly, and wondered where this stranger, that had saved her, had appeared from.

"You had better hurry if you are to get there before they close the gates. The guards will tell you the way," continued the woman not allowing Matilda to answer. She helped her to her feet and walked with her slowly to the stairway. He watched them slowly climb the stair then turned and headed out of the door, snatching up a piece of bread left on the table as he went. He picked up his staff and asked the innkeeper who stood watching him to look after his bags. Then he stepped out into the rainy afternoon.

The road was muddy and running with rich brown water. The land appeared awash. The grey sky swamped the daylight making the afternoon appear like dusk. Slipping and sliding he stepped out as fast as he could, leaning forward on his staff, his cloak wrapped tightly around him, his liliripe pulled down and twisted tightly about his neck. The rain lashed down on him remorselessly.

Mud-ridden and leaning heavily on his staff he reached the gate three hours later. Darkness now closed in upon him. His muscles ached, his body felt raw and tender from the movement of his wet woollen clothes.

The guards stood in the gatehouse eying him uneasily, hands resting on their sword hilts. One side of the gate was already closed and he had seen they were about to close the other when they had noticed his approach.

"What business brings you out in this?" called one of the men.

"I come with news for the master of the house of Gobion." He saw them relax slightly. "How do I find him?" Thomas pulled himself into the shelter of the gates archway and leaned against the cold damp of the sandstone wall.

"You alright?" fear of disease once again put them on their guard. They stepped back. "You look pale and ill."

"It's just tiredness. I have come a long way today. You would look rough if you had gone as far! My message is urgent. Which way must I go?" impatience showing in his voice.

"Hold your horses we don't have to let you in you know."

"Do you want to have to answer to Master Gobion?" He did not know the man but had not forgotten the effect his name had had on the tavernier's wife. It seemed to have a similar effect on the guard, who muttered under his breath and stood aside. Water dripped from the end of Thomas's nose. He realised he could no longer feel his feet. His calf muscles ached painfully. "Which way?" he almost shouted at the retreating guards.

"Alright! Alright! It's over there. That wall goes round his house. If you walk along Abington Street you'll see the entrance." The guard turned abruptly away and began to close the gate.

Thomas stepped out into the rain. The night closed in around him. He walked fast, not concerned about the mud-ridden puddles that splashed up around him. He quickly arrived at a large gate, closed tight for the evening. After a moment's hesitation he lifted his staff and rapped it against the oak. He listened intently, hearing just the sound of rain, then a curse further up the street that made him turn, tense with staff at the ready. He saw a shadowy figure further along the street picking itself up from the sodden street. Turning back to the door he swung his staff at it with more force and urgency. The sound echoed down the street. Still he was greeted with silence and he began to wonder what he should do. A very bedraggled rat ran over his feet as it negotiated its way along the wall's edge. He cursed and kicked out at it in frustration. It gave a squeal and darted off. He hit out at the door again.

"Alright, alright, I'm coming. It better be important!" A little hatch opened and Thomas let out a sigh of relief. "What is it? What do you want?" A pair of eyes surveyed the bedraggled figure.

"I have news for Master Gobion regarding his wife. I have come a long way. Will you open up?"

"I do not know you Sir;" the face looked concerned. Thomas wondered at his appearance and knew he did not look the picture of trustworthiness. "Wait" The hatch suddenly closed. But the door did not open. The rain lashed down.

He leaned on his staff, the exertions of the day beginning to catch up with him. He had come full circle. His physical and emotional strength had virtually ebbed away. He felt cold and began to shiver uncontrollably. He did not know how long he stood there or when he actually fell. He came to as he was being half carried, half dragged into a large well-lit hall. People bustled round him, took his clothes from him and threw a blanket over him. He was placed in a chair by the large central fire. A drink was put to his lips. It burned right through him and shocked him into a coughing consciousness.

An older man sat in front of him; behind him stood a grey haired woman. They were well dressed, as was the large bug eyed young man who leaned heavily on the back of the chair. He guessed they must be the Gobions.

"You have news of my daughter-in-law sir. Are you in a fit state to communicate it? I can see you have had a hard journey." There was concern in the old face that looked at him. He noticed it was not mirrored in the others. Slowly Thomas's shivering faded and he gained control of his vocal chords.

"I have come from Ecton, where your daughter-in-law is staying the night." He went on to explain the day's events. They listened quietly when he fell silent the older man stood up.

"You have done very well and we are indebted to you. I will send some men out directly. We shall follow in the morning." He looked up at the man behind him.

"Oh father!" he replied looking annoyed.

"She is your wife!" the older man retorted angrily. He turned back to Thomas. "Eat and rest; I will see you in the morning, when hopefully you will be able to ride out with us." With that they all left via a door at one end of the hall, which led into their private solar. The servants soon came with food and a mattress. Thomas quickly fell into a deep sleep by the crackling fire, wondering over the beautiful young girl's choice of husband.

He woke early to the sounds of screams echoing through a dark cold forest. His eyes snapped open silencing the fear of his nightmare. It was a while before the image of death and the girl being dragged away left him. He sat up; the fire was now embers, which crackled softly, his dried clothes still hanging next to it. The servants were all awake and busy tidying the hall around him. The shutters were pulled open, letting in the full force of the dawn. He shielded his eyes and watched the light splash through the dancing dust that floated in the air. The sight finally destroyed the horrors with which he had woken. He stood and pulled on his clothes. The aches in his body made him slow and awkward.

Heading outside, he looked up at the clear sky; puddles of water filled the courtyard. In a small building on his right he heard voices and saw smoke rising up through the roof. He wandered over and looked into the manor kitchen, to see a couple of men, one busy at a table, the other by the fire. Their chatter stopped the moment his shadow crossed the hearth. They nodded greetings and after he had enquired the whereabouts of the well he headed out again, got a bucket of water and washed himself down. The cool water instantly refreshed him.

He returned to the kitchen, to the amused smiles of the two cooks who had come to the door to watch his water antics. It seemed to have eased their reticence and soon he was sitting in the kitchen eating bread and cheese with a mug of weak ale at his side. The cooks then set off for the Gobion's in the solar with food piled high on trays. Thomas ate in quiet contemplation, then picking up his leather mug of ale he wandered out and sat in the courtyard soaking up the morning sun's rays.

He heard the creak of the large oak entrance gate and turned to see a knight with four men-at-arms, all mounted, ride into the yard. Thomas recognised the knight as the constable of the castle, Ralph Bassett, whom he had last seen at Lucy's wedding. Grooms suddenly emerged from the stables, rubbing sleep out of their eyes and held the horses. The knight dismounted and headed for the hall's entrance. Old Master Gobion himself met him at the door. Thomas could not hear their words but he recognised that they were well acquainted. They disappeared into the hall.

After time enough to share a drink they re-emerged with Gobion's young son. Stopping in the yard the old man looked around, his eyes finally resting on the seated Thomas. He beckoned him over.

"Good morning Thomas, how are you feeling?"

"Better sir, thank you." Master Gobion nodded, accepting the answer, knowing that Thomas would say nothing else.

"This is Ralph Bassett. He is the constable of the castle. I have told him what has happened and he is coming with us. He wants to visit the place of the attack. Can you ride?" he did not wait for a reply. "You will ride my daughter-in-law's palfrey to Ecton for her; then you can continue on your journey to the church of St Peter of Burch." He turned and called at the grooms to bring out his horses. Thomas had ridden very little but had dared not admit his lack of proficiency to the authoritative face of the old man who seemed to exude power.

He soon found himself bobbing uncomfortably through the East Gate on a grey, which thankfully for Thomas, was content to follow the others with little leadership from the rider. The guards at the gate looked nervously at him, recognising the company he now travelled with on this new day. The constable stopped and had a word with them; then they were heading out at a trot along the Wellingborough road.

They were quickly up to Ecton, where Thomas dismounted and rubbed his buttocks, glad to be off the beast. A crowd of villagers soon gathered around the inn. They entered to find Matilda sitting at a table waiting for them. She smiled but Thomas was sure he noted a touch of fear in her eyes. He had seen fear there before and knew its look.

"I'm glad to see you well," greeted old Gobion, once again taking the lead. Her husband nodded grumpily at her then sat his large bulk on a bench and called for ale. Old master Gobion and the constable sat opposite Matilda. "We have heard from the man, Thomas. They all turned their gazes towards him and he cringed inwardly under their combined stare. "Is what he has told us correct?" They had now turned their attention back to Matilda and he saw her colour and wring her hands. Her eyes flickered up towards him looking for reassurance. At that moment she looked so weak and alone. He felt he wanted to hug her and tell her it was all right. That it was only a dream. His eyes caught a movement from her husband and he suddenly realised that her nightmare had not come to an end.

"I think he has probably told it accurately." She once again glanced up at him. Her look reached right into him. "But perhaps what he has not said is that he saved my life at great risk to himself."

"I had guessed as much." This time the old man eyes turned on him and fixed him with an appraising stare. Behind his shaggy white beard his mouth twitched in a slight smile. "Perhaps you had better tell us what you saw happen Matilda; Just in case Master Thomas has missed something else." He turned to the landlady. "Food and ale for us and take some to the men outside." The woman bobbed and shot off.

Thomas sipped his ale and listened to Matilda as she told her story. The constable asked her some questions and also turned to Thomas with a few queries.

"I think as a witness you must return to Northampton. We will need you for the identification of these criminals when they are apprehended." Thomas opened his mouth in protest but knew that such would be hopeless. He nodded glumly towards the constable. Suddenly Matilda spoke up.

"Thomas is on pilgrimage to Saint Peters Burch. I think that we should not interfere with a journey set by

God." The constable turned towards her momentarily confused. He was not used to his commands being queried. Before he could reply Matilda continued, "I can identify them as well as anyone. Surely constable you do not intend to hold this man from his holy journey? I believe his intention is to return to Northampton afterwards. Is that not right Master Thomas?" She turned to him and he nodded, then she turned to the constable and gave him an appealing look. "I owe him my life. I do not wish to be responsible for him not fulfilling his pilgrimage." The constable hesitated and stroked his sharp chin with his hand in thought.

"Thomas Millerson, you are to return to Northampton and report to the castle in thirty days or earlier if you return before that date." He suddenly turned his piercing authoritative face towards Thomas. He appeared like a hawk circling prey. Thomas nodded, his heart lifted. He could not wait to leave this place and these people of power. The constable stood up, still watching him "First you will take me to the scene." He turned to Matilda. "He will ride your horse my lady, if that is alright with you. We will then return with the horse to escort you home and then this man may continue on his way." Matilda nodded her consent to the constable's plan. The constable also turned to Master Gobion; he too, consented.

"I need a rest before I return, so go find your clues Ralph." He turned to Thomas and beckoned him over. "Here this is for your trouble. If I can be of further service you know where I live." He gave him a small leather purse.

"I also thank you and will not forget what you have done." He looked around at the Matilda's pale round face and nodded his thanks, picked up his bags and headed out.

Once outside the door he took a deep breath of morning air, glad to be out of the tension-filled room.

One of the men-at-arms passed him the horse's bridle and he groaned not wanting to return his aching rear to the saddle. He bobbed out of the village in the company of the soldiers and the constable.

The sky was bright and clear, a contrast to the previous day. They trotted into the woodland and down to the brook. Images shot through his head and he searched the trees, his body tense, waiting for the first arrow to strike. They reached the small bridge bathed in sunlight and dismounted. The soldiers fanned out and headed off into the trees looking for clues. Thomas pointed out to the constable where each incident had happened. He stared down the stream seeing the running Matilda, hearing the screams and shouts of laughter. He shivered and clutched at his staff with clammy hands.

A call from the woods made him start. He felt his heart beating faster. He held his staff in readiness.

"Come on," called the constable. They headed round the edge of the bridge and walked a little way into the wood. Thomas noted that they followed a trail of flattened grass and ferns. They came up to the white faced guard and looked down at his discovery.

The naked bodies of three men and a woman lay tangled together. Their skin a mottled purple, and hair sodden from the previous night's rain. The guard prodded them with his pike then bent down and pulled one of the men over. His rigid body turned as one. His swollen blue face contorted in a hideous grin. A black slug sat on his eyelid. Thomas turned away having seen enough. He felt his stomach contracting and bile in his throat. He walked quickly back to the road and sat down. Closing his eyes he rested his head on his knees. He searched his thoughts, finally grasping at an image of Eleanor, which he tried hard to create in an effort to banish the picture of the dead, which still seemed imprinted on his retina. He heard footsteps.

"Here," the constable approached him and handed him a wine skin. He drank deeply. "The dead are never pretty." He turned and walked towards the bridge and one of his men. Suddenly stopping he looked back at Thomas. "Leave when you wish. We will stay here and search the area some more. Mind you return in thirty days." Turning back he shouted to the soldier on the bridge, "Ride back to Ecton. We need a cart for the dead. Take the Lady Gobion's pony with you and escort them back to town." The man nodded and scuttled off.

Thomas got up, picked up his bags, which were leaning against the bridge parapet, and without a word or look back made his way unsteadily up the road. When it finally left the wood he stopped and took a deep breath, in an effort to dispel the tension that gripped his body. He felt that he wanted to shout and scream. He began to run. He ran on and on and did not stop until his legs gave way. Throwing himself down on the grass verge he sobbed as the reality of the last day and a half broke over him like a wave. His fist hit the ground and tore up sods of earth and grass. Finally spent, the emotion ebbed away and he rolled over and looked up at the blue sky dotted with great cotton wool cumuli. He determined to enter the next church he saw and pray for the souls of the four dead. His chance came that evening when he arrived at the small town of Wellingborough.

Chapter 7

Three days later Thomas entered Peterborough. He found himself in a large square. It was busy with stalls and hawkers. Townsfolk and pilgrims bustled about. Houses, many of which were inns, surrounded the square. In front of him at the end of the square stood the gatehouse, towering up behind which Thomas could see the three great arches of the abbey portico and the huge pyramid capped central tower.

Thomas stopped, unable to move. His heart pounded as he attempted to take in the breath-taking view before him. Never before had he seen such a sight. In his wildest dreams he had never imagined a building of such dimensions. It reached skyward allowing the essence of heaven to flow in, a house surely majestic enough for God. Mesmerised he walked across the square and under the arched gatehouse stopping again as the whole west front of the abbey was before him. The figures of the saints peered down from the great arches. He knelt in the earth before the great stone edifice and crossed himself, humbled by the immensity of this construction.

"It is a thing of wonder is it not? It never ceases to amaze me." Thomas looked up to see a monk holding a bucket looking at him. "I'm sorry I disturbed you. It's just that people round here just take it for granted. It's nice to see someone as awe inspired as I always feel when I look up at it. When I first saw it, like you, on a pilgrimage, I knew I could never leave." Thomas got to his feet, still looking up at the carved figures in the gables. "That's Saint Peter." The monk pointed to the apex of the central gable "and that's Saint Paul and the other is Saint Andrew." Thomas's gaze was eventually drawn away from the church to the monks smiling face. "I was a builder," he was saying. "How could I ever leave such a beautiful building? Now I am a lay brother. Stephen is my name."

"Thomas of Buckbie."

"Have you travelled far, Thomas?"

"Not too far. Buckbie is the other side of Northampton." The monk nodded sagely. To Thomas home certainly felt a long way off even if geographically it was not. He studied the monk in his simple brown robe and sandals. His hair was cut away neatly to reveal his tonsure. His face was well tanned and craggy from a life spent out of doors. His forehead deeply lined. He had a strong jaw. He had a large powerful frame. Stephen was a man used to hard work but Thomas noticed a certain depth in his gaze.

"Well I must be off. If there is anything I can do for you?"

He looked intently at Thomas, who hesitated, finally saying, "I have some water from the well of Saint Thomas in Northampton. It's for my ill father."

Stephen thought for a moment. "Yes, I know the one. Saint Thomas is supposed to have drunk there on his escaping from Northampton after his trial." Thomas nodded.

"I was hoping to have it blessed or touched by the relics of the Blessed Saint..." Thomas now fell silent unable to continue, not sure quite what he had intended for the water and certain that as a humble commoner he would be allowed little. The monk smiled at him.

"I may be able to help you there. I must go now, but meet me here tomorrow after Nones." He touched Thomas's arm, then walked off. Thomas watched him go and began to wonder why the monk Stephen had really picked him out of the milling crowd in front of the abbey. It could not just have been because he had knelt. He felt certain that the place was truly holy and God had played a part.

The abbey bell began to chime, waking Thomas from his reverie. The sun was setting and Thomas realised this must be for the service of Compline. Geoffrey had taught him about the eight services that monks in particular would follow assiduously. He felt too dirty and dishevelled to enter such a holy site and decided to look for a bed for the night. Rest and food were a priority. Then he would visit the church in the morning for the service of Prime.

The next morning he rose at dawn and washed himself thoroughly in the back yard of the small inn on the square that he had chosen for the night. This was much to the amusement of the innkeeper and her children, who danced around him as he stripped naked and splashed water from a bucket over himself then shaved his face with his knife. He felt refreshed and cleansed.

He had prayed for the souls of the four dead and the thief, whom he was sure he had killed, in a small church in Wellingborough but he still had the dirt of that day on his body and in his clothes. He dressed himself in a fresh tunic and hose, then headed out towards the gatehouse, followed a short way by the giggling children. They stopped at the gatehouse and he went on alone, once again enthralled by the rising portico that grew higher as he approached its entrance in the central arch.

He joined a small group of pilgrims and towns people who were entering for the service through the large oaken doors. Thomas found himself inside a vast cavern.

Staring upwards he saw a highly coloured wooden ceiling, animals and figures seemed to dance in the candlelight surrounded by bright golden triangles.

He stood still allowing the others to walk around or push past him. Great circular arches, piled upon each other, shot up along either side of the nave. He saw light from the rising sun shine through huge coloured glazed windows, sprinkling the altar with rays of rainbow light.

The monks entered and were taking up their positions. Thomas walked up the nave and listened to a monk intoning Latin prayers at the altar.

"'Tis Abbot Robert." He heard a local tell a pilgrim. "If he's about, he likes to attend Lauds or Prime." Incense rose from the altar, mixing with the smoke from the many candles, making the air rich and heavy with scent. Soon the monks were chanting psalms, which floated through the cavernous chamber, echoing along the arches, so that the sound appeared to be from heaven itself. Thomas and many others dropped to their knees, crossing themselves. Thomas felt ecstatic, as the power of God seemed to rush through him.

At the end of the service, he determined to find the holy relics that were within the abbey. The knowing parishioner pointed him towards the southern transept where already a small queue of pilgrims waited to enter the small chapels there, especially the first, which contained the relics of Saint Oswald.

A monk arrived and silently opened a wooden gate that guarded the chapel entrance. He then went up a short stair to a small watchtower. Thomas saw his face over the top looking down at the pilgrims with a bored expression. Thomas entered the tiny chapel. Upon the altar he recognised the shape of a hand and forearm wrapped in a white linen cloth, which was held in place by a golden clasp. When Thomas's turn arrived, he knelt and reverently kissed the shrouded hand, feeling the power of the four hundred year old saintly bones flood through him. He offered up a prayer for his father and for those that had lost their lives at Ecton.

In a further chapel, with fewer visitors, that was dedicated to the virgin saints of Kyneburga, Kynswitha and Tibba he prayed for his mother, for Eleanor and also for Matilda. He knelt, allowing the mysterious presence of God overwhelm him.

The ring of a bell, which signified that the service of Terce was about to begin, eventually disturbed him. Thomas jumped up in amazement. He had been at prayer for a full two hours. He waved an apology to another pilgrim who he had disturbed and went into the nave for the service, after which he left feeling enriched but hungry.

In the square he ate a pie, purchased from one of the many hawkers who made their trade before the abbey. From another stall, he bought a lead pilgrims badge, which depicted the keys of Saint Peter, as a memento of his visit.

Thomas spent the afternoon walking around the town. Visiting the river, he stood on its impressive stone bridge and watched a boat, load up and sail off. He prayed in the small church to the east of the abbey and then, coming full circle, found himself back at the gatehouse as the bell rang out for Nones. Once again he entered the abbey for the service, listening in awed silence. Then he quickly returned to the gatehouse.

As if from nowhere, Stephen appeared at his side, a smile on his weathered face.

"Come," he said after a quick greeting. "Let's visit the Becket Chapel." Stephen led Thomas to a small chapel just outside the gatehouse. It was busy inside. The air heavy with incense and candle fumes. Upon the altar Thomas espied the beautiful reliquary that Geoffrey had mentioned. He was amazed at its meticulous workings of gold inlayed with deep blue and turquoise. Stephen whispered, "It depicts the martyrdom of the Saint." The pilgrims queued, as did Thomas and Stephen. When they got to the altar Thomas saw that the reliquary was open. He looked in, seeing the thin remains of a shirt, two glass phials of blood and a part of a stone flag. Stephen pointed to the bloodstains. They both knelt and kissed the gold figure of Thomas upon the box's outer decoration. Stephen then led Thomas to the side of the chapel and whispered; "Do you have money?" his face was now serious. Thomas studied him warily.

"Why?"

"For the monk in charge." Stephen nodded to a monk standing by the altar watching the pilgrims. "He owes me a favour. But it will cost a sizeable donation to have your water tinctured with the Saint's blood." Thomas gasped. "Nowadays it is usually reserved for high ranking visitors with huge donations."

"I have some money," Thomas said quickly and pulled out the leather bag given to him by Eleanor. Stephen took it and looked inside. He appeared impressed. Thomas knew it was a large sum; enough for him to live well on for a couple of years. But he also knew that Eleanor would be happy for him to use it in this way.

"Your looks hide your wealth. Can you part with so much?" Thomas gulped then nodded nervously. Stephen took the leather bag up to the monk by the altar. After a moment of heated whispered debate he beckoned Thomas over.

"You have the water?" Stephen hissed quietly. Thomas quickly drew the flask from his bag and opened it. The monk studied it for a moment, then he lifted the phial out of the reliquary removed its stopper and added a drop to the flask. Thomas watched the thick dark red blood ooze out of the neck of the flask and fall heavily into the water; a collective sigh went up from the watching pilgrims. Replacing the lid the monk crossed himself, as did Stephen. Thomas quickly followed suit. The monk then muttered a short prayer in Latin nodded to Thomas, replaced the phial in the reliquary and put Thomas's leather pouch in a large iron banded box behind the altar.

Stephen handed Thomas the small bottle.

"Here take a sip before the altar. It will protect you and give you health." Thomas knelt, his hand shaking; the warm liquid trickled down the back of his throat. He felt as though his insides were on fire. Clutching the flask to his chest, he prayed.

Chapter 8

Winter 1263/64

Christmas had passed. His pilgrimage to Peterborough was already just a memory. Thomas massaged his tonsured scalp. Even after four months he had still not got used to it. The tight bristles caught at his fingers. He looked down at his robes. He appeared every bit the student and was enjoying his studies and the new company he kept, though every now and then he yearned for the quiet village he had left, the clank of the millwheel, the timelessness of its turning, an ale at Margery's. He still felt like the miller's son inside and wondered at the conflict of interests that flickered constantly through his thoughts.

For now, he was the student. He sat in a corner of the Austin Friars Hall listening to one of the friars lecturing on rhetoric.

The University at Northampton was in its infancy and was not established around college buildings. Lectures were given by clergy at their respective establishments, or by secular teachers in hired rooms. The students signed on with the lecturers they preferred. To attain the sought-after degree in the arts they must make sure that they studied the Dividium, which consisted of Maths, Geometry, Astronomy and Music and the Trivium, which were Latin, Rhetoric and Logic.

Thomas had wished to study medicine but he had soon discovered that to study medicine alone would be frowned upon and that those who did had already achieved their Arts degree. Even so Thomas spent as much time as he could at the Franciscan Friary where an old friar called

Peter lectured on medicine. He had trained abroad and appeared to Thomas the epitome of the knowledgeable physician. The Franciscans also seemed to possess the largest collection of medical books in Northampton. Thomas had only ever seen bibles before and only ever read from the old battered one at Saint Gregory's church in Buckbie. So he looked upon such collections of knowledge with amazement. Friar Peter would proudly show them the text by Galen called Tegni, Hippocrates' Aphorisms and Regimen Acutarium, and Judaeus's De Febribus. Telling them that these books contained all you needed to know to become an excellent physician.

Thomas had less interest in Rhetoric and soon found his thoughts once again drifting back to his return from Peterborough. He had visited his father who had been ecstatic at the sight of the flask and had carried it with shaking hands to the small church where on bended knees, before the alter, he had sipped some. He now carried the rest in a small phial around his neck.

Thomas had also reported to the castle the day after his return. Nervously entering through the large oak gates, he had walked into the impressive inner bailey. He felt the impregnable power of the huge rust coloured walls that surrounded him. He looked up at the men-at-arms who walked importantly up and down upon the stone parapet.

He soon found himself before a clerk who took his details and then left him. The clerk returned after a short while saying that his presence was not needed at the moment, as the villains had not yet been apprehended, also that he was not to leave town and would be sent for when required. With a contemptuous nod of his head the clerk dismissed him.

He shivered as the winter wind echoed through the building and pulled his black students robes closer around himself. When the lecture finally finished he breathed a sigh of relief and leaving the hall walked the short distance across to St. John's.

Thomas had been returned a while from his pilgrimage, and already attending lecturers, before he had felt confident enough to approach the gatehouse of the Hospital with his letter from Geoffrey.

He had left it, convincing himself that it would be a pointless exercise as he was already enrolled in the university and had enough in his purse from his father and the Gobion family to maintain him for a few years of study. But one day after a visit to his father he had fingered the letter still secure in his pocket and on an impulse, feeling empowered in the fresh autumn sun, had turned into Saint John's.

At the gatehouse he was stopped by a Benedictine lay brother who directed him to a wattle and daub thatched building in the grounds of the hospital. He entered and once his eyes had acclimatised to the smoky gloom he saw an old white haired monk grinding some dried leaves in a pestle and mortar at a trestle table. A small fire burned in a hearth in the centre of the room. The smell of drying herbs took his breath away.

The old monk looked up. "Can I help you?" he enquired, smiling. Thomas gave him the letter from Geoffrey. The monk peered at it carefully moving towards the door to allow the light to hit the parchment. He stood silhouetted.

"Geoffrey…Gosh, I have not heard or seen him in a long time." Thomas watched him carefully. The monk eventually looked up. "He values you it seems and asks me to assist you." He felt the monk's eyes studying him. His gaze seemed to pierce through his outer defences. "I see you are already a student. Geoffrey says you are keen on medicine." Thomas told him that he was attending the lectures of Friar Peter when he was able. The monks faded eyes seemed to light up as they focused upon him. Thomas scratched his head nervously. "Why medicine?" he asked astutely. Thomas told him of the death of his mother and the loss of his father, who was his reason for coming to Northampton, and the leprosy that he so wanted to cure. He fell silent.

After a moment the old monk nodded and came over to him taking his hand. "My name is Robert. Come, let us have some ale. That will give me time to think and allow you time to tell me more about yourself." He mumbled as he led them to two stools by the hearth and then wandered off, coming back with two pots of ale. Handing one to Thomas he sat down with a grunt and quietly listened to Thomas's much edited life story.

"Yes, interesting, interesting," he mumbled. "Geoffrey thought much of you, I think." He scratched the grey hairs upon his chin. "Now let's see. How can I help you?" He looked up but did not expect an answer. Thomas sipped at his ale. The ale was good he thought. "I am the hospital's apothecary, Thomas. Did Geoffrey tell you this?" Thomas shook his head. "I have been looking out for an apprentice, someone to help me with the garden, growing herbs and mixing unctions and electuaries for the patients. Unfortunately the monks are either too highborn or too stupid. Perhaps you would be interested. You could move in here also. That would make things much easier. I don't think the Prior over at St. Andrews would mind." Thomas quickly agreed, excitedly gulping at his ale.

Within a week Thomas was living at the small hospital and working with Brother Robert whenever he was not at a lecture. Robert had given him a corner of the small cottage where he placed a palliasse and a wooden trunk for his belongings. He immediately felt at home and was glad to be away from the confines of the inn with its fetid stink and rats. A herb garden and trees surrounded the cottage. It had a country feel to it, which refreshed Thomas and reminded him of his roots.

With each passing day Thomas's friendship with the old monk grew. He visited the patients, dug the garden, helped prepare the masses of dried herbs and mix medicines and in the quiet of the winter evenings he sat and read. Slowly he worked his way through the hundred and seventy-five recipes for the production of electuaries and other compounds by Nicholas Salerno from his book the Antidotarium, which Robert had cajoled out of the Priory library.

Every now and then he crossed the road and walked up to the inn to sit and discuss the latest theories with Heycock and his friends. At present politics was the main topic as all the students were up in arms at the fact that Louis of France, who was acting as arbitrator between King Henry and the barons, had on the twenty-third of January in the new year of twelve sixty-four pronounced in favour of the King against the Barons.

Thomas would take a back seat and sip at his ale as he listened to the talks of civil war and other treasonous acts. As these discussions had grown more heated and serious he had become alarmed and he began to visit the inn less and less.

On a cold night in late February Thomas sat with Brother Robert before the hearth of their small cottage.

The fire burned with little smoke, for which they were both grateful. In the gloom of the cottage interior the fire was a haven of warmth and escape from the shadows full of unimaginable evils that surrounded them. Thomas shivered, his thoughts turning to the political troubles.

"What do you think will happen, Brother?" Thomas said as he sat contemplating the crackling logs glowing in the heat of the fire. Robert looked up at him disturbed from his own contemplation.

"I don't think the Barons will settle for the decision of an arbitrator who quite frankly is keen to have our king in the pockets of foreign courtiers. They have gone quiet for the moment but as the weather improves…" he fell silent and looked hard at Thomas. "I think there will be civil war before the year is out." He shook his head sadly. "It will mean suffering and anguish; that I do know, and not just for those involved in the fighting. It'll be the poor peasants that suffer in the long run; you mark my words lad. I can remember the debacle of twelve fifteen." He tailed off again and shook his head slipping into his memories. The flame danced and crackled between them. "Tread carefully Thomas. The students are for the Barons and Ralph Bassett is one of De Montfort's henchmen. But if they stand against the king and drag the town into it and the king wins there will be little mercy shown to the common man of Northampton, of that I'm sure."

"But the Barons are right!" Thomas burst out and then after a bit of thought, "aren't they?"

"I must be careful what I say as I'm sure the priory will back the king. We are a Cluniac Priory after all. The prior and many of the monks are French." He looked around and lowered his voice. "The Barons have a good case I guess but is it worth dying for? I would suggest you don't show your hand to soon Thomas. There will come a time when you will have to decide where you stand but leave it as long as you can."

There was a knock at the door which made them both start with surprise. A young lay brother entered.

"Hello Brother Simon. How can we help?" The monk bobbed his head at Brother Robert and stared at Thomas. He looked anxious his eyes bulging. Quickly he blurted out the reason he had disturbed them.

"There are some men Brother Robert, men-at-arms from the castle, two of them. They want to speak to Thomas. They are waiting in the gate house." Robert joined Brother Simon in staring questioningly at Thomas, who shrugged nervously.

"I wonder what they want," he mumbled

"The Gobion incident?" suggested Robert.

"Maybe," Brother Simon began to back towards the door. "I'd best not keep them waiting I suppose." He grabbed his cloak and a liliripe and followed Simon out into the cold February night. The cool fresh air cleared his head, calming his nerves as he made his way across the garden to the gatehouse. He entered the building, which stood by the large gates to find two soldiers warming themselves by a brazier. They turned to face them.

"Thomas the miller's son from Buckbie, now student of the university?" one of the men said questioningly; Thomas nodded. "We are to escort you to the castle." Panic rose in his chest. He felt his heart race.

"Why?" he replied hoarsely his throat suddenly dry.

"The constable, Ralph Bassett wants to speak to you."

"Why?" he said again his voice quivering.

"Who do you think we are, his chief advisors?" said the other soldier, smirking. "Some clerk comes down and says leave your lovely warm barracks and get your arses out in that cold night and get Thomas Millerson. So off we dutifully trots, but we ain't happy Thomas, and we want to get back to our ale and warmth. Whatever you done we ain't got a clue and we doesn't care. So let's just get a move on, hey!" His smirk had faded and the more he reminded himself of the place he had left the more agitated he became. Thomas said no more and nodded, following them quietly out of the gate, one soldier behind and one in front.

They made their way quickly through the quiet town, crunching on the frozen earth of the moonlit streets. Frost glistened on wooden house posts and thatch. They arrived in Chalk Lane; the dark mass of the castle loomed threateningly upwards. Shadows creeping out from its cold walls blanketed with shining crystals. Thomas shuddered as they entered this darkness, coming finally to a small postern gate.

Once inside, they went straight across the outer bailey and into the inner bailey and thence into the main hall. Thomas blinked as he entered the room ablaze with light from braziers around the edges, a big fire in the hearth and sconces in the walls.

The soldiers had stopped at the door and he saw that they expected him to go on alone. He walked hesitantly and slowly across the rush covered floor. Absently he noticed how clean they were compared to those at the manor in Buckbie. At a table at the far end he saw some clerics busy writing. People seemed to be moving around the room purposefully.

He noticed a small group to one side, still amongst the movement. An old man raised his hand in recognition. He smiled with relief and headed across to Master Gobion, who stood with his son and daughter-in-law. She smiled toward him and he bowed. She appeared small and pale next to her obese husband. She turned her gaze nervously toward the big man who grunted and did his best to ignore Thomas. Thomas's heart went out to the lady but he could not stop himself from studying her shapely demeanour in the tight frock.

"I am glad you're well and now a student, I see." The old man's eyes looked him up and down. Thomas nodded, uncomfortable before his gaze and amongst the well-dressed nobles and merchants that seemed to fill the court.

"Was your pilgrimage successful?" He turned to the Matilda, who watched him closely, her face flushed.

"Yes thank you." For a moment they looked intently into each other's eyes.

"They have caught one of the scoundrels," said Master Gobion, his watery eyes looking hard at the two of them. "That's why we've all been rounded up." Thomas was forced to forget the look he had seen and think back to their past meeting on the road to Peterborough.

"Is it always this busy here at this time of the evening?" Thomas said nervously looking around. He had tried to hide what had happened and had all but forced all thought of the incident out of his mind. The pilgrimage had helped and since returning, he had lost himself in his study and the work at the hospital.

It was warm and he had come in from the cold. He felt the sweat trickle down his back and wiped his forehead with his sleeve.

This time, when he looked at Matilda he found himself back on the riverbank. There she lay, her attacker over her. He heard again the thud of his quarterstaff as it hit the man.

"Are you alright?" Her voice was tremulous with concern and he felt her hand touch his arm. The delicate fingers slowly came into focus.

"Oh, yes, I'm sorry; it's the heat in here." He looked at the roaring fire in the centre of the hall.

"You were saying, father." The heavy jowled son scowled at Thomas.

"Yes I was just saying that the young De Montforts have apparently just arrived, Simon and Peter. I believe they weren't expected until tomorrow. Ralph Bassett will have little time for us now, I'm thinking." They stood in silence watching the commotion in the hall. Half an hour passed; Master Gobion stood patiently, obviously used to such waits. His son, who was less patient, paced up and down. Thomas leaned up against the hard cold stone wall and tried to relax.

There was a commotion at the far end of the hall behind the clerics at the table and three men emerged from behind a tapestry screen. Thomas recognised Ralph Bassett and knew the other two were the De Montforts, the Earl of Leicester's sons. He recognised Simon who had attended Lucy's wedding and wondered how advanced their plotting had now become. Northampton was tense and waiting for a sign. A cleric walked over to them from the group and after bowing to Master Gobion asked them to approach the front of the hall. Thomas felt his heart beat faster as he approached.

He watched as the constable took Master Gobion's hand and apologised to him for bringing him out in the night. He introduced his guests who gave them a cursory glance, their eyes lingering on Matilda.

"As you are, I believe aware, we have apprehended one of the trail bastons but we need a witness to confirm that he is indeed one of the guilty party."

Ralph Bassett was looking tired and agitated and was obviously keen to have justice done as quickly as possible. The two brothers had turned away and were talking to some well-dressed noble men.

"As you can see I am very busy, so hopefully all can be settled immediately," he continued in a quieter tone, giving a meaningful glance at his two guests. As soon as Master Gobion had nodded he shouted at a clerk who ran off down the hall and out at the far end.

Almost immediately some men-at-arms dragged in a manacled man. All eyes turned to watch his sad progress across the wooden floor. His feet dragged in the rushes. Ralph Bassett sat down in a large chair behind the table. The prisoner was made to stand before him. His hunted eyes roamed the room, his face gaunt and full of fear.

"Mistress Matilda, is this one of the men?" Ralph Bassett spoke, his voice loud so that all could hear, although his eyes kept wandering to the two brothers who seemed to be ignoring the proceedings.

Thomas looked into the face of the prisoner, knowing that he too would be soon asked the same question. The man's hair was matted with grease and the filth of the dungeon, his face lost in ingrained dirt. The smell emanating from his clothes made Thomas want to gag. Matilda looked unsure and turned to Thomas nervously, then looked back at the constable.

"I think so, but it's hard to tell…." Her voice trailed off.

"Thank you. Thomas Millerson?" He did not look at him but continued to look across the room at the De Montforts.

"I too am unsure Sir. He is unkempt. It may have changed his appearance. It could be... I was not close to all the attackers."

"There is some similarity with the man who dragged away my maid." Matilda's voice shook as she began to remember the scenes by the brook.

"Thomas?" Thomas looked closely trying to remember the scene and the faces.

"Yes, perhaps..." as Thomas looked at the prisoner he no longer saw him but was once again in the wood. He heard the crunch of bone as he struck out with his staff. He closed his eyes trying to blot out the vision of the clear bubbling water changing to a bright rich red.

"It is enough." Ralph Bassett finally faced the prisoner, "for the crime of assault, murder, rape, and robbery, I sentence you to hang." The man's legs gave way and the men-at-arms quickly grabbed him to hold him up. Thomas saw absolute fear in his face, his eyes bulging. "Take him away." Thomas felt rooted to the spot. He wanted to speak for the man. He could not believe that it was all over just like that. The man was now going to die. Was he the right man? He must be. But he was not sure no matter how much he tried to believe it. Matilda had seemed sure and she had seen them close up.

He knew he should feel glad that someone was being punished for that heinous crime but he just felt lost and drained. He opened his mouth and took a faltering step towards the table. For a brief moment Ralph Bassett turned to him questioningly. His mouth was dry. He found he could not speak.

"But…" he managed to mumble. He felt a hand on his shoulder.

"We will take our leave now Sir Ralph," said old Master Gobion.

"Yes, thank you all for coming." He gave the briefest of nods. "I must return to my guests. I hope you will excuse me." He turned and left. Thomas felt the old man gently squeeze his arm in an effort to remove some of the tension.

"The decision is made Thomas. Whether it is right or wrong we must accept and move on." Thomas turned on him.

"Do you think it's right!?" His voice was raised and brought a few stares and an angry look from Gobion's son. Master Gobion did not remove his hand but gripped it more tightly.

"Quiet! Let us walk towards the door." They began to move slowly down the hall. It settled Thomas. He concentrated on his passage across the hall and as he did so he became aware of the faces watching them.

The old man did not speak until they had exited through the large oak doors and were walking across the inner bailey. "As it happens," he said stopping, "I agree with the constable. The man was guilty. I have seen the evidence. Your identification was not all that convicted him." He turned and looked meaningfully at Matilda then back to Thomas. "I was discussing the matter with the constable before the arrival of the De Montforts." He said the last impatiently, releasing Thomas's arm.

Thomas suddenly realised that this old man was richly dressed perhaps more so than those that they had just left and though a merchant, he was certainly as noble and very respected by the gentry of the town. With his heart suddenly racing again he realised how dangerous it would be to upset this man who had so far shown him only good will.

"I apologise for my outburst sir. The decision; it caught me by surprise coming like that." Thomas knew his face was flushed. The old merchant nodded and walked on. When they reached the postern gate he stopped and said,

"You will be expected at the hanging tomorrow, at midday. It will be outside the East Gate on the road to Ecton as a warning to others." The Gobion party's horses had been brought round and they mounted up outside the gate and rode off. He saw Matilda give him a glance over her shoulder and he raised his hand then they were gone into the dark. The gate slammed shut behind him and he felt suddenly cold and alone. The night closed in around him and he hoped that no footpads were lurking about looking for the unwary traveller. The sound of rats raiding the day's refuse made him quicken his pace across the town back to Saint John's.

He breathed a sigh of relief when he finally reached the gate at Saint John's and was let in by a sleepy Brother Simon. When he reached the small cottage he found Brother Robert still up and sitting by the fire where he had left him.

Thomas sat down and drank deeply of the warm spiced ale that the old monk gave him. He then recited all his news. Robert listened in silence.

"I am sure that the decision is in all probability right even if the process is a bit uncouth. I think Sir Ralph has little time to dwell on justice when he is most likely plotting treason. I do not like the news you have brought about the De Montforts. It can only bring trouble, especially for us."

"How so?" Thomas looked across the fire questioningly.

"As I said earlier, my order will back the king. Let us just hope they can stay quiet and not get involved!" He stood up. "You must get some rest Thomas. You have had a trying day and tomorrow too will test your emotional strength. We must rise early to pray for the soul of this man. Drink the rest of the ale. It will help you to sleep. Good night." The monk slowly walked out of the circle of light and slipped out through the curtained doorway then across to the hospital and the monk's dorter. Thomas drained his mug of ale in one gulp then went out and urinated up the back wall. He returned to the cottage and collapsed onto his pallet exhausted.

Sleep came easily but it did not last. As the effect of the herbs in the ale wore off Thomas drifted in and out of consciousness, slipping through nightmarish dreams.

At dawn all pretence of sleep finally slipped away and he sat up feeling hot and clammy, even in the cool February morning. He quickly rekindled the fire and busied himself breaking the night's fast. Today there would be no lectures, just the prospect of a hanging. He rubbed his forehead, trying to massage the creases out, to remove the tension that was threatening to increase the headache already present. Brother Robert arrived and after a moment at the workbench handed him a tisane of willow bark.

"Here, drink, it will numb the growing pain in your head. We have a lot to do before you go." Robert kept him busy until an hour before Sext at midday, not giving him a moment to dwell on the approaching event. They made up various poultices and other medications, which they took into the hospital where they visited patients with the Infirmer.

Thomas usually enjoyed such activities but even this busyness could not completely hide the reawakened thoughts of the Ecton road and the villain's face. It was almost a relief when he found Brother Robert telling him it was time to go.

They walked together through the cold streets. Thomas comforted by Brother Robert's silent assurance. At the East Gate they met a quiet but expectant crowd full of the sense of approaching death. They joined the queue and filed through the gate. Just outside the road divided; between the roads stood a small wooden church.

"Saint Edmunds," muttered Brother Robert. In front of the church stood the gaunt skeletal gibbet. A small crowd was already gathered at its base and the roads were filling with excited spectators and hawkers. As they got closer Thomas found himself mesmerised by the gibbet, which towered threateningly, its rope hanging limp, waiting, below the outstretched crossbeam. It seemed to be calling quietly. The crowd in their nervous excitement felt its power and held back from approaching too close to the man-made terror that preyed on human necks.

Thomas shuddered, feeling goose bumps across his body. The cold day seemed suddenly colder and hostile. He felt the reassuring steadiness of Brother Robert's hand upon his arm as he guided him across the frozen rutted earth through the crowds to a small roped off area at the front.

"You will have to stand in there." He saw the Gobion family already gathered. The old man gave him a nod. Matilda's pale face gave him a wan smile of recognition.

He stepped over the rope with Brother Robert and immediately felt that he had stepped onto a stage. He felt the eyes of the surrounding crowd upon him eating into his soul. He felt sure of the man's guilt but hated the thought that part of the responsibility for this spectacle sat upon his shoulders.

The sound of horses crunching the crystalline earth made him turn and in the pale noon light he saw the constable approaching with the De Montfort's.

"The crowd is bigger than usual. There are many here keen to catch sight of the two brothers." Master Gobion spoke to those around him in general. A ripple of cheers moved with the horses to be followed by jeers and shouting as the prisoner was led by men-at-arms behind.

The horsemen dismounted and stepped over the rope. Ralph Bassett exchanged pleasantries with Master Gobion and greeted his family, then turned to watch the approaching prisoner, ignoring the student and the monk. Thomas felt Matilda move to his side.

"Come on man, walk a bit faster, we haven't got all day!" Peter De Montfort shouted at the unfortunate prisoner. The crowd cheered.

"Yes it's a bit cold for standing still. I can't wait till we're out hawking. As soon as that halter is tight on this peasant we can be off." Simon said to those around him. "I can't wait to fly that peregrine. She's a beauty, Ralph." This last was directed to the constable who nodded in return. Peter blew on his hands and rubbed them together.

Thomas's attention was now drawn to the approaching prisoner. He shuffled slowly along looking at the ground not even attempting to dodge the refuse and clods of frozen earth, as they came flying at him. When he reached the space between Thomas and the gibbet he was swung round by the heavy-handed fist of one of the soldiers. He staggered but remained on his feet.

Suddenly he looked up at them. His stare seemed dead; an emptiness seemed to have taken over. Spittle dribbled down his chin between his cracked brown teeth. His hose were soiled.

The constable stepped forward and, unfolding a piece of parchment, began to read the charges in a crisp voice. His words hung in the air as clouds of water vapour. The crowd were now silent. The prisoner seemed oblivious to his surroundings and stared, uncomprehending. As Ralph Bassett fell silent the crowd began to jeer. A priest moved across to the prisoner, to try to get a last confession, but the man seemed to not notice his presence. The priest turned, shook his head to the crowd behind the rope and made the sign of the cross.

The soldiers now grabbed the man and dragged him towards the gibbet.

"Don't let him drop." came the cry, which grew in intensity until the whole crowd were chanting. Thomas turned questioningly to Brother Robert, who whispered back.

"If he drops he will break his neck and it will be over quickly. The crowd want a spectacle. They want him to hang slowly. It will take much longer because he will die of suffocation." Thomas nodded. He had never seen a hanging before. There had been one in the village but his father had not allowed him to watch.

Thomas found that his anxiety had now turned to a curious detachment as he watched the man be bodily lifted on to a barrel by two of the soldiers. The rope was placed around his neck and tightened. Once again the crowd fell silent, waiting in tense excitement. The soldiers looked across at the constable. Thomas saw him nod. The two men immediately kicked away the barrel. The wretched man fell, his body began to dance, his eyes bulged, his mouth opened in a silent scream. Thomas found he could not look away. He felt transfixed by the animal stare of fear as the realisation that death approached finally took hold.

Simon began to stamp his feet and mutter to Peter with impatience, neither of them were looking at the hanging man. Ralph Bassett, noting their agitation, made a pulling motion to the two soldier executioners. They looked at the victims soiled hose with distaste, but knowing they had no choice they grabbed a leg each and pulled down using all their weight. It was enough. With a final shake the life went out of him and his dead unfocused eyes rolled upwards towards the cold grey cloud-covered sky.

The crowd silently began to disperse, drained by the intensity of what they had witnessed. Horses were soon brought round. Thomas noted the birds of prey being carried by the attendants. The constable and his two guests were quickly in the saddle. Ralph pulled his horse round to Master Gobion, bent down and after a quick glance at the two brothers began to speak, his voice low. Thomas took a surreptitious step forward.

"… You have been a good friend sir, but I advise you to leave the town for a while at least."

"Thank you. We are intending to visit our country estate soon anyway."

"Good, good, farewell then. May God protect you and your family."

"You also, Sir Ralph." The constable nodded towards Matilda then quickly turned his horse around and led his guests away.

Thomas wondered over these words as he watched the horsemen disappear into the countryside. Master Gobion approached him with his daughter- in-law. His son did not move but scowled across at them.

"It is over now. You two must put it behind you and move on."

"What of the others. He was not the only one." Thomas's eyes were drawn back to the swaying figure, its face now purple in the pale winter light.

"I think they are long gone and best forgotten. If they are caught, well…"

"We'll deal with that if it happens." Matilda looked into Thomas's grey eyes. The depth of her look affected him. She took her father-in-law's hand. "Thank you, you have helped me through this."

"We must not forget, Thomas." He knew she had not. "We shall not forget what you have done. This family is indebted to you. If you need anything you know where I live." He looked at both Matilda and Thomas and sighed. "Farewell. Come on Matilda." He did not bother turning to his son but began to walk slowly towards the East Gate, his retinue falling in around him. He watched them for a while then turned back to the swinging corpse. He was used to bodies but this was different.

"Isn't it incredible how the complexity of an individual life which takes years of creating can be snuffed out in the blink of an eye, and then forgotten as if it never existed." All who passed, apart from giving an occasional glance, now ignored the corpse and gibbet. It had become part of the background.

"Perhaps not incredible; I would use the word sad, though God does not forget." Robert crossed himself. "Yes, thanks be to God, at least we know our souls will go on to a better place."

"Do we?" said Thomas sharply turning to Robert. "It is hard to accept that with what we have just witnessed." He waved his hand at the corpse, "…and been party to it." Robert took Thomas by the hand.

"Come, it's best we leave this place." Thomas shivered turned and walked towards the gaping gate in the dark wall. Once through, Thomas felt the weight of his burden fall from his shoulders. "Do not doubt the church too openly Thomas. It is a powerful beast. I understand you but many would not." Thomas nodded glumly.

"I do not doubt God's kingdom."

"That I know." They slipped into a thoughtful silence as they weaved their way through the streets back to the hospital. As they reached the gatehouse Robert said "Do not dwell on it Thomas. You must move on and put it behind you."

"No, it is not that. I was thinking of what the constable said to Master Gobion."

"Oh" Robert looked at him in surprise. "And what was that Thomas. I did not overhear them."

"Ralph Bassett told them to leave town. They said that they already had plans to. Why would that be, Brother?" Robert thought for a moment as they walked across to the cottage.

"Yes, I think I know and it could be a bit worrying. The Gobions follow the king, and I have just heard from one of Bassett's clerks that the king is in Oxford and is gathering an army.

Chapter 9

It was early morning a week later. Prime had just finished at the small chapel in the hospital. Thomas walked out into the cold crisp air and pulled his black student robes around him. He walked quickly across the earth yard to the front gate and then out into the street. He turned up Bridge Street, his leather shoes crunching through the snow.

The town was slowly coming alive with the quiet steps of tired students leaving their lodgings and the hurried movements of the town's workforce gathering momentum for the day's labour.

Thomas walked with a spring in his step as he made for the Franciscan Friary nicknamed Grey-friars. The hanging had been cast into the pit of unwanted memories and ahead was a lecture by Friar Peter. As he passed the steps of All Saints Church he caught up with Kyftyll and Heycock; the fellow students who he had met on his first night in the town. Kyftyll was also heading for the lecture at Grey-friars. Heycock was going over to the town hall on Scarlet Well Street, where a learned scholar from Oxford was holding a debate on Logic. He was also full of the latest information from Oxford and Heycock was keen to discover what he could.

Heycock left them as they passed across the market square, where merchants were busy laying out their wares. They went on up Newland and entered the Grey-friars building where they were ushered into a cold airy room with large shutters thrown wide open.

"The cold will stop us dozing and the light will let us learn. Come on in and sit down," called out Friar Peter. Thomas and Kyftyll sat on a bench with a growing number of students. Friar Peter's lectures did not attract the numbers that attended the core curriculum of Dividium or Trivium but it contained many serious scholars. Thomas drew out his wax tablets in order to write any necessary notes.

Friar Peter started with a reading from a book entitled Tegni by Galen, and then began to discuss his ideas on treatment. Thomas noted on his wax tablet as the discussion progressed. '...Keep patient in balance/look at opposites for treatments.'

"So," continued Peter, "if the woman arrives with a cold, Galen would treat with warming herbs and spices such as ginger and pepper." Soon discussion moved on to diseases and their opposites. Thomas suggested Leprosy, but to his disappointment they could not agree.

"They feel no pain so apply pain," said one.

"Their skin is dry and rotten so apply moisture and leeches to try to balance the humour," said another.

"Your ideas follow Galen's teaching but I fear you would have little success. But if there appears to be no known cure then new ideas based on established knowledge are always worth trying in my point of view, though there are many learned men that would disagree with me so take care." Friar Peter took a deep breath and sighed. "Still, that is the beauty of medicine, there is always something new to find out." The discussion moved on. Thomas wondered on the suggestions he had heard and decided it would be worth further thought later on. He soon lost the thread of the discussion and felt the cold slowly creep up through his feet. He pulled his cloak about him.

Noise from the window began to disturb the scholars. Thomas and Kyftyll looked up.

"Sounds like another riot building up," said a student.

"That's a surprise. I haven't heard of any disputes," said another.

"Who do you reckon," said Kyftyll, "students versus townsfolk or…" his eyes glistened with excitement.

"Oh bother!" Friar Peter called out loudly and walked over to the window. "We can't work with that racket." The next minute the door burst open and in flew Heycock. His eyes bright and face flushed. As one the whole group turned and faced him.

"Well sir, explain your reason for disturbing my lecture. For I'm sure you have one!" Friar Peter said loudly resting his hands upon his hips in agitation. Haycock's eyes shot from the friar to his friends then back. He began to talk excitedly to the room in general. "Slow down boy!"

"Oh yes, right." Heycock managed to look slightly calmer. "It's the council; the De Montfort brothers and Ralph Bassett the Constable have been to the town hall. The burgesses…" he paused looking around excitedly.

"The burgesses have what?" called out an exasperated Friar Peter.

"Well they've voted in favour of the Barons and De Montfort."

"They have officially rejected Louis of France's decision and the Mise of Amiens and declared against the king." Friar Peter stared incredulously at Heycock.

"Too right!" shouted one of the students. "No longer shall we be ruled by the king's foreign friends!" A cheer rose from the gathered scholars and they had all soon left to join the milling crowd of students and townsfolk in the square.

"Come on!" shouted Heycock. Kyftyll was already up with him. Thomas looked across at Friar Peter. Thomas found himself keen to know the man's views.

"I'll catch you up!" Thomas was soon alone with the Friar. "You do not seem so pleased Friar," said Thomas, walking over to where the lecturer stared out at the gathering crowd through the window. He turned, surprised that he was not alone and then looking almost vacantly at Thomas, he rubbed his palms on his grey robe and walked over to where the book by Galen lay.

"Simon De Montfort is already fighting the Marchers in Wales. I fear that soon our medical skill will be much needed," he said to the room in general.

"Why so, sir?" said Thomas who was now becoming eager to join his friends, but could not drag himself away. Friar Peter now looked up at him.

"The king, as you know, I'm sure, is at Oxford, which is barely fifty miles away. He will not allow Northampton to stay in the hands of the Barons. It is too important a town." He looked down at the book before him. "Too important," he mumbled again, then opened up the book before him. "Go, join your friends." He began to read.

Thomas turned and dashed out into Newlands his mind full of the news and the friar's comments. It was as if the whole town had come out. The square was crammed with people shouting and calling out. The inns and alehouses were doing a roaring trade. Thomas pushed his way through and on past All Saints church, its steps and entrance crowded. He headed down Bridge Street to the inn, where he knew he would find his companions.

The inn was bulging at the seams with scholars, all intent on having their say. The air was filled with noise, shouting, and laughter. Ale flowed by the jug full.

Heycock saw him enter and waved him over. He struggled through the crowd to their table and was soon drinking ale and listening intently to the students' excited babble.

"At last! It's about time someone stood up to the king and his fancy foreign courtiers. Here's to De Montfort." Heycock took a long drink.

"It'll be civil war," replied Thomas. He then went on to relay the friar's thoughts.

"Nonsense, King Henry is as weak as water once he sees important towns like Northampton challenging him, he'll back down."

"His son, Prince Edward, doesn't seem so weak, besides even Louis of France who's the Arbitrator has sided with Henry."

"Well he would. He's a foreigner too." They were determined not to let Thomas dampen their spirits. "Hell! Let'em come anyway! There's an army within these walls. Every student here's for De Montfort. There are thousands of us, plus the castle garrison, and a good number of townsfolk."

"Against an army of trained knights and men-at-arms?"

"The town walls and defences are so good our skill is easily good enough to hold off an army. Besides if the king comes the Barons and De Montfort himself will have the perfect excuse to rise up with an army against him."

"Ah, so we are the bait so that De Montfort can have the excuse."

"God, Thomas you are so full of questions and pessimism. You must be the only scholar not jumping for joy."

"Not for the king are you?" muttered another scholar darkly.

"No, no." said Thomas holding up his hands, "but I came here to study not to fight."

"Oh heck, there you go again, you're not going to fight, you'll see. Drink this Thomas." Heycock filled his pot up from the jug. "You might see some fighting though. The De Montfort brothers are going to send another challenge to Henry's foreigners to come and fight in a tournament here at Northampton."

"Didn't they try that before?"

Yeah, the king's always stopped them in the past."

"He will find it hard to stop them this time."

"It'd certainly be a tournament worth seeing if it happens."

Soon Thomas was lost in revelry, his concerns washed away by his excited colleagues and the ale. He found himself staggering the streets, chanting and shouting. He watched fascinated as a royalist's house was looted, its occupants beaten. Another house was burned to the ground. The students danced in the fire's light.

When he awoke his head was thumping badly. He tasted vomit in his mouth and smelled it around him. He was lying on the filthy floor of an inn on the market square. His comrades lay heaped around him. His robes were dirty and torn. He smelled of ale, vomit, sweat and smoke. He felt the bile burning his throat and staggered to his feet. Stepping carefully over his friends he almost fell through the door and into the light. He immediately vomited, which made him feel better.

He began to gingerly make his way back to St. John's and thought of the comfort of his pallet. His pace was slow as he crossed the square through a ground-hugging mist. The air felt cold and damp. He shivered as it touched his bones. He passed the smouldering remains of the burnt out house and quickened his pace guiltily.

He needed to confess and realising he would not sleep until he had done so he walked slowly down Gold Street towards Saint Gregory's which he had visited one Sunday because it shared the same Saint as his own village church at Buckbie. Since then the small church in the weavers' district had become his most regular place of prayer and confession outside the chapel at Saint John's hospital.

Turning off West Street he approached the church via a small lane. The eaves of the houses encroached in on either side. The church had no tower. It was a rectangular shaped stone structure surrounded by a small graveyard.

The cold air and the exercise had freshened Thomas and apart from the occasional pain in his forehead he felt much improved by the time he entered the church. Thomas soon found the priest, a slender man about the same size as Thomas. He was not much older. His eyes shone with passion, a love of God and keenness to help his parishioners. The priest looked up and placed his broom aside.

"Ah, Thomas, what brings you here at this hour? You look weary and worn. I see the nights revelries had you in their grasp."

"Yes father. It is for that I need confession." The priest nodded and walked up to the altar where an old bench leant against the wall. They both sat and Thomas told him of his part in the night's activities.

"Give them alms and pray for them each day for a week. Pray also for the town. I think it will need our prayers. Now go Thomas and rest, then start your penance."

He crept slowly back to Saint John's through the cold waking streets and crawled onto his pallet, not daring to look at Brother Robert who grunted and walked off to the hospital building.

Chapter 10

Through the rest of February and March there was little change in the scholars routine apart from a daily meeting at the newly erected archery butts at Saint Peter's Church, where each day they were trained by men-at-arms. It gave Thomas a chance to improve his archery and practice with the Quarterstaff, with which he proved the most skilful of the students that regularly gathered there.

The burgesses of the town had been busy repairing the town walls. The extra work meant that everyone was employed. The constable at the castle busied himself with the garrison and with entertaining the growing number of knights that began to arrive in support of the cause. He had announced that the tournament would be held at Easter; as the celebration grew closer the practice field became more frenzied. Brother Robert commented that it was more to keep the knights and soldiers out of trouble, as Henry's knights would never show up. Thomas had laughed as everyone was looking forward to the spectacle.

On Maundy Thursday, Thomas attended all the services at Saint Gregory's. He always found the Tenebrae service moving; and at Matins when the candles are slowly extinguished and darkness takes over.

On Good Friday, he headed quickly to the church again for Prime and listened reverently to the service but was surprised at the priests exhortations against the Jews who filled the next street, Gold street and were also numerous around Silver Street.

"On this day did they not nail our lord to the cross and now they have brought their evil ways to our shores." Thomas unused to such provocations in church, having only experienced the mild mannered Geoffrey, looked about him to see the crowd soaking up the recitation expectantly.

He left the church feeling bemused and angry. The priest had turned on him when he had approached him about the subject, saying, "This is the time for them to repent. They are heretics and must be brought to salvation. It is our duty. All good Christians in this town will see to that this afternoon."

"What do you mean?" Thomas asked. The priest's lean features were now twisted in a sort of fanatical arousal.

"Then they shall be herded to the church for mass and there shall repent of their sins." Spittle began to dribble down his chin; the man seemed to have changed into a fanatical demon. A small crowd of parishioners who were listening began to cheer. "I expect to see you all there!" he called out to the crowd in general.

Thomas walked away, cutting across to Horseshoe Lane through the ramshackle weavers' houses that ran along the town wall, until he came to the South Gate. His mind was astir with the contents of the priest's sermon.

He arrived at the leper hospital in time for Terce and found his father in the church of Saint Leonard's knelt in prayer; many other lepers were there. Thomas joined them closing his eyes to hide from their disfigurements. He listened to the chanting of the priest whose quiet intonation calmed him and enabled him to refocus on Christ's sacrifice and love.

When the priest had finished, Thomas and his father ambled down to the river with ale, bread and two fishing rods. The air and earth were fresh with the first touches of spring, budding leaves had appeared in the trees and crisp fresh shoots full of verdant colour put new life into the damp grass.

As they sat munching the bread and sharing the ale from the leather flagon, their rods over the slow flowing river, Thomas studied his father. He had visited him regularly every week. He was thin; his skin, a pale leather that wrinkled around his wiry well-used body. His eyes shone with an expectation of life. Thomas knew his condition had certainly not worsened. He had searched through all the available texts in Northampton and questioned his lecturers and those at the hospital. He had turned up regularly with new and varied concoctions, which he applied to his father. Walter bore it patiently but told his son 'if cure there is it will come from God.' At such times he would kiss the small vial of water that Thomas had brought back from Peterborough and which hung around his neck. He continued to drink daily from the well of Saint Thomas.

"I believe you're cured father." Thomas said as he studied the old man. He had not meant to say it, but the more he studied him the more he became sure of it. The old man did not turn to face his son.

"I have been thinking so too for some time, may be it is so. I have great faith but, well, you never can tell." Now he turned to face Thomas. "If I am, what of it? My life is here now. I could not go back to the village. It has changed; you know that. They would not accept me. No, quiet, listen to me." He held up his hand to stop Thomas interrupting. "You know in your heart that they would fear the disease whether it is in me or not. There can be no return to things past. Nicholas, who I cared for and nursed through infancy and made a man, has rejected me and accepts neither you nor I as his kin."

"The mill is yours by rights, is it not."

"Yes."

Their thoughts turned to the village life they had lost and they sat silent for a moment.

"The mill could be yours." Walter studied the water gently moving his line causing ever-growing circles of ripples. "Do you want it lad? You also have a new life now." Thomas pondered the ripples.

"Life would be difficult there with Nicholas as future lord of the manor. It is my home, my inheritance. I don't know, father. I long for the stability of the past."

"Turmoil is in the wind, not just for the likes of towns like Northampton. It will reach the villages too. What news do you have from the town, Thomas? We hear all sorts of rumours here." Thomas filled him in on events as they fished. At noon they walked back to the entrance of Saint Leonard's compound, Thomas carrying two fish.

At the gates Walter said his farewells "If you wish to return and can prove that I am cured, we will return Thomas. I would dearly love to pray by your mother's grave." He released Thomas and turned away, leaving him with his dilemma.

As he returned to Saint John's Hospital, he decided that he would at least prove his father was cured. His first step would be to get a testimonial from the priest at Saint Leonard's. He would also get Brother Robert to examine him and try to persuade Friar Peter to visit. If their evidence was positive he may stand a chance. If only the Gobions were still in town he felt sure they would have helped his cause.

"Thomas there you are! Come on!" He was broken from his reverie by a call from Bridge Street. He recognised the voice of his student friend, Kyftyll. "Come on, we're off to the service at All Saints. You're just in time." Thomas quickly dropped off his fish at the hospital gatehouse then ran up Bridge Street after his friends.

At the top of the street they joined a large crowd gathered before the steps of the church. The crowd seemed to stretch down Gold Street. Most of the townsfolk, clerics and resident students must have been there. The senior clergymen of the town stood on the steps of the church along with the senior town dignitaries and many of the noble men and women that were in the town. The air was full of jeering and shouting, which was rising like a wave along the street. Thomas pushed forward and looked down Gold Street. Suddenly he made out the object of their derision. A large body of people were walking sedately up the street.

"Here they come! Here they come!" The shouts grew louder all about him. The priest's words from the morning filled his head and he felt himself fill with anger towards his companions and the crowd that surrounded him, as the Jews approached; gentle folk who kept to themselves, and with whom most of the town seemed quite happy to do business with. He looked about him in amazement as the crowd became more frenzied and had to be held back by the soldiers that lined the streets.

They now approached the front of the church at the top of Bridge Street. They seemed to be dressed in their best clothes and looked well turned out in comparison to the motley crowd. Each one bore two yellow rectangles of coarse material sewn upon their chest. The group gathered before the church steps; the crowd grew quiet, as they fell under the proud scrutiny of the Jewish elders. The whole group appeared un-intimidated by the proceedings and held the gaze of any that continued to shout.

A young woman of Thomas's age stood nearby, her long silk jet-black hair tied down her back. Thomas looked into her dark Eastern face. He caught the full blaze of her green eyes. There he saw no humiliation, just anger. He quickly turned away ashamed, his face flushed red. He walked rapidly down the street, the sound of the crowd receding into the background.

Entering the hospital grounds, he went straight to the chapel where he lay prostrate before the altar and prayed for forgiveness.

He was disturbed sometime later by footsteps; rising, he saw Brother Robert. "You look melancholic Thomas, what has touched you so?" Thomas gestured towards the town.

"The ceremony," he spat out once again, feeling his face flush.

"Ah, the humiliation of the Jews. Yes, it can touch the few sensitive souls amongst us. It has become a popular Easter event over the last few years. At least they have not yet been thrown out of their homes and expelled from the town, though now we are under the influence of De Montfort who has already expelled them from Leicester, I expect that will happen soon enough."

"But why Brother? Coming from the country I am unused to Jews. I have heard stories of course, but they seem harmless enough. How can these Jews be blamed for the death of Christ twelve hundred years ago?"

"Oh Thomas, it is not just that. It is a way of removing the guilt that we all feel for the sins we have committed. The wrongs we have done can be conveniently blamed on these people, the poverty, the sickness, and famine. If it can be heaped on the Jews, the rest of those good Christians in the crowd will feel infinitely better and more holy."

"But that cannot be right."

"In the eyes of God who is to say what is wrong and right?"

"You feel it could be."

"I cannot judge the decisions of the Church. I am a Benedictine monk." He shook his head with indecision, which surprised Thomas. "Come let us find a remedy for this melancholic. Tomorrow is the parade and on Monday the tournament starts. They surely shall be great occasions to cast away the shadows of today."

Brother Robert and Thomas were away early the following morning of Holy Saturday. After a short service at the chapel they headed up to All Saints, where Thomas came across his friends, yawning and rubbing their eyes. The knights, lords, burgesses and high-ranking clerics of the town, plus those that had arrived to support the Barons' cause were to attend the morning service of Prime.

In the afternoon the tournament was to start, which would last for the next three days. Thomas had entered himself for the Quarterstaff competition. There would also be wrestling and archery but the main events were a game of camp ball between townsfolk and students and the knights' mêlée to which the foreign knights had been invited. No message had come from the king but rumours that he was gathering an army at Oxford filled the taverns.

The streets were busy, as much of the town clamoured around the great church. Thomas and Robert did not expect to gain entry to the church as like the rest they had come to see the parade of knights and their ladies. The church today was reserved for dignitaries only.

Brother Robert had said they would complete their Easter devotions that afternoon with a visit to the priory of Saint Andrews, the Clunaic Priory in the northern corner of the town to which Brother Robert belonged. He had visited the priory on a few occasions to see and pray before the holy relic of Saint Andrew's finger, but this would be Thomas's first as the monk's guest.

Thomas once again pushed himself to the front of the crowd at the top of Bridge Street, his stomach churning with momentary 'déjà vu' as he remembered the previous day. He was soon distracted by the approach along Gold Street of the town's Wait, the minstrels all dressed in the livery of the town. They walked along blowing their trumpets and banging kettledrums, acrobats leaped about in front of them.

At the church steps they stopped. They had been followed by a troupe of men-at-arms wearing the castle livery. Behind these came the leading families of the town and surrounding country, knights and their ladies, merchants, the council of twelve burgesses and the mayor plus the knights that had arrived at the call from the De Montfort's. Leading the whole procession were Simon and Peter De Montfort and Ralph Bassett. The crowds clapped and cheered at the splendid display of wealth and power.

Thomas looked on with amazement at the courtly splendour of the knights and their ladies, the knights dressed in velvet and fur of the highest quality, swords of great value at their hips. The women were clad in expensive surcoats and kirtles, their hair plaited and decorated, some wearing wimples. Both men and women were adorned with impressive gold rings, chains and brooches studded with jewels that glistened multi-coloured in the spring sunlight with flashes of ruby, sapphire and garnet.

Thomas touched his rough scholar's gown, tied at the waist with a belt and scratched at his unshaven chin as he recognised the class divide between himself and this rich display of wealth and nobility.

Amongst the slow moving throng, a well-dressed priest caught Thomas's eye, his garments of the finest quality. Thomas went pale.

"Henry of Leicester," he mumbled.

"What? Who's that did you say?" came a shouted query at his side.

"The priest there, he is Henry of Leicester; the Earl of Leicester's priest." He felt eyes on him and turned to see Brother Robert watching him. He smiled faintly and turned back, listening to a man in the crowd naming some of the lords as they passed.

"That there's Baldwin Wake and he's Adam of Newmarket. That's Thomas Menhill of Hemington and John of Buckbie." Thomas looked up recognising the two names his heart racing. He picked them out and there she was. He stepped back into the arms of Robert, who felt the tension in his body.

"What is it Thomas? Are you unwell?" Robert had moved to his side and was holding his arm looking with concern at his pale face.

"It's Sir John of Buckbie and..." He stumbled slightly over his words, his mouth dry, " ...and Eleanor his daughter."

"Ah, the liege lord of your village." Robert nodded, his face full of understanding. Thomas watched Eleanor. She seemed distracted, searching the faces of the crowd. He knew she looked for him. He felt his heart speed up. He breathed deeply. She must see him. As they grew closer he leaped forward. He heard shouts around him as he dodged the soldiers lining the street. She and her father stopped. He felt her eyes momentarily lock on to his. He smiled, still now before her. He did not notice the soldiers as they approached and hardly felt the pike handle as it crashed into his chest. He dropped to his knees, his eyes not releasing hers. She took a step towards him. He saw her father reach out and take her arm. Thomas Menhill had drawn his sword. He felt hands grab him under the arms and drag him back. He turned to see his friends around him. On turning back he was faced with the bellowing pike man who Brother Robert was trying to calm. He looked away towards Eleanor as Sir John pulled her on, irritated at the disturbance, no recognition in his eyes. Her hand reached up and pulled something from beneath her tunic. He caught a glimpse of it just as he was pulled away. He turned to Robert, his eyes bulging and face flushed as he pulled him back through the crowd.

"She wears it still brother! I saw it."

"Thomas, calm yourself, and let's get back to Saint John's."

"The medallion I gave her, she wears it Brother!" This time Robert looked at him strangely, and then with a quick glance at the others about him, who all stared questioningly he whispered firmly.

"Say no more Thomas, until we are at the hospital."

He gripped his arm and pulled him away, waving the others back with thanks. Soon they were walking slowly down the deserted street, the crowd cheering at the procession behind them.

Back in the quiet safety of their small cottage in the hospital grounds, Brother Robert made Thomas a tisane of chamomile, which he drank quietly without much thought as he sat by the small hearth in the centre of the room.

"Well, " Robert began, sitting opposite him. "What was all that about then?" It was not long before Thomas had explained, his face now flushing with embarrassment.

"It is best that you keep quiet about this and no more crazy stunts. John of Buckbie and Eleanor's ward Thomas Menhill have powerful friends. I have heard that Menhill knows the Earl of Leicester well. John will crush you if you interfere."

"Of that I'm sure. He has never liked me. But it is hard. I never thought I would see her again you know and here she is walking back into my life. I have been trying hard to forget her." He thought of Matilda. Robert nodded understandingly.

"Put her out of your mind." He cut some bread and cheese. "Come on eat up, we are to be at the priory this afternoon. It will soon be time to leave."

That afternoon they crossed the town and entered the secluded realms of the Clunaic priory of Saint Andrews, which occupied a large swathe of land in the northwest corner of the town. Its monks were seen little but its wealth was felt throughout the town. Many of the homes and much land were under the control of the prior, a Frenchman, like many of the monks that lived there.

Having come through an imposing gatehouse, Thomas found himself on a lane that led to the monastic buildings. Around him, lay brothers, in brown habits, toiled in the fields and animals grazed. The fields dropped down towards the river, which was hidden by a large wall that surrounded the grounds.

Robert led Thomas into the large stone priory. Smoke from the many candles floated in the air. The smell of incense burned at his nostrils. Towards the altar, rows of darkly robed and hooded monks chanted the liturgy. Their melodic tones filled the building, reaching into Thomas's soul. The hairs on his arms stood up and he felt his blood rush with the thrill of the holy music. The extended service of nones stretched on, leaving Thomas weary but exhilarated by its end and loath for the Godly music to cease.

The monks filed out for a short break before they returned again. Thomas walked out with Robert and they walked around the priory perimeter. The church itself was the most northerly building so they headed south passing down the outer walls of the Chapter and Frater. Turning left at the bottom they passed the kitchens and refectory and then walked up the eastern side of the great square of monastic buildings, past the least impressive of the buildings, that of the lay brothers' Dorter and Frater.

"Within are the cloisters. Few monks wander far from these buildings. They spend their time reading, writing, in choir or prayer."

"But not all; you have escaped its confines."

"Yes, such buildings need their officers, those who must work without to make sure all runs smoothly within. Besides…" he smiled wryly to Thomas, "I'm not French, so they are happy to have me out of the way."

"Do you miss it?"

"The silent calmness of the cloister, the regularity of the day, that feeling of closeness to God; Oh, yes, I miss it but I cannot hide away the skills God has placed in me."

"The tranquillity and security is tempting indeed." Thomas looked into the church wistfully, remembering the sounds and smells of the service. Brother Robert looked at him.

"You would make a good monk. You would also make a good chirugeon and a good husband to the right woman. Escaping to the cloister can often be the easy way out. Think carefully on the subject. God does not intend for all of us to be monks, but if your heart is there…" he smiled at Thomas. "I must return to my place. Vespers will be starting soon. I will stay tonight and pass the last part of the Holy Week vigil here. Good luck in you competing. I will see you back at the hospital." Thomas thanked him for taking him round the priory and said his farewells, then left, the quiet temptation of the cloister filling his head as he walked back though the bustling streets.

He could think of little else as he sat in the small cottage at the hospital eating his pottage. He saw the chance to escape his yearning, anger and loss, but even as he thought about it he knew it was not for him; such problems would still be there.

There came a tap on the door, which disturbed his thoughts. Brother Simon the gatekeeper entered.

"You have a visitor." In the darkness of the night Thomas caught the movement of another figure. He put down his spoon and bread and stood as a cloaked figure entered the small dimly lit room.

"Alfred!" exclaimed Thomas.

"Hello Master Thomas." Alfred's face beamed. Thomas turned to Simon.

"He's an old friend Brother. I will show him back to the gate later." Brother Simon nodded but did not wish to leave. Thomas finally had to shepherd him out and close the door.

"Alfred come, sit and have some ale and pottage. Tell me your news? What brings you here, so far from home? How is the mill?" He overwhelmed the slower Alfred, who sat and sipped the ale gratefully.

"One thing at a time Master. I came with Sir John as one of his men-at-arms. Master Nicholas and my young brother tend the mill. As you know, there is little work at this time so they will cope. I dare say…" Alfred began to ramble; Thomas became impatient.

"But what of the Lady Eleanor?" He coloured immediately. "I saw her in the parade," he finished lamely, by way of an explanation. Alfred smiled at him through black cracked teeth.

"It's warm in here." He removed his old leather coif and sipped his ale. Thomas could not contain himself and stood up. "It is she that has sent me, Master." Thomas turned to Alfred in surprise. Alfred fumbled in his Gypciere and finally produced a small scrap of parchment, which he handed to Thomas who quickly unfolded it. He recognised the rough hand of a street scribe. He read the short note quietly.

"Saint Peter's after Nones."

"The Lady Eleanor said for me to say 'tomorrow'." Alfred looked at him, confused. Thomas dropped the note into the fire and watched the flames take hold. His heart raced. He took his mug of ale and gulped it down greedily, his hand shaking with excitement.

Chapter 11

Spring 1264

After the Sunday morning service, Thomas grabbed his quarterstaff and hurried up to the inn. He shook his friends awake and they staggered out into the cold grey morning, grabbing bows and crusts of bread as they left. They headed out towards the castle, becoming more boisterous as they went. The archery was at the Butts at Saint Peters. After practicing with his friends Thomas knew he did not match their skill. He had been good in his village but they surpassed him. He waved them goodbye and turned in the direction of the castle where the quarterstaff competition was to be held.

As he entered the outer bailey, the huge milling crowd of hawkers, spectators, beggars and competitors, momentarily confused him. The entire town seemed to have been attracted to the castle and the field just south of Saint Peters. The air was full of shouting, bustling and laughing. The smell of humans and animals flooded Thomas's nostrils as he pushed his way through to the roped off area. He noticed that the wrestling had already started at the far end of the arena.

He gave in his name and sat back on his haunches with the growing group of competitors. Shutting his eyes he tried to prepare his mind. His thoughts were constantly jostled aside by his latest image of Eleanor.

Suddenly he felt somebody nudge him and then he heard his name being called.

"Do we have Thomas Millerson here or not?" he opened his eyes to see the competition judge dressed in the constable's livery. Thomas quickly jumped up. He realised other bouts had already started. "What's up lad? Are you deaf? I was just about to scratch you out. Right, here's your opponent. First to fall or receive a serious blow is out. Ready?"

Thomas quickly threw off his cloak and grabbed his staff, studying the man opposite him. He was older and was carrying more weight than his body was designed for; his face was ruddy. A man who liked his ale, Thomas decided.

The man was not slow and immediately went on the offensive. Thomas parried quickly and danced sideways, skipping away from the continuous blows. The man was good but the more he struck out the more he puffed and the redder his face became. Thomas decided to take his time. He goaded the man on to strike and quickly jumped away. Then as Thomas saw his eyes glazing he parried a blow, skipped inside the other's staff and swept away his opponents legs with his own staff.

He became aware of the sound around the arena, cheering and jeering. He turned and waved to the crowd and took his place with the others who had won their fights.

He had some time before his next bout so as he sat he studied the castle around him. At his back was the keep and inner bailey, which towered over all, making its presence felt and reminding everyone of the power of the constable. In front of him the great outer walls stretched away in each direction. On their battlements he saw men-at-arms looking down at the crowd below.

He was called out again and found himself facing a small wiry student whom he remembered seeing at the Bridge Inn on a few occasions. He quickly realised that he would not be so easily worn down as his previous opponent. They stalked around each other, attacking quickly, defending, feinting but neither could get an opening. Thomas soon became aware of the jeers around them but held his concentration. They were close to the rope and soon found themselves being pelted with rubbish.

"Come on, at'em. You're not mummers." Thomas saw his opponent flinch nervously at the taunts and dodge a chicken bone aimed at his head. He momentarily looked away towards the crowd. Thomas seized his chance and feinted a strike at the man's feet, then spun and gave the man a blow across the head, which felled him and left him out cold on the ground. The jeers turned to cheers and Thomas felt his heart race with the excitement of victory.

His opponent was quickly carried away to the town physician who had set up camp in the inner bailey and was doing a roaring trade, along with numerous barber-surgeons, their fees all paid for by the De Montforts. Thomas had attended lectures given by Richard Norton the towns leading physician. He was a great believer in the study of urine, and had recently given some excellent lectures on the study of the four humours as described by Hippocrates and Aristotle.

As Thomas watched his unfortunate opponent being carried away, the judge noted down his name, and then quickly turned away to watch the other matches still in progress.

Thomas stood for a moment wondering what he could do before the next round. He was disturbed by a shout from behind and turned to see Heycock and Kyftyll. He wandered over and climbed over the rope. They pounded his back congratulating him on his wins. They had not done so well in the archery and Thomas commiserated with them. They decided to watch a fellow friend and student nicknamed Small, who was built like a bear, in the wrestling. They arrived to see him throw his opponent to the ground with ease and he came over to them wiping sweat from his brow.

After more congratulations they wandered off through the stalls chatting happily. Finally they ended up with pies sitting at an ale seller's up against the castle wall.

"Stretches right round Saint Peters and up Gold Street to All Saints where there are plays and mummers and acts of all kinds going on."

"There's a bear," said Small to a round of laughter. "It's in the square."

"Dogfights and cockerels there too," chipped in Kyftyll. Thomas did not know whether to continue his competition or go and explore. Kyftyll and Heycock promised to see their two companions through the next round.

When Thomas arrived back at the arena he was regretting the pie and ale. He felt heavy and sluggish as he faced his next opponent, a villager from a small settlement to the north of the town. He was fit and quick and was soon raining blows at Thomas, who found himself hard put to defend against them. It was not long before he had suffered a blow to the shoulder, this was rapidly followed by a whack in the chest and then the legs, which left him down and winded.

Instead of attending the long queue at the physicians Thomas and his compatriots found the apothecary's stall. Thomas bought himself a poultice to ease the swelling of his shoulder and had the apothecary make up an infusion for his chest. He drank this down before being half carried half dragged over to the wrestling, where they found Small facing up to an even bigger bear-like creature in the final.

It was not long before they were dragging Small over to the apothecary's stall where Thomas ordered him a 'pick me up' and something for his aches and bruises.

They were soon making their way through the crowds towards the square, pushing through the noisy, colourful, smelly streets, full with people lost in the momentary pleasures of this short Easter holiday.

When finally they arrived at the square they stopped in amazement, for every corner of space was filled with stalls, mummers, musicians, contortionists, acrobats, cockfights and dogfights. In comparison, the fair in Buckbie, which had amazed Thomas every year, now faded into insignificance. But the greatest attraction was at the centre by the pillories. They pushed their way through until they came to a rope. Before them, standing on his hind legs towered the bear; the first that any of them had ever seen. Thomas had never imagined such huge beasts actually existed. He had heard ballads and stories from passing storytellers in the village but had as a youth assumed that they were just mythical.

The great shaggy animal stared out at them mournfully from huge doe eyes. It seemed gentle and sad; its fur was mangy and skin red with sores. Its master played a fiddle and a small boy banged a drum. It slowly turned its gaze upon them and gave a guttural growl that reached into Thomas's soul. The crowd gave a fearful cry and as one stepped back. It was full of animal anger and hopelessness. The bear master just yanked on a chain that was tied to the bear's muzzle. He pulled again and slowly the bear began to move its legs and bells on its muzzle began to ring. Thomas and his friends roared with excitement along with the crowd and threw coins at the bear's feet. The boy with the drum scampered around collecting them.

"Amazing," shouted Thomas unable to take his eyes from the slowly moving creature.

"Yeah," cried Kyftyll, "it makes you want some refreshment, I reckon. Look I see barrels over there." Grabbing his friends, he dragged them over to an ale stall, which was doing a roaring trade. "Got to celebrate your successes especially Small here." As they arrived at the counter Thomas heard the All Saints bell chiming; he stopped.

"Nones," shouted Heycock above the noise around him.

"Nones! What already! I've got to go," returned Thomas. The others looked at him quizzically.

"But..."

"Haven't got time to explain; must go." And with that he dashed off towards Saint Peter's. As he ran, dodging through the crowd, he realised with some amazement that he had not thought of Eleanor since the start of his first fight, early that morning.

He was exhausted when he arrived and the service had already started. He crept in genuflected and stood quietly against the wall at the back. The church was crowded, as many people had come in from the festivities. A haze of steam rose from the damp woollen clothing of the congregation that stood upon the hard stone floor of the nave. He studied the walls around him as the priest intoned the Latin service. The rugged aisle walls were gaudily painted with bible scenes. Circular Norman pillars held up the wooden roof, their rounded arcades intricately carved with heads, circles, foliage, animals and winged creatures.

His eyes now began to search the congregation. He could see little but the russet tunic backs of the poor at the back of the church, dirty from continuous wear, but he anxiously continued his search for the figure he knew so well.

The service was soon over and everyone was keen to return to the pleasures that the town had to offer on the Holy Day celebrations. Thomas moved to one side and stood with his back against a pillar watching the crowd file out, all chatting and shouting loudly, some looking seriously inebriated. He smiled at one particular parishioner who sat against a pillar opposite him snoring loudly, a mongrel dog licking at his drunken features.

Suddenly he noticed a cowled figure by the side of him, clad in a well-made green cloak. She smiled at him and took his hand. Holding her other hand to her lips, she bade him to be quiet. She led him quickly to the shrine of Saint Ragener, a quiet place hidden from the bustle of parishioners in the nave. As they knelt before the intricately carved tomb, Thomas noticed the familiar shape of Alfred step between the great Norman pillars behind them to turn away any would be disturbances to their secluded rendezvous.

She said an Ave Maria, then stood and quickly removed her hood, pulling him up she took hold of both his hands.

"I tried to forget, Thomas, but I am surrounded by selfish fools at court who only love themselves. My wards are good to me and they try their best to find me suitable company, but..." She gazed across at him her eyes searching his body. His ruffled black hair silky and matted, his tonsure all but grown over, grey eyes and pronounced cheek bones covered in stubble, his nose slightly awry from a break in his youth. He had a small cut over his eye from the morning's competition; blood congealing along its line and his tunic was stained with sweat. She could smell his strong musky aroma. "When I saw the soldiers knock you down I was afraid you were hurt. I knew then that we had to be together. I know that you feel the same way about me. I had to see you." Thomas squeezed her hands, his mouth dry. He could not speak, overwhelmed by the emotion. He swallowed and tried to moisten his lips.

"As you can see I am well and you look..." he smiled at her and his face coloured, "radiant". He quickly looked down embarrassed at speaking from his heart. He felt her squeeze his hands so he continued. " I did not forget you either."

"I know." They looked at each other for some time, not wanting to break this moment of intense unity. A cough from Alfred finally broke their bond and they released hands.

"Why have you come here Eleanor? It is a hotbed of rebellion here. The king is more than likely preparing and army. So the gossips say anyway."

"I came with my ward at the request of my father. They both felt that the womenfolk ought to be seen. I think they want to show people how confident they feel about the cause. I worry for them. My father is out of his depth, I am sure. Thomas Menhill, my ward, he at least has the contacts and knows what's going on."

"Your father, he's a small fish in a big ocean."

"He feels so grand with his soldiers wearing his livery and being courted by the lords and knights up at the castle."

"You came from London?" Eleanor nodded "Are you returning there?"

"The Lady Menhill is returning to their manor at Hemmington after the festivities of Holy week are over. I have not thought what I should do. Do you want me gone?" She pouted at him her eyes soft and inviting.

"Of course not but you should not stay here. If the gossips are right and the king does come this way, all hell will be let loose. Besides is it not better that we stay apart? What future do we have?"

"My father wants me to stay. Anyway, he says the king won't come because he's more worried about the Earl of Leicester who is in the South. He says we are just one of many towns including London that have rejected the Mise of Amiens and sided with the Barons. He says I'm safer here than London."

"But..." Eleanor once again knelt before the small tomb. He knew she was stubborn and that she would not listen. His eyes were drawn to the mystical carvings of beasts and plants flowing from the mouth of the bearded face of Ragenar the martyr who was tortured to death by the Danes but refused to abjure his Christian faith. He placed his hand upon the cold stone, and muttered a short prayer.

"What are we to do Eleanor?" he said finally.

"Pray with me Thomas." He knelt next to her. She took his hand and for many minutes they stayed locked in prayer.

Then she turned to him, "Do you wish to be alone with me?" She turned, looking him full in the face, anxiously. "I mean fully alone, together?" he studied her, unsure, but his heart began to pound. He had dreamt of such an occasion.

"Is it what you want?"

"Yes." He took her hand and pulled her up. She whispered to Alfred who followed at a distance behind them as she pulled Thomas quickly through the church and out onto the street, where she quickly covered her face with the cowl of her cloak.

"My father has rented lodging for me at Bearward Street between Marehold and Sheepmarket. I complained of the lack of privacy in the castle." She smiled to him coyly. They were soon heading up the Horsemarket and it was not long before they arrived outside the front of a large three-story wattle and daub timber framed building. Many such buildings crowded the street, which contained the houses and workshops of wealthy merchants.

"Everyone is out at the fair. Come, I have the top floor. My maid, Clarice is out at the fair too." She beckoned him in through a side door and up to the top floor.

It was dark when Thomas finally slipped down the stairs that led directly to the back entrance. He walked quickly out onto Sheep Street, turning towards the hospital. His mind a blur, his body warm with the pleasure he had lost himself in. Crowds still filled the Drapery and Market Square, loud with drunken laughter. He was aware of little as he jostled and bumped his way through towards the hospital.

The next day Thomas woke late at the sound of Brother Robert pushing open the wooden door.

"I can see you had a good day yesterday. Up you get, it's already after Terce. We need to make up the medication and get over to the hospital. Brother James will be wondering where we are."

Thomas groaned and closed his eyes and sank back into a reverie of Eleanor. His head thumped slightly and he remembered being dragged into the Bridge Inn, the student's hostelry, and having large quantities of ale with Kyftyll, Heycock and Small. The place had been heaving with students many too drunk to stand.

"Here drink this. It should help with your alcoholic over indulgence and cleanse your blood. It's nettle juice and syrup of hops." Brother Robert put a tisane in Thomas's hands and he slowly drank the warm liquid. "Well how did you get on then?"

"Got through two rounds," said Thomas sitting up.

"Enjoyed the fair afterwards too, I think."

"Mm," muttered Thomas sipping his drink remembering Eleanor's smooth white skin, her long black hair framing her face neck and shoulders as she lay beneath him; his hand upon her breast. Feeling a stirring in his groin, he quickly tried to push the images out of his mind.

He got up and staggered out into the damp air. A mist had climbed up through the streets from the river during the night and its remnants clung to the open space of the hospital garden. Going around the side of the cottage, he urinated onto a large manure heap then staggered back in and began his morning duties assisting the monk. He was an automaton, his thought on the afternoon and his secret liaison during the Camp Ball game, which was to occur in the large meadow that ran down to the river from Saint Thomas's Well.

"Are you coming to the game?" Thomas said over his pestle and mortar.

"No, I don't think so. Watching the townsfolk and students take all their anguish out on each other. I would spend all my time repairing you all!"

"The Physician Richard Norton will be there I believe, along with a heap of barber surgeons and apothecaries," replied Thomas.

"Well, that leaves you all well covered then." Brother Robert laughed. "No, I thought I'd go and see your father." Thomas stopped pounding at the roots in his mortar. "You wanted me to check him over. It would be nice to meet him too. Maybe we'll watch your melee from the other side of the river."

"Thank you Brother. I appreciate it."

"It's nothing Thomas. Come, hurry up let's get this done. I'll visit the hospital; you get off and enjoy your day." Thomas smiled and pounded even harder at his root.

He was soon off towards the Bridge Street Inn and his friends where tactics were discussed over ale and hot pies. After much debate and a few too many early ales, they decided to head for the town wall to survey the terrain of the impending game and to await its start. They headed off past All Saint's church and along Swinewell Street towards the tower and then to Derngate. The road was muddy and busy.

"I reckon we'll have a few hundred on our side," said Small.

"Well you're equal to at least twenty!" replied Heycock, laughing and expertly side stepping away from Small's grasp only to find himself directly beneath some falling refuse from an upper window, which brought a roar of approval from Small and the others and curses from Heycock who picked up some of the rotten mess upon the ground and threw it up at the window, then kicked out at a mangy mongrel that happened to come to close.

They were soon past the Tower and at the Dern Gate. Thomas, who had been careful to stick to watered ale during the morning, still felt light headed and warm with the glow of companionship from his fellow students, who were raucous.

They climbed the thick stone steps up onto the parapet of the wall, usually out of bounds to students and townsfolk but open for the camp ball game. Along the parapet workmen put the finishing touches to a large wooden stand that jutted out over the wall and upon which the town's dignitaries and visiting lords and ladies were to sit. Eleanor had said that she would be there with her father.

Soon the two teams were gathering on the field below. At the well end stood the townsfolk in their rustic work tunics and down by the river, swollen by recent rain were the students, clerics and friars in their scholar's robes and habits. The group on the wall were soon forced to leave by some agitated men-at-arms keen to clear away the rowdy bunch before the town's dignitaries arrived to take their seats.

They spilled down the steps and out through the Dern Gate, hurled some friendly abuse at the townsfolk along the lane and ran down to the river.

Thomas stood on the edge of the growing group and watched the dignitaries arriving, led by the mayor and members of the council. The castle delegation led by Ralph Bassett, along with the town's high-ranking merchants and priests, followed them. Thomas recognised the De Montfort brothers and their priest, Henry of Leicester. He also saw John of Buckbie. Realising he was holding his breath; he took in a great gulp of air. John was alone.

The teams gathered under the wall in a hushed excited silence. The mayor held up the pigs' bladder filled with peas and threw it down between the opposing teams. With a sudden roar the mass of bodies sped towards the ball. Mayhem ensued. Thomas standing against the castle wall saw the ball fly out of the fighting group down into the field, to be followed by a few hundred shouting, charging figures. Hidden in the shadow of the wall he made his way south, slipped through the crowds of spectators and entered the town through the small Cow Gate.

He began to run leaving the cries of the game behind, up Cow Lane, past the All Saints Church once more, eventually arriving at Bearward Street breathless. He slipped into the alley at the side of the house and knocked on the heavy oak door.

That evening as Thomas slipped out of the door he felt the cool air across his cheeks but was oblivious to the cold. Lost in his lover's dream once more he made his way to the Bridge Inn where he sat in the shadows drinking ale and listened to the students' victory stories. Their win had come about by some clever passing which had allowed a group of students to break free with the ball and carry it through to the townsfolk's goal at the well.

Thomas found Brother Robert waiting for him when he reached the cottage. It had begun to rain heavily. It drummed on the thatch. Robert sat at the table carefully writing on a piece of parchment in the dim candlelight.

"Ah, Thomas, here you are. A great victory for the scholars. Well done! I'm glad to see you suffered no injuries. Come over here and sit opposite me. I'm writing a report for you." He saw Thomas's quizzical look. "About your father. I saw him today, remember." Thomas nodded and smiled.

"He is well?"

"Very. I see no signs of the leprosy in him. I have checked his urine and pulse and given him an examination. He is sensitive to pressure and heat in all his toes and fingers. He has no new lesions or damage to his skin. I am writing this down. But here, you will want to read this also." The monk handed Thomas a roll of parchment. "Your father has written a Will. He is leaving you the mill. I have witnessed it, along with the priest at Saint Leonard's. If you can prove your father is well to a gathered council, then he may return to Buckbie and the mill will be yours, if you want it that is? Brother Robert studied Thomas. "I will visit Friar Peter and see if he will also write a report. Your father has a good case. You will also need to get a surgeon, or perhaps Richard Norton if you can afford it, to check his blood to search for signs of sediment or grease."

"Thank you Brother. Yes I think I can; I will see him." Thomas blushed feeling ashamed. He had thought little of his father recently and even now found it hard to focus on Robert's words. His thoughts kept returning to the vision of Eleanor naked before him on the bed, arms outstretched her pale skin almost white in the filtered daylight coming through the window. Brother Robert watched Thomas carefully.

"You have seen her again?" Thomas blushed even deeper and looked away into the flames crackling in the hearth. "Be careful Thomas. I warned you before and I will do so again. You would not stick your hand in that flame and yet you play with fire!" He turned back to his work.

Thomas listened to the crackling of the wood and the drumming of the rain up on the roof. He could not face Robert. He could only think of Eleanor. He knew he could not stay away.

On the following day, even as the horses charged toward each other and the knight's fought sword to sword before the excited crowds of the town, Thomas stole away, muffled in his cloak against the biting cold wind and to hide his visage from passers-by.

He had looked forward to the highlight of the holiday, the knights melee and did stay to enjoy the first few jousts, but his heart pulled him away and he could not resist its yearning. He was soon ensconced in the warmth of the house on Bearward Street and thoughts of the tournament were just a distant memory.

After the festivities of the Easter Holy Days it became harder to arrange their clandestine meetings. Thomas found it difficult to study and keep his thought focused on the words of his lecturers. He spent little time with his friends, seeing them socially only during archery practice at the butts.

Eleanor had rebelled against her father's wish that she should go to Hemmington and he had not pushed her, enjoying her presence and the attention it brought him from the younger knights in the castle.

Friar Peter had visited his father and returned with a very positive report, which he wrote up and handed to Thomas, saying he would be happy to act as a witness at any appeal. Thomas had also used some of his money to get a written opinion from Richard Norton, the town's physician, who visited Walter, lanced his arm and tested his blood. Thomas had kept away from his father, as he knew he would not approve of his relationship and had felt unable to go and not tell him.

One evening, Alfred arrived at the little cottage at Saint John's with a message. Thomas immediately abandoned his studies from the Aphorisms of Hippocrates, a book that Brother Robert had managed to prize out of the priory library on a short loan. Apart from Salerno's Antidotarium that Brother Robert already had at the hospital, it was the only other medical book at the priory.

Luckily Brother Robert was not at the cottage so Thomas did not have to explain where he was going. He left quickly with Alfred and they made their way to Saint Peter's church, now a regular destination for his clandestine meetings. Eleanor was already at the small shrine. He found her pacing up and down with agitation. Even at his approach she was unable to sit. Alfred took up his customary position between the pillars and immediately Eleanor rushed into his arms.

"Oh Thomas, I've been so agitated. I was at the castle all day. A messenger came. He was dirty and tired. He had been injured too." She breathed in quickly not wanting to stop. "He said that Henry has left Oxford with a huge army and that he is heading for Northampton; not London as everyone thought he would. He will be here in a few days. What's going to happen Thomas?"

"So the king is finally making his move. Did you hear what your father or any of the other knights said?" Thomas held her hands trying to calm her and led her to a bench against the chapel wall.

"The De Montfort brothers clapped their hands and cheered, calling for wine, saying the Earl their father would soon follow and anyway they could beat their father in destroying the king. Bassett looked more sombre but he did say that the town and castle are impregnable."

"They're probably right but it won't be very nice with the king's army camped outside the town walls. You must leave the town. Go to Hemmington."

"No! I'm not going. I will not leave you now that at last we have some time together." She stood up. "If you stay, I will stay."

"I don't know what to do. If I go, I could never return to study. If I stay I commit treason. I cannot stand aside and watch. Anyway as a student I will be automatically tarred with the brush of revolution. I cannot force you to go but I will fear for you here. Your father is well and truly tied in with the rebels."

"I am going to stay and…" she knelt before him. "I want to see you as often as possible. We must see each other; for each day I feel our time grows shorter."

"Tonight."

"Yes."

"I will come after Compline."

"Be careful."

"I will. Now we must pray, then I must see my father and warn him. Saint Leonard's is outside the town wall." They both knelt before the shrine and said the Ave Maria and Pater Noster then knelt in silence holding hands. Finally Alfred coughed. Eleanor jumped up, and with a quick look, she brushed his cheek with her hand, then she turned and disappeared out into the nave.

Thomas sighed feeling the turmoil of emotion run through his body. After a short while, he too left the church and went out through the west gate intent on walking around to Saint Leonard's via the fields outside the town's wall. At the castle gate he turned south passing the hermitage and headed along the river towards the mill. His feet squelched through the water meadows. Set back from the river, the town walls, on his left, towered upwards, looking powerful and invincible. The sight of them raised the foreboding from his heart and he walked with a lighter step. He knew it was not his studies that kept him. He had become gripped by the excitement of the impending confrontation.

Pondering these thoughts he soon arrived at the gate to Saint Leonard's. He knew his only quandary was whether he should be standing on the outside with Henry the third and his son Edward, who was already a formidable warrior and leader, or on the inside with the De Montforts, full of the zeal of righteousness and revolution. With a sigh he realised that there was only one side he could conceivably be on, and knocked on the hospital gate.

He studied his father as they sat in the church, warming themselves at a brazier set up in the aisle. He would tell him about Eleanor he decided, but first:

"I have all the medical reports I need father. When this political mess blows over I will try to convene a hearing."

"Thank you Thomas, though I will probably not leave now. Unless perhaps for a short visit to your mother's grave and one last look at the village. But I would return here. This is my home now. You saw my Will that is in Brother Robert's keeping?" Thomas nodded. "So will you return?"

Thomas looked down.

"I don't know… my studies."

"I understand. It would be useful to fall back on if you ever need it." Thomas nodded. His father smiled, "So carry on with your endeavours to prove me cured. Now to more important matters, what news have you for me? The tournament and the Holy Week celebrations have been the talk of the hospital." He chuckled, "you'd think from the way some of them talk that they had been there and took part. They take every visitor's view as their own here. Brother Robert said you did well with the quarterstaff." Thomas nodded, "and did you get to touch the ball in the game. It was a great victory for the students. We watched from the river bank." Thomas blushed and shook his head, quickly changing the subject.

"King Henry is on his way from Oxford with his son and a huge army, father." He saw Walter's forehead crease up, cracking the permanent wrinkles and pulling his bushy grey eyebrows together and sighed.

"He is heading for Northampton?" Thomas nodded. "It is a shame it has come to this. There will be bloodshed before the month is out. You will stand with the town?" Thomas saw the frown was now directed at him.

"I do not wish to argue, father."

"But you will?"

"It is my place. Not perhaps of my making but I cannot leave it now."

"Destiny can be a cruel bedfellow." Walter looked away. Thomas knew he must continue to release his burdens.

"There is something else father…" Walter turned his grey eyes upon his son with concern, hearing the quiver in his voice. "I have been seeing…" he looked away, "Eleanor." Walter continued to watch him and placed his hand upon his son's knee.

"I know, Thomas." Thomas looked at him surprised. "Brother Robert," Walter said by way of explanation. He looked at the cross upon the altar. "We need to pray, son." He knelt and Thomas knelt with him.

After some time Thomas rose and helped his father to his feet.

"Will you be able to come into the town father?" Thomas now held his father by the arm.

"They will not allow it. Our priest has already made a representation before the town council. He was told that we would be fine where we are and there was no need to go upsetting the townsfolk by letting us in. I would have not gone in anyway. I remain a king's man Thomas." They smiled sadly at each other. "Go with God my son, I pray you will be alright, I think we will not get another chance to see each other before King Henry arrives, if your news is correct." Walter took Thomas in his arms. Thomas felt the emotion well in his chest. He saw moisture in the old grey eyes of his father. He felt strangely as though he were losing him all over again but this time he must be the one to walk away. His eyes too became blurred with moisture but he knew he was stronger this time. He turned and walked out of the gate.

Chapter 12

The next morning the news had spread throughout the town. Student and town volunteers made up watches along the ramparts of the town walls, armed with an odd assortment of weapons. Most of the scholars carried bows.

It was early the following morning that a cry went up along the walls and the church bells began to sound. Brother Robert and Thomas were halfway through their morning round at the hospital. They rushed outside and headed for the town wall that ran along the back of the hospital. Some ladders had been put up, along with a pulley and platform for lowering injured to the hospital. Thomas shot up the ladder and Brother Robert followed behind more sedately. The parapet was filling up with townsfolk and scholars alike.

Thomas looked out across the river to where the land rose up towards Hunsbury, just to the west of Saint Leonard's. The fields were full of ant-like soldiers busy setting up camp. Fires burned and bivouac shelters were scattered across the whole hillside. A large unit of horsemen, fully armoured, cantered along the Nene's opposite shore surveying the wall.

"Look there's the Royal Standard!" came a shout from further along the wall. "The king must be down there amongst those riders." A murmur ran through the gathered crowd. The air buzzed with momentary fear. Thomas felt butterflies in his stomach as he looked out at the proud well-armoured warriors.

"That must be him, there, with the great robe over his mail," he whispered to Brother Robert. The folk on the walls fell silent as they came to the bend in the river just to the west of the gate and reined in. During the moments of tense silence on the wall, Thomas wondered at the decision they had made to face this all-powerful king and his son the great warrior Edward. The cavalry suddenly wheeled and galloped off along the river in the direction of the castle. The crowd let out a collective sigh and many quickly and quietly left the wall, returning to their dwellings.

Thomas looked on, transfixed by the purposeful movements in the fields. He watched as a great troop of soldiers crossed the bridge and began to loot and burn the vacated houses at Coten End just outside the South Gate. By midday the whole street was ablaze. The air was full of smoke. Other fires could be seen to the west around Saint James End. The smoke drifted over the walls and into the town on the southerly breeze. It stung Thomas's eyes, which watered, and caught the back of his throat. He found himself unable to leave the wall and the terrible sight before it and was still there at dusk, listening to the rain hissing as it hit the fires.

Brother Robert found him in much the same spot he had left him eight hours earlier. He handed him a cup and poured some ale from a jug. Thomas drank deeply washing the smoke from his throat but he refused the food.

"It is a terrible sight." He said meditatively

"It is war. They are posturing. It is why the king rode along the riverbank. They want to show us what can happen. What will happen if they enter the town? They are trying to frighten us."

"It scares me." He looked at the monk who smiled sadly at him.

"Me also."

"Will you return to Saint Andrews?" Brother Robert looked away across the wall.

"We have been recalled. The prior wants no part in this revolt."

"He is a Frenchman, like most of your brothers. They would be happy to see us fall." Thomas spat some of his ale over the wall.

"In any war there are always two sides and both believe they are right." After some hesitation Robert continued. "Your heart is not totally in this I know. You could come with me to the priory." Thomas looked across the wall at the fires.

"No Brother Robert I am here now. It is a strange path that has led me here but I have made my choice." He looked along the parapet at his friends. "Whether right or wrong, I cannot leave my friends and besides, I could not live with myself if I walked away." The monk nodded in understanding. "Anyway, what an opportunity to practice some medicine," he smiled. Another perhaps stronger reason was that he knew that locked away in the abbey he would not see Eleanor again.

"Unfortunately in war it's usually the surgeons who are most busy. You may have to turn your hand to that! Some of the patients have left today and some have been moved, a few to Saint Andrews. There are still a few left. You will continue to care for them Thomas until I and the other monks return.

"I will do what I can." Thomas grabbed Robert by the arm. "Take my father's papers with you."

"Take care, I have come to value our friendship." Thomas smiled and squeezed Roberts arm but said nothing. He watched Robert clamber down the ladder and disappear into the shadows of the hospital.

At dawn Thomas rose and busied himself first with a cold wash, then some bread and ale, then with the preparation of medication for the few hospital cases left. The Franciscans had provided some food and were helping with basic care. Friar Peter had also been down to offer his support when casualties arrive. Thomas moved from patient to patient as he had done before. He was used to their ailments and administered Brother Robert's prescriptions where necessary.

When his duties as the new hospital infirmarer were finished he found himself unable to sit without knowing what was happening, so headed up to the wall, to watch the stirring king's army. They began to take up position, fanning out either side of South Gate in a great array of strength.

Thomas felt a touch on his arm and saw Heycock. He noticed that the walls were now full of scholars armed with bows swords and slings, and men-at-arms. He felt the ripple of tension run through his body from the touch of Heycock's hand. An eerie silence hung across the wall. Archers notched their bows and slingshots were loaded with stone. Thomas gripped his bow tightly and felt for an arrow in the quiver at his side.

A commotion along the wall made him turn. He saw the young Peter De Montfort striding along, smiling and talking to those he passed. With him walked the more severe Ralph Bassett. Tension became a nervous excitement with their passing.

From his vantage point near South Gate, Thomas saw the arrival of the King's Standard and a great gathering of knights on the south road. After some moments a group of knights broke away and began to ride down the road towards the gate.

"A parley," muttered Heycock, "look." Thomas turned and saw Peter De Montfort, Ralph Bassett and a mounted escort preparing to leave through the gate.

The two groups of knights met amongst the ruined remains of the suburb. The meeting was short and both sides were soon galloping in opposite directions. De Montfort and his knights cantered straight through the gate and on towards the castle without stopping.

Realising it would be a while before they returned, Thomas headed back to the hospital where he visited the patients and then went back to his small cottage.

As he sat at the trestle table, an unnatural silence hung around him. He studied the room in the light from the window opening. This room had been his home for the last six months. A small fire crackled in the hearth, a cauldron above, as it had done every day. Herbs hung from the beams, drying and releasing their scent to fill the room with a strong heady aroma, a smell, which now reminded him of his home. Shelves stacked with storage jars filled one end of the room. Thomas's bed lay along the other end, on an uneven earth floor.

He kicked at the dirt. Here was home. It was safe, warm, and had been full of friendly conversation. Yet he felt once again that he stood upon a precipice even as he looked about him. He thought suddenly of Eleanor and knew he would not see her that night.

Drinking his ale, he picked up his bow, and a small leather satchel packed with bandages and poultices for wounds and tinctures for pain relief. With one last look round he walked out and closed the door.

To his surprise he found the parapet crowded with folk all chattering and looking out. He pushed his way through the crowd and found Heycock.

"What's happening?"

"Oh, hi Thomas. They're going to hold a conference out on Cow Meadow. Look, there's Peter De Montfort, Ralph Bassett and the Mayor, John Le Spicer coming down from the Derngate. The king is there in the meadow already." He pointed out to a group of horsemen out in the meadow. Thomas looked across the meadow crowned above by grey heavy low clouds, which moved silently across the sky but looked menacing and heavy with rain.

"Do you think they'll reach an agreement?" he felt his heart thumping faster, unsure of what reply he really wanted.

"Last time the De Montfort's took up arms they did reach an agreement." They fell silent and watched the two groups getting closer but even as the town delegates closed with the King and his representatives, they mounted their horses and rode fast across the meadow to the small tributary bridge, crossing it they entered the smouldering remains of Coten End, their cloaks and standards streaming behind them as they rode back to their troops. Shouted insults and jeers came from the watching crowd on the wall as they flew past.

The town delegation had stopped unsure what to do. The clouds suddenly released their rain, which lashed down with force almost blotting out the view. Thomas felt its hard cold bite on his cheeks. He wondered at the scene, feeling momentary fear. Turning away from the rain, he looked across the town.

As he did so a large a large plume of dust and smoke rose up to meet the oncoming rain. It was instantly followed by a great rumbling sound.

"What's this? Is the devil come upon us?" shouted Heycock. The jeering had stopped to be replaced by silent shock as the gathered crowd turned as one to look at the rising dust. It was being carried up in the air currents and was drifting across the northern end of the town. The rain slowed and a strong wind swept across the wall. "This is not good."

"No, let us pray that God has not deserted us." Thomas replied, his fear mounting. Anxious cries echoed along the wall as spectators jostled for a way down, keen to return to the invisible safety of their homes. A roar came from behind them causing those left to turn and stare over the wall. The town delegation had disappeared. The king's army approached.

"Archers to the front, non-combatants clear the wall," came the shout from an older man-at-arms in charge of the section. Numb and shaking with adrenalin, Thomas made ready his bow.

"Fire!" a hail of arrows sped out from the wall falling on the long ranks before them. Raised shields and the earth took many but not all of the falling arrows. Thomas saw men fall, heard their cries. Then chaos broke out on the wall as the army below released their arrow storm. The crowded walls meant that many arrows found targets, indiscriminately hitting scholars, men-at-arms and the towns folk still stuck on the wall. Thomas shut his ears to their cries and fired off his arrows.

As quickly as they had advanced they began to retreat; the defenders stopped firing and watched in confusion as the kings army began to march rapidly to the west leaving their wounded along the river bank. Thomas did not have time to ponder this move.

"Come on Thomas, you're the medical man," came a cry from a fellow student. Thomas turned to see casualties lying along the parapet. The student who had called him was holding another student with an arrow in his shoulder. Thomas dropped his bow and took a deep breath. Brother Robert's lessons in dealing with wounds and what he had gleaned watching the surgeon on the few occasions that he had been called to the hospital, running fast through his head. Even as he worked on the injured along the wall, shouts of panic reached them, from below.

"The wall is breached in the north. We are betrayed!"

"The French bastards at the priory. They have done for us!" Thomas ignored the shouts as best he could and cut away at a young peasant woman's tunic before him, revealing an arrow embedded in her left breast. He looked at her imploring eyes. Heycock knelt opposite him.

"If they are in the town Thomas, all is lost. We cannot fight men-at-arms and knights." Thomas felt his fear. "They tricked us. They never intended to parley did they?" Thomas shook his head and picked up his knife. He looked from the woman's terrified gaze to his hand, which shook.

"Hold her, Heycock." Quickly, he cut out the arrow. The woman soon fainted. He bandaged the wound and together they carried her down to the hospital. Even as they entered they could hear cries of fighting to the north echoing down the streets.

The hospital was already filling up. Thomas watched one of the towns barber surgeons hard at work removing arrows from patients. Friar Peter moved around applying physic and bandages, assisted by some of the other friars.

"Hello Thomas, things not going too well out there?" Thomas shook his head by way of reply. "We are in need of you here," Thomas nodded. Friar Peter bent over the peasant woman. "Not a bad bit of surgery Thomas."

With that the friar moved on, humming to himself. Thomas looked around him, dazed at the chaos.

"Shit, he seems to be enjoying this."

"No, I don't think so. I think he's just trying to pretend it's not happening out there." Heycock picked up his bow.

"You staying here?" he asked. Thomas pondered for a moment, keen to see what was happening, but he knew he must stay, and nodded. Heycock turned to go, hesitated then came up to his motionless friend and hugged him quickly before running off. Thomas watched his disappearing back as he ran out through the door. He never saw him again.

The small hospital seemed to be bulging at the seams. Cries and moans came from every corner; Thomas did not know where to start. Each moment a new casualty staggered in through the doors, letting in the sound of the fighting outside. Each time the noise seemed louder and closer. Thomas began to move around stitching, repairing, bandaging, removing arrowheads, and doing what he could with his limited knowledge to help the injured as he went, losing track of time.

He was administering to a fellow student who was dying, his eyes slowly misting over, chest heaving and rattling with the effort of life's last breath. He began to pray for the departing soul but as he closed his eyes the only image he could see was that of Eleanor at the house on Bearward Street. He uttered a quick prayer for the dead boy, and then prayed that Eleanor was at the castle. Surely her father would have got her there. But as he continued to move around the moaning bodies on the floor his doubts grew and he knew he must find out. With a quick glance about him he moved to the door retrieved his staff and left.

He ran up Bridge Street fighting his way through fleeing townsfolk. The smell of burning filled his nostrils. The air was electric with terror and adrenalin. It gave him strength.

At All Saints church he grabbed hold of a terrified merchant, his hands full of materials and moneybags, his wife beside him.

"What's happening?" he shouted into the uncomprehending face, wide empty staring eyes looked at him.

"Let him go!" shouted his wife hitting out at Thomas with her fists. "They are coming. They have taken the north end of the town. The Marehold is full of corpses!" he released the man and watched them hurry off, shoulders bent like scurrying rats.

Heading into the market place, he found it full of people looking aimlessly about, unsure of what to do or which way to run. As he reached the pillory at its centre there was a sudden commotion at the entrance to Sheep Street. A herd of loose sheep came charging into the square followed by a clatter of shouting horsemen, their swords swinging as they reached the confusion in the square. Soon the general panic turned to terror as the townsfolk scattered. Thomas used his staff to fight his way through the crowd and out of the Square, feeling terror rising within him as he struggled. Reaching the buildings along the edge he forced his way into one and ran through it, past its cowering occupants and out the back into the Drapery. He made his way up Silver Street feeling calmer but holding his staff in readiness. It was quieter; there were a few running students and some Jews coming out of their houses with as much as they could carry. Recognising one of the students he called them to a halt.

"What's happening?"

"We fought them in Marehold," panted the boy. "We did well, our arrows inflicted a lot of casualties but once they reached us we could not hold out against their knights. Prince Edward leads them. They are still holding out down at Black Friars and down the horse market I think but it won't be for long." He stopped, taking a deep breath, his face damp with sweat and grime.

"They are already in the market place," replied Thomas.

"Then all is lost I fear."

"What will you do now?" Thomas studied the exhausted students.

"Try to reach the forces on the horse market, I guess." Sudden cries ahead alerted them to a group of approaching men-at-arms. He watched as they hacked down a Jew and began searching him.

"The fight is here as well by the look of it." Thomas felt his nervousness turn to unexpected anger as he watched the soldiers who seemed unconcerned at their presence further down the road. As he stood fuming, he watched as one of them pulled a woman from a doorway and tear at her dress with his mauling hands. Without really realising what he was doing, Thomas began to run towards them, yelling at the top of his voice. An arrow shot past him and hit a soldier in the chest. He saw another drop from a slingshot. He realised that the students behind were joining the fight. As he flew forward he caught a glimpse of a sword raised and about to strike out at him. Quickly without stopping he swung his quarterstaff in an arc and caught the man in the chest. With a quick second blow he hit his opponent across the back of the head. He felt the shudder pass up his arms with the intensity of the blow, but he did not stop to think. The girl was his goal and like a stoat he would not be deterred. Now with her bodice ripped open, her raven black hair whirling in the wind, blood running down her face, she fought her assailant, her hands clawing at his face. Thomas knocked down another soldier but felt a burning across his shoulder as the man's blade bit into it as he fell. Cries and shouts echoed in the streets as more joined the fight.

The man-at-arms pushed the girl to the ground and drew back his sword, realising it was too early for rape and pillage. Thomas gave a shout and was upon them. He looked from the rugged face of the soldier to the wide green eyes of the woman. With a start he realised he knew her. He remembered her standing proud in the Good Friday tormenting of the Jews, how those eyes had made him run from the crowd ashamed.

Thomas closed and lashed out at the soldier. His staff was expertly parried, but the man had forgotten the Jewess who kicked out hitting the soldier in the groin. Thomas swung again, crushing the man's skull as he bent forward. Pain shot through his arm with the force and his staff cracked. Blood spurted from the man's nose, mouth and forehead as he collapsed first to his knees then slowly he toppled forward.

"Behind you!" came a shout from the girl. Thomas instinctively ducked, turned drawing his knife. The soldier's sword cut the air over his head, causing him to go off balance. Thomas stepped in close and drove the small blade deep into the man's kidneys. He felt the warm sticky blood spurt over his hand and arm as he pushed the dying man away.

The girl grabbed his hand as he stood staring down at his groaning victim, and pulled him back into the dark doorway. The short fight was all but over. The few surviving rebels were in full flight back towards the market place, with the soldiers in pursuit. He knew there was no escape for them that way.

In the enclosed doorway he felt her hot breath, her naked back against his arm. Her raven hair blew across his face. She pulled him into the building and closed the door. He felt the sobs break from her and knew that he too was shaking. He pulled her to him and she came into his arms, he ran a hand into her dark coarse hair holding her close, trying to stop both their bodies shaking with shock.

When he was finally able to gather his thoughts he looked around the small room, taking in the table covered with papers and an open chest, a fire burning in the hearth. On the table he noticed a jug and letting go of the girl he went across and drank straight from it. The wine calmed his nerves. He offered it to the girl who drank and spluttered.

She was lost, he realised, unable to think for herself, still suffering from the shock of the incident. Her eyes stared back at him, unfocused. Thomas peeped out of the door. The street was now full of men-at-arms. The looting would begin again soon.

"You must hide."

"Father," she said, eventually pointing at the door. Thomas remembered the old Jew falling under the sword blow.

"You must look after yourself now." He knew that neither side cared much for the Jews nor would they care what happened to them. "Is there somewhere for you to hide?" He shook her gently. Slowly comprehension of her situation dawned on her. Her green eyes sparkled once again. She pulled up her bodice, covering her breasts and blushed slightly. Thomas smiled at her sudden modesty.

"What about you?" She said suddenly.

"I must get to Bearward Street."

"You can get there through the garden." They heard shouting in the street close to the door. "My father built a secret cellar. He always feared there would be trouble for us. I will hide there." Her pale face smiled at him. She took his hand and led him into a back parlour. Sensing his uncertainty, she pointed to the door. "Go on, they will be in here soon."

"But…"

"I will be fine now. You have done enough for me already." She picked up a cloak and wrapped it around herself. "Go!" He opened the door, and then turned back to her, starring once more into those powerful green eyes.

"When you can, find Brother Robert of Saint John's Hospital. He will help you if you tell him Thomas sent you." She nodded and smiled. Then pushed him out of the door and he heard her bolt it.

After a moment's indecision he turned and ran across the garden, climbing a fence at its end, his body alert and tense. He entered the house that backed onto the Jewess's and which opened up onto Bearward Street. It had been ransacked. The body of a raped woman lay on the floor, her husband, his throat cut, at her side. He tasted bile as he stepped across them, and eased open the front door.

He looked across the street to where Eleanor's lodging should be. The street was full of running figures silhouetted against a great fire. He felt the heat hit him in the face.

Throwing open the door, his fear gone, he rushed out into the street and cried out in despair. Her house, their house, those beautiful moments, they blazed; roaring flames shot upwards, timbers crashed inwards. The whole side of the street was an inferno. He dropped to his knees, oblivious to the movement around him, tears falling down his face, his hair singeing.

The knight rode past at a canter. Thomas did not even see the mace that crashed into the back of his head. He fell forward into the sodden earth of the road.

Chapter 13

The kicking slowly seeped into the recesses of his unconscious mind. He heard a groan and knew it was his own. Slowly he began to feel the pain. The boot hit him again.

"That's a penny you owe me. I told you he was alive."

"He won't be for long though, I'll wager. The bastards'll soon be strung up you see. Old Henry's hopping mad." The soldier turned to a huddle of prisoners. "Pick him up!" Thomas felt himself lifted as a man supported him on both sides. He had no strength of his own. He opened his eyes. Pain ran through his head.

He glanced at his two aides. They looked dishevelled and dirty, their spirit broken. One was a scholar the other a man-at-arms wearing the tattered remains of a surcoat bearing the De Montfort Arms. He looked around at the silhouettes of other prisoners. There images flickering in the glow of the fire, which was all that remained of Bearward Street. He stared at the pile of ash and timber that marked Eleanor's house, then felt himself being tugged along, his feet dragging in the mud and ash.

"Thank God for rain." He heard the guard's voice. "I reckon we would have lost the whole town to fire without it."

"Yeah and all our pillage to boot!" came the reply from the other.

When Thomas woke again he found that he was staring up at a great domed wooden ceiling. He lifted himself up as best as he was able and leaned against a huge pillar, above which a mighty arch reached across to another Norman pier. Thomas recognised this heavy circle of columns as the nave of the Holy Sepulchre. He groaned with pain, which seemed to shoot from every corner of his body. Lowering his eyes, he focused on the mass of humanity crowded into every corner of the church: scholars, townsfolk, men-at-arms, priests, and friars, all battered and weary, clothes torn and dirty. Their faces were expressionless, lost in their own private agonies. Cries rose from the wounded that lay amongst them.

He slowly turned his head, pain shot across his skull and shoulders, a crushing pressure inside his head threatened to burst his eyes.

As the pain faded he made out the figure of a soldier in the livery of Thomas Menhill. The man nodded to him. Thomas tried to speak but his throat, dry and swollen, would not respond. He moved his cracked lips, feeling a sudden terrible thirst. The man held up a leather pot and poured a small amount of water onto his lips and into his mouth.

"Thought you were dead when they first dumped you down. Don't speak, conserve your energy. You look like shit by the way." Thomas recognised the man as a professional soldier. He had a rugged unshaven face caked in blood from a cut now crusted over on his cheek. Thomas closed his eyes. It was some time before he opened them again.

"So we lost then," he croaked. The man laughed a deep-throated cackle that echoed around the dome. Thomas smiled feeling the dirt and dried blood crack on his cheeks.

"So you've surfaced again. You're right there though, that's for sure. Still, we had a good fight along the Horse market." He rubbed his hands together. "Haven't had a fight like that for a long time. Shame we lost, still that was a forgone conclusion once Edward beat Simon De Montfort and his knights in the breach at the priory." Thomas looked at him questioningly so he continued "Yeah, the monks let Edward and his knights in and they destroyed the wall, so gaining access to the town. The De Montfort's put up a good fight there apparently but could not hold them."

"Oh I had heard some but not the whole story." Thomas settled back against his pillar trying to relax his painful body. "How bad do I look?"

Oh pretty ghastly, mind I've seen worse. You have a nasty gash in your shoulder and your head looks a mess."

"I have some stuff in my bag, a poultice and some bandage."

"I'll give it a try. I've got some water here. Let's see if we can clean you up a bit first." the soldier busied himself with the task gently humming to himself.

"You're one of Thomas Menhill's men?"

"Oh aye, I wear his livery that is. He hired me in London just before he left for here. Last time I saw him was in the horse market. We were making a good stand from what I remember. There were too many of them though. Then I got clobbered." He pointed to his head. "Must've dropped like a stone cause I don't remember anything else." Thomas struggled round to face the man.

"You know of the Lady Eleanor?"

"Oh yes, a pretty one she is. Very distant though, as though she always had something pressing on her mind."

Thomas persisted, "Have you any news of her?" The soldier looked quizzically at him.

"Her father fell at the breach. I saw him go down under a pile of knights, but the lady…"

"Was she at the castle, do you know?"

"Not that I know. We came out of the castle. I haven't seen her there much at all this last week; has lodging in the town apparently. I hope she's managed to keep away from the king's men. They don't hold much with honour by the look of them." Thomas sat back and closed his eyes, trying not to picture the horror of Eleanor in the clutches of the king's men. He prayed that she had escaped somehow.

Throughout the next day Thomas lay dazed in the church slipping in and out of consciousness. The soldier continued to care for him, tending his wounds and feeding him small gulps of water whenever he woke. As the light slowly faded from the small church windows, their guards announced the collapse of the castle and the capture of Ralph Bassett and Peter De Montfort. Throughout the night sounds of the victorious armies plundering celebrations echoed through the church.

"Sounds like they're taking the town apart," Thomas mumbled.

"Aye, there won't be much left I reckon. Thank God we are locked in this church. It won't be safe to be out there." Thomas thought of Eleanor once more.

On the third day the prisoners were forced to their feet. The soldier grabbed Thomas and pulled him up. He was a big broad man with immense strength.

"Now we go to find out whether we live or die. My name is Henry by the way." He chuckled at that. "Never thought I'd fight against the king I was named after."

"Thomas," he mumbled, "my name is Thomas."

They staggered slowly out of the dimly lit circle of the Holy Sepulchre and joined the column of broken men that made their way through the battered streets of their town; Stepping over bodies and the shattered remains of houses and their possessions as they went. Those prisoners who were townsfolk wept openly at the demise of their once great town, when such a short time ago they had stood at the pinnacle, filled with confidence and success.

They crossed the Marehold, past a great pile of rat-infested bodies, scholars, soldiers, townsmen, their congealed blood mixing with the dirt in pools of rainwater. The smell of death crept in through Thomas's shattered nose. He felt the acidic bile rise up from his empty stomach.

They were herded across the bailey of the castle, where corpses hung from a quickly erected scaffold, to the prison tower. There, they were forced down steps underground into a crowded dark room. The odour made Thomas feel faint and he retched, his stomach tight with cramp. The acrid taste of human waste, sweat and fetid wounds overwhelmed his senses.

Henry carried Thomas over to the only cot bed and mattress in the crowded room, upon which sat a priest. Henry pulled him off with a grunt and lay Thomas carefully down.

"Do you know who I am?" the priest moaned angrily from his new position amongst the fetid straw. Though his voice was full of anger, he was wary of this giant powerful soldier, who had usurped him without a thought.

"I don't care priest. This man needs a bed." The priest's face filled Thomas's vision.

"Henry of Leicester," he mumbled as he slipped into sleep.

He dreamt of Eleanor calling out to him, while the dead at Marehold rose and watched him with cold empty eyes, Sir John, on a dead horse rode at their head. His brother sat on the large chair in the hall at Buckbie laughing at them and constantly the priest Henry of Leicester circled him, walking round and round, his head down. Thomas felt dizzy and sick.

Waking, he vomited. His eyes focused at a pair of feet now spattered with puke. They were good leather shoes. He looked up wincing to see the thin face of the priest with his pronounced Norman nose. He still had some of his old arrogance but there was also a haunted look and fear in the depth of his eyes. His clothes were tattered and dirty. He stared dumbfounded at his spattered shoes.

A chuckle and a shuffle at the bottom of the rickety cot bed made Thomas look down. Henry, the man-at-arms picked his teeth with a bit of straw from the mattress.

"Hello Thomas, glad you could join us. You've been out so long I was beginning to worry you'd got lost and couldn't find your way back." He smiled. "Here have some water. It'll clear the vomit out."

"Thanks," Thomas looked at the two men watching him. He mopped the sweat from his brow and knew he was running a fever. "I have a fever. It's these damn wounds. It will probably get worse. I could do with a posset of feverfew and borage to lower my temperature." The soldier shook his head gravely.

"They don't care for no one in here unless you have plenty of money." Thomas looked at the two men.

"Henry, man-at-arms meet Henry of Leicester priest to the De Montforts and the bastard that falsely pronounced my father a leper. The consequences of which led to my presence in this pit of Lucifer." The priest looked around at him in surprise and confusion. The soldier chuckled.

"How can you laugh at everything." The priest shouted at the soldier. Then he turned to Thomas his eyes wide and staring. "You know me. That I can accept, but what is this about your father for I know you not." Thomas, now becoming weary explained the events of the previous year and watched the recognition appear in the face of the haughty priest.

"Yes, I remember that case."

"He does not have the leprosy, priest. I have proof, yet I cannot get him released without the churches permission. You are no physician or surgeon. Yet you pronounced against him. Why?" The priest went quiet for a moment and looked at the floor.

"Speak priest, we are all equal in this squalor," said Henry. Finally the priest looked up.

"I do not perceive myself as an evil doer Thomas, though I see that you believe it is so. Everything I have done I have done in the belief that the end result is right in the eyes of God." The priest struggled on with his conscience, not used to having to explain himself. "The symptoms were there. There was enough evidence…"

"And yet!" Thomas said, coughing with overexertion "There is more priest. Speak!"

"I knew Sir John wanted your father out of the way. It seemed very convenient that he was a leper. If Sir John had other reasons it mattered little to me, for, as your father was a leper, I had to perform my duty. Sir John's reasons did not interest me. My focus was the cause." He finished lamely.

"What do you think now, Henry of Leicester? Now that you sit with his son in this squalor."

"The mouth of Hell," muttered the priest and crossed himself.

"Yes, a good place to repent of any sins, I would say," chipped in Henry.

"If what you say is true then I have done wrong. Would that this was my only sin, to allow myself to be blinded for this cause." He looked at Thomas as he lay on the bed, feeling remorse rise. "I did have some doubts, so I made some enquiries when I returned to Odiham castle. The Earl was there, as was his physician and surgeon. The Earl had taken a fall and broken his leg. I spoke to them about your father. They said that there are many herbs and poisons that will have similar effects while they are being administered. You said that your father has not had any symptoms since leaving. I fear that this could be an explanation."

"Yet you did nothing."

"I was busy with this business." He waved his hands vaguely about. "It was a small matter in the scheme of things at the time. Besides, it meant that Sir John would give us his full support."

"He did that! He died at the breach!" returned Henry. The priest shook his head.

"So many deaths. I did not dream it would be like this." Thomas pulled himself up as best he could and grabbed the priest's tattered robes.

"You could help right this wrong that you have done." The priest looked at him nervously. "I have letters from an eminent secular physician, a learned Franciscan physician and the infirmarer at Saint John's hospital. All of them state that my father no longer has the symptoms. You can rescind the judgement that you made or call a council that can." Thomas looked pleadingly at the priest for a moment then fell back on the couch.

Finally the priest said."If I get out of here I will do what I can but I have it on the authority of the sergeant in charge that we are all to be hanged. The priest finished with a resigned sigh and began to mutter a Pater Noster.

"Haven't you pleaded for a clerical trial?" said Henry with a sneer.

"They would not listen." The priest mumbled full of self-pity. Thomas closed his eyes and shut them out and tried to overcome the dull constant ache of his cracked head. He felt dirty, and hot. He realised he had not eaten since the day of the attack. He touched his face. He had grown quite a beard. It was matted with dirt, blood and vomit. His scholar's robes were in tatters. His hose and tunic chaffed at his skin underneath. He itched all over.

"Bed's a bit lousy I'm afraid," said Henry, noticing him trying to scratch. "Still it was the only one and you had need of it." Henry scratched at his beard. "Still I don't think it matters whether you're on the bed or not, I'm covered in them too!"

Thomas pulled himself up again and surveyed the writhing mass of humanity packed into the small room. The only light came flickering through the bars in the door and a small recess high in the wall, through which crept the faded light of a grey spring day.

"God what a hell this is! What is to happen to us Henry?" Thomas felt despair.

"First they will ransom off those who can pay. Then those that are left, well…" He fell silent. "You'll be alright I guess, priest. You must be worth a bit I should think." Henry of Leicester pulled himself from the damp floor and brushed his robes then sat at the other end of the bed. Thomas looked at the two Henry's who were like chalk and cheese.

"They threw me in here and refused to recognise me. Said for all they knew I wasn't even a priest but a rebel who put on a priest's robes for protection," he said despondently.

"Just another meddling priest, hey." Soldier Henry laughed. "Don't worry they'll get you eventually. Hopefully before any prison contagion that is!" he chuckled again. The priest looked away his face ashen.

Later that evening buckets of water were placed inside the door and bread thrown in. Thomas's guardian angel, Henry got them bread and a mug of water which the three of them shared. Thomas ate little, his fever once more raging.

When the priest thanked the soldier and asked him why, he said.

"I'll not have my conscience fettered as yours is."

Later, as Henry mopped his sweating brow, Thomas asked. "Do you think she's dead Henry? I feel I should know but my heart feels only despair."

"I don't know Thomas. We can just pray and hope. From what I saw of her she was a resourceful lady. I'm sure she would be okay." He tried to make his voice sound convincing for the sick man.

"The following morning when Thomas finally woke from his feverish sleep, he discovered the priest had gone.

"Took him while you were sleeping," Henry said by way of explanation. "Looks like his value was realised after all, lucky bastard. Those that cause all the aggro always get off and leave the likes of us to get the shit."

During the day more and more of the prisoners disappeared.

"Well its ransoms or hanging. What do you think? My guess is ransom. Fat chance I have. I ain't got any family and I can't imagine Thomas Menhill being in a position to ransom his men even if he wanted to. That's if he survived. I guess it'll be the noose for me."

"You sound calm about it Henry," Thomas answered, closing his eyes. He had been continually surprised at Henry's calm jovial attitude.

"For the likes of me, it's either a steel blade or the noose. Though can't say I'm too happy about it now it seems so close. What about yourself? Anyone likely to bail you out?" Thomas thought for a moment.

"I too, have no family here. But there is one, a monk who might be able to help; that's if he ever discovers I'm here." He had tried not to think of his own death but he began to feel despair.

They slipped into silence, perched on their bed like a raft among the flotsam of waste, filthy rushes and humanity that drifted about the chamber. As the day wore on Henry became more morose. Thomas did not like to see Henry quiet and felt guilty for having made him face the reality of their situation. He too felt the depression of their circumstance overwhelm him. Tears welled up and mixed with the dirt and sweat of fever on his cheeks.

It was another day before Henry woke him with a shake and said his name had been called. At first he felt tense unable to move.

"I'll help you to the door. Come on lad," urged Henry, but Thomas was so weak he could not lift himself up so Henry pulled him from the bed and dragged him to the door. He felt light headed and weak, his body was wasted from his injuries, fever and lack of food. The guard held a lantern to his face and nodded.

"You, Thomas Millerson of Buckbie?" Thomas nodded. "Come with me."

"Hang on mister, if I let go he'll hit the floor." The guard looked perplexed for a moment.

"Okay, you bring him, but no funny business alright?" Henry nodded, just glad to leave the stink of the cell behind him. Looking back, Thomas noticed that the shape of another already filled the coveted spot on the bed that he had so recently occupied.

They shuffled slowly along the corridor. It seemed to them an age since they had come in the other direction. Finally they reached the guardroom, well lit by a number of arrow slits. Thomas felt the breeze coming through and smelt the cool air. He heard Henry give a large sigh. At least he felt that he was to see the sky once more, even if it was to be the last time. He felt Henry grip his arm tightly.

"Thomas, scholar of this town and millers son from Buckbie?" this time the question came from a serious looking man who stood behind a table covered in papers. Once again Thomas nodded. The man looked across at two other figures that Thomas had not noticed. Brother Robert stepped forward, his eyes wide with pity and concern. The other figure also came forward. He smiled at them, feeling relief overcome him; knowing now it was not the gibbet that he was heading for.

The other person threw back her cowl and came towards him.

"Oh, Thomas you are in a state!" he saw tears in her eyes. She touched his cheek.

"Thank the Lord, Thomas you have survived. We had thought you lost." Brother Robert crossed himself.

"Thomas you are free. These people have paid your bond."

"Free…" Thomas mumbled to himself, the word echoing on inside him, slowly sinking in.

"Come on," said Robert, "let's get you to the hospital. He began to take his weight. But Thomas would not release Henry.

"I cannot go without this man, Henry," he whispered to the monk's lowered head. "He saved my life. I cannot leave him in there. It is Hell Brother. I have money at the hospital…" Sweat broke out on his pale brow with the effort it took him.

"I have not the capital Thomas. It was not me that paid for you." He looked at the lady who stood before them.

"Matilda…" he stumbled lost for words. "I owe you much but…"

"I owed you a life Thomas, I have not forgotten that." She watched him, her eyes full of compassion. She turned to Henry. "And any man that has saved you is worth saving too."

"Thank you my lady." Henry attempted a bow and brushed his free hand through his rough matted hair.

"I thank you also. I had thought you would have forgotten me by now."

"Oh, no," she smiled her face reddening slightly. "I have thought of you often, especially through these troubled times. Now talk no more. We must get you and your friend out of here and back to the hospital where we can care for you properly."

Thomas shielded his eyes as they stepped out into the bright crisp April day. He breathed in deeply, almost overcome by the cool air. The Lady Gobion had a carriage waiting which carried them slowly to the hospital through the broken streets of the humbled town. The hospital had been left untouched by the victorious army. It was full of injured townsfolk. Many homeless victims squatted in its grounds. Fresh graves were scattered around the chapel. Thomas was carried into the small cottage, which was unchanged from that fateful day when he left it. It felt safe and homely as he lay down on his palliasse. Brother Robert busied himself, re-bandaging and washing Thomas's various wounds and prepared a tisane of feverfew and borage to help reduce his fever. Henry collapsed on a bench by the hearth exhausted from his exertions.

"I should return." Matilda said hesitantly as she watch the monk at work.

"Oh yes, yes, forgive me, my lady. I will escort you to the gatehouse."

"No you carry on Brother. I will be fine. Thomas needs you more than I. I will return in a few days to see how you are faring." She looked at the two men, her gaze lingering on Thomas.

"Your money my lady. I have not repaid you." She waved a hand.

"Later. It is not important at present." Then with one last look, she turned and left.

He felt the fire surrounding him, soldiers shouting, Eleanor watching him from amongst the flames, the soldiers beating the Jewesses father. The flames grew closer, licking at his clothes and face. Eleanor and the soldiers began to melt.

He woke with a start. His body sweat soaked. Henry was sitting up watching him, and scratching at his beard.

"You Okay? Nightmare?" he did not wait for an answer but rose and went across to the table where Robert had left a jug of wine. He poured out two cups and passed one to Thomas. "It won't be the last," he said sitting on the bed. "But at least you're conscious enough to have dreams and your fever has finally broken."

"How long…?"

"Oh a few days. After we arrived in the night you dropped into a deep fever. Brother Robert has been caring for you every day. Only taking rest when either the Lady Matilda or myself have been here. He said last night that your fever had finally broken and that the wounds would heal well."

"The Lady Matilda, she has been here?"

"Oh yes, most days she has come by." Thomas lay back, surprised.

"That is good of her."

"She thinks a lot of you. Told me what you had done. Rescuing her." Henry stoked up the fire and sat by the hearth drinking his wine.

"I saw the Lady Eleanor in my dream," said Thomas from his bed. "Has there been any news?" He looked across at Henry silhouetted by the fire. Henry shook his head.

"We have had little time, what with you… anyway the Lady Matilda made some enquiries. Nobody has any idea what happened to her up at the castle. Get some more sleep. You can do nothing now. We will see what we can find out tomorrow." He came over and made Thomas drink the wine. It flowed quickly into his body, making him drowsy and dropping him back into a deeper sleep.

The next morning, with the help of Henry and Robert, he raised himself and washed outside, enjoying the cold air on his naked flesh. Henry drenched him in cool rainwater from a bucket, washing away the dirt and stink of fever and prison, which still clung to him. His body ached and his shoulder was stiff from the sword wound but he felt more revitalised. It had been many days since the defeat and he needed to see what had happened to the town, his friends and Eleanor. Inside they helped him get dressed in hose and a tunic. Brother Robert had taken out and burned all the clothes they had arrived in, from prison.

They all sat at the table to break their fast on bread, cheese and ale. Thomas ate slowly and carefully. He had hardly eaten in over a week. They had said little to each other since rising so Thomas broke the silence. He was desperate for news.

"What is happening out there, Brother?" He turned to the monk.

"The town is badly looted and damaged. In the end the king was persuaded not to hang the prisoners, though many still linger in the castle. He has closed the university and ordered the scholars to disperse. Those that are not locked up have already left for Oxford and Cambridge. It is a sad quiet place out there. By the way," he looked at Thomas. "A Jewess came to me asking for help. She mentioned your name. It was the morning after the attack. I had just returned."

"Was she alright? Did you help her?"

"Of course. You knew I would. I protected her here for a couple of days, and then the Lady Matilda escorted her out of the town. One of Lady Matilda's servants then escorted her to some relatives she has in a town on the coast. It is lucky she did not head for London. News has just arrived that the Earl of Leicester has had all the Jews in London put to death." He stopped for a moment and chewed meditatively on a piece of bread.

"What is it Brother, there is more I can tell?"

"I have some news which pertains to you Thomas. I have been unsure how to tell you." Thomas went pale.

"Eleanor…"

"No, it is not the Lady Eleanor. As yet I have no news of her. It is your father, Walter."

"Father." Thomas realised that he had not thought of him since his last visit. "How is he Brother? Have you visited him?"

"No, Thomas but I have news from a fellow monk who went out to Saint Leonard's." Robert paused and drank some ale. "The community was destroyed Thomas. It seems the king did not want the leper colony so close to his camp."

"What of the inmates? My father where did they go? I must go and see him."

"They are dead Thomas; all slaughtered, your father amongst them, as was the priest. They burned the bodies and the buildings. I'm sorry Thomas." Brother Robert rose and put his arm across Thomas's shoulders.

"He's dead. It cannot be! Not now! No! He was not even a leper; of that I am sure! Oh God!" Tears began to fall down his cheeks. "He even supported the king!" He put his head in his hands "Have I lost everything?" His body shook with grief.

It was sometime before he looked at the other two men, his grey eyes pleading through the moisture. He stood up. Wiping his face. "I must find Eleanor."

Henry rose.

"I will come too. You are not yet that strong."

Using a staff and Henry as a prop they made slow progress up Bridge Street, past the inn, which contained only king's men who looked menacingly at them as they stood in the doorway. Henry quickly pulled him away and on up to the town centre. Few shops were open and even fewer stalls stood in the square. Townsfolk moved furtively, their eyes darting suspiciously at every passing person. Men-at-arms stood dotted around in groups and occupied most of the taverns and inns.

They made their way slowly into Bearward Street. It was empty; a charred and barren wasteland of blackened wood and stone, patrolled only by animals, rats, dogs and scavenging cats. Thomas moved slowly, memories flashing before him, the flames, soldiers, Eleanor naked upon her bed. He stood before the shattered remains of the house.

Henry moved amongst the ruins. He stopped finding a blackened corpse at his feet. A dog pulled at one of its limbs. He cursed and kicked it. It gave a yelp and moved back a few feet and started growling not prepared to leave its prize. He looked across at Thomas and wondered if she lay before him.

"There is a body here," he said tentatively "Under the beams. It's badly burnt so don't..." he did not want Thomas to see the corpse but it was too late. He had climbed across. He knelt down and pulled over the rigid cadaver. A rat ran out, making him fall back with a start. He returned quickly forcing himself to continue.

The corpse stared back at him with a burnt grin of teeth, its skin blackened and tight, its hair and eyes gone. It was unrecognisable. Thomas could tell it was female. He vomited up his breakfast, and felt faint from the fetid aroma. Tears fell from his cheeks onto the body.

"It cannot be her Thomas, come on." Thomas shrugged off his arm.

"We cannot go until we know. Besides even if it isn't we cannot leave her here." Taking his cloak he carefully lifted the body onto it. As he laid the corpse down he noticed an object clutched in the remains of its fingers. Carefully prizing them open he recognized the glint of gold and precious stones. It was a brooch. He held it up and carefully began to clean it. His heart raced.

He stared at the gold ring brooch set with red rubies and blue sapphires. Each gem surrounded and linked by delicate punched decoration in the gold. He knew it. He could not speak. It was hers. She had told him it had been a present from the Menhill's on her betrothal to their son. She had worn it in the parade. She had looked beautiful that day. The vision had not left him. Henry once again put his arm upon Thomas's shoulder, feeling his pain.

"It's hers," he croaked eventually to Henry, holding out his hand.

Henry carried the body wrapped in Thomas's cloak back to the hospital and laid it in the chapel. Thomas knelt before it. Brother Robert came in at a rush and went over to the body carefully examining it.

"It is a dark haired woman," he muttered quietly as he knelt at Thomas's side.

"It must be her then. There can be no doubt. Oh my poor beautiful Eleanor. Look at her now Brother. How can God be so cruel?"

"It is man that has done this my son. Let us pray that we can overcome the pain and that she will find peace in heaven."

"I have lost everything Brother, my father, my lover, the university. What is there now? It is over." With a cry of despair he threw himself down before the altar. The brooch still clutched firmly in his hand.

His face touched the cold stone floor. "God has forsaken me. What have I done? One moment I have hope, love and happiness then," he watched the light filtering across the small chapel, filling it with a dusty haze.

Suddenly a dark cloud cut it out. "It is there one moment and like a speck of dust in a beam of sunlight, but when the darkness comes it slips away." Robert found himself unable to reply. He began to pray. Thomas lay amongst his tears listening to the soft Latin chant.

The following morning Lady Matilda arrived at the small cottage to be greeted by Henry and Brother Robert who was preparing medication for the many injured and sick in the hospital.

"How is our patient today?" she enquired concerned at his absence from the palliasse which he had occupied on her many visits. The monk quickly explained the happenings of the previous day.

"So physically he has been recovering well but now with what has happened I fear that his humours are now imbalanced. He has too much yellow and black bile. I think he may soon need lancing. Hopefully he will pull through and restore the balance but he will need his friends. You have some feeling for the lad?" she blushed and nodded. "Good, he needs to know there are people about who still care for him. Now come, for we must bury the Lady Eleanor." Henry rose and they all left for the chapel. "He has remained in the chapel since he brought her back yesterday," the monk said as they walked across the yard, to its entrance.

The bound and shrouded remains lay before the altar on a trestle table. Thomas knelt before it. Brother Robert performed a short service then Thomas with Henry's help carried the light corpse out to the small hospital cemetery and lowered it into the grave.

Lady Matilda stayed with Thomas at the graveside when the others had left. They knelt and watched the shadows from a weak spring sun slowly move across the disturbed earth in front of them; neither spoke. Eventually Matilda rose, her legs shaking with weariness. She stood behind him and placed her hand upon his shoulder. She looked down upon his black shiny hair, its tonsure all but grown out.

"What will you do now Thomas?" she whispered, she felt him give a shudder.

"I do not know," he mumbled in reply. His eyes still fixed on the pile of earth before him.

"You have your life. The Lady Eleanor and your father would not have wished for you just to give up and fade away." He turned on her, his eyes fiery. His brow furrowed.

"How would you know!" he all but shouted, then looked away embarrassed at his outburst. She went to withdraw her hand but he grabbed it quickly. "I am sorry Matilda. Forgive me. You deserve better. You have been good to me. It just doesn't seem that easy at the moment."

"It is never easy but you do not give up on life." She looked away from him and he remembered the struggles that she lived in daily with her husband. "Come Thomas, we will go to Saint Leonard's. You have not yet visited the grave of your father." He rose, nodding and they made their way silently out of the hospital and out through the South Gate past the destroyed suburb and to what remained of the Lazar Hospital.

Little remained but the chapel, all the small huts and cottages had been destroyed. A large mound of earth lay to one side of the chapel. Brother Robert had told him that this was the burial site of all the inhabitants. Thomas knelt in the earth taking some up in his hands once more he prayed and again tears flowed down his cheeks dripping into the damp loam. Matilda again knelt beside him; her presence began to erode his pain. His nostrils slowly filled with the scent of her instead of the burnt wood and freshly dug soil.

"I have lost him twice now. Just when I thought all was well and that I could get him released from the bonds of being a leper. Now I have to grieve again."

"You are not alone Thomas. Do not forget that." She dared not look at him.

"Thank you," he muttered, "I will try." Matilda got up and walked away; sitting at the entrance to the chapel to wait. She looked at his gaunt figure and sagging shoulders and sighed. She listened to the song of a skylark drifting across the damp meadows.

Each day for the next week the Bridge Inn drew Thomas in until he no longer went back to the hospital, to the concerned faces of Henry and Brother Robert. He would instead collapse in his cups on the damp empty mattresses, now vacated not only by the students but also the soldiers who had headed north with the King, towards Leicester and Nottingham, where they were to join up with another Royalist army.

Early one morning Matilda entered the inn. She stepped in the entrance, the smell of decay, filled her nostrils, unchanged rushes on the floor, full of stale ale, old food and vomit. She saw the huddled shape of Thomas on a bench near the empty hearth. As she moved slowly towards him, rodents scurried off in different directions, a thin dog darted out of the door already tense waiting for the blow from a well-aimed object.

She sat down opposite the slumbering shape and studied his dishevelled countenance. His hair was greasy and matted and full of lice as was his beard. His clothes too seemed alive with fleas and filth. She felt moisture fill her eyes. Fate was a cruel bedfellow, she knew. Before her on the table was a scholar's wax tablet amongst the crumbs of food and pools of ale. Thanks to her brother she had some skill at reading. She was not an expert but slowly she interpreted the words in the wax. She muttered them quietly.

"Roaming, listless in the wild sea
 Of agony, without the pain.
 God has deserted me.
 My soul lies dead in this earth."

The rest was smudged and unreadable. She could make out only a few words that filled her with dread, "…anger… hate…"

She jumped as he stirred and dropped the tablet, which clattered, onto the floor. He opened his red-rimmed eyes and sat up.

"I tried, but all I saw was emptiness," he said looking at her, seeing the pity in her eyes. "So you have come to see my downfall." He saw the flash of anger.

"No! I have come to help someone I care for!" he rubbed at his stinging eyes. The stench of him hung in the air. "This place, it…"

"Once it was wonderful, full of laughter, dreams, excitement. That has gone; it is empty and decaying, like me." she heard his stomach rumble.

"Come, let's get some food and you need a clean-up."

"Does my smell upset you!" he chuckled to himself. She rose becoming even angrier.

"You stink!" He shrugged about to lie down again. She stood unsure but not prepared to give in. The last two words on the tablet came to her. She smiled slyly.

"So you give in so easily. I'm sure that would impress your father and the Lady Eleanor."

"What can I do?" he mumbled closing his eyes, trying to ignore her.

"Fight!" she shouted into his face. His eyes popped open. "The king did this to you, didn't he?" He pulled himself up.

"That bastard, he destroyed me and he doesn't even know or care."

"Is not a king meant to care for and protect his subjects." She saw how much his mind had slipped. His ability to reason had gone. He looked at her like a lost child. "Why don't you make him realise what he has done." She saw how much his subconscious wanted to grasp at a purpose to go on.

"How can I, a commoner, affect the affairs of a king?"

"Perhaps you can't in a big way but you can still do your bit. The Earl of Leicester is gathering an army along with Gilbert de Clare and the rebel Barons."

"So?" he grunted, his gaunt face watched her, his ale soaked brain uncomprehending.

"So! Join them, you fool, fight back." Her heart fluttered at the thought, but she could not watch him sink slowly away. He leaned on the table his head in his hands.

"I don't know." She saw his despair and failing courage flickering in his bloodshot eyes.

"Hold on to their memory. Show King Henry how important they were to you. You can't do that sitting here!"

"Why are you saying this?" He could not look her in the face now. "You are with the king aren't you?"

"The Gobion family are," he heard her give a sob and turned to see tears in her eyes. "You can fight for me too." She held his gaze now. "Will you come?" she stood and held out her hand to him. "The Gobions' are away. Come with me and we will make you ready." He hesitated, unsure but finally got to his feet and took her hand.

He allowed her to lead him across the town to the Gobion Manor. She led him straight through the hall into solar where she stripped him and sat him in a great barrel filled with water heated over the hall's hearth and carried in by one of the servants. She washed him, scrubbing away the grime. The servant returned and shaved him. Then she helped him dress in some of her father in law's clothes and they sat together to eat. He had not spoken since they had left the inn, allowing her to mother him.

"Why are you doing this?" he said at last as he finished his stew and bread, the life's energy once again beginning to flow in his veins.

"Apart from my brother and my father-in-law, you are the only other person who has cared for me as a person rather than an object. I have not forgotten that or you." She blushed, her round face going scarlet. Her eyes sparkled with the pleasure her words brought to her. He did not reply but took more stew and bread and continued to eat ravenously.

"Am I really worth all the effort?" he finally said standing. He rubbed his eyes unable to look at her.

"Yes." He hardly heard her reply, but turned to the bed and walked over.

"I must sleep. I feel so confused," he mumbled. Lying down he quickly fell into a deep sleep.

He awoke in the night to the touch of soft warm skin under his calloused hand. His heavy eyes focused on the naked female form, pale in the moonlight through the half open shutters.

"Matilda…" she put a finger to his lips and began to pull off his tunic. He felt the sexual urge rise within him. She pressed her body down on his and kissed him passionately.

When finally he climaxed, spent and exhausted. Their bodies entwined, held together with sweat, the name 'Eleanor' slipped from his lips and a tear dripped from his eyes upon her warm belly. She held him as he wept.

"Why?" he finally uttered.

"We both have needs. Though her name is on your lips, I know we care enough for one another to value what we have done. I for one will treasure this moment long after you have left here. I will remember what true pleasure can be and…" she looked into his damp grey eyes. "What love is, for now as you have lost your love I will surely lose mine." She smiled sadly up at him.

"What now, then?" said Thomas, unsure what was happening, his emotions in total chaos.

"Tomorrow you ride south, to join De Montfort's army. He is in London. Henry and his army have also gone south."

"But…"

"You cannot stay here. What is there for you here?"

"You."

She smiled as tears trickled down her cheeks.

"You know that is not possible for me and not true to your heart. You are clutching at straws in the wind that blows you south. Let's rest now." They did not rest but loved once more.

It was late in the morning when they rose to furtive glances from the servants. Thomas gave Matilda a worried look.

"Don't worry. They all hate my husband. He bullies them as well as me," she said as they broke their fast with pottage, bread and ale. "Did you know I've asked Henry to join the staff here?" Thomas shook his head. "Yes, I could do with someone strong who I can trust, and who will not be scared of my husband as the other staff are. Henry will not be frightened by him I think."

"Has he accepted?"

"Provisionally, but he has returned to Thomas Menhill at Hemmington. Apparently Menhill survived and escaped the town. Henry is still contracted to him but he will return here when he can." She smiled and put her hand on his. "Come on, let's see what kit we can find you. Old Lord Gobion keeps a stock of weapons in the undercroft. I don't think he'll miss a few."

In the candle lit undercroft to the great hall Thomas picked out a sword, a dagger, a small shield and a helmet. He rolled them up in a padded leather tunic and they headed out into the light of the courtyard.

"You must go now." Matilda clutched his hand.

"I need to see Brother Robert before I go. I want also to visit the physician Richard Norton." She looked at him quizzically "It's about my father." He did not elaborate any more.

"The army will not stay in London long." She felt tears once again welling in her eyes. "Come and see me when you return." Thomas nodded.

"Thank you for everything. You have made me see…" he felt lost for words; she touched his face.

"Go now; say no more." She watched as he walked across the courtyard and through the gate. It was a long time before she finally turned with a sigh and entered the hall.

Back at the hospital the discussion raged long into the night. But Thomas would not be persuaded from his new direction. Since Matilda had planted the idea, he had grown more and more eager. Eventually Brother Robert accepted his decision. Conversation turned to Thomas's thoughts of his father.

"The priest Henry of Leicester will hopefully rescind his previous decision, though I think I will have to find him to remind him."

"That is, if he will even see you now that he is back in De Montfort's court," chipped in the monk.

"He also said that herbs and poisons could be used to simulate such affects as he had. Have you heard of such things?"

"Do you think Sir John would do such a thing?"

"Maybe, I don't know but I do not trust him or my half-brother. To think he is now Lord of Buckbie and the surrounding lands and manors that Sir John held. They both had much to gain getting my father out of the way; gaining the mill back, plus removing the main connection to my half-brothers past life. People will soon forget where he originated."

"I also have heard that it is possible to produce the effects of Leprosy but I have never seen a case and do not know how to do it." The monk shook his head. "If you really think it is a possibility, then yes, go and see the physician, he may know. He is still in the town; did rather well from all accounts following the fall of the town. Charged a lot for his services, treated the wealthy injured on both sides apparently. Have you the money to pay for a consultation," Thomas nodded. The money he had kept for his studies would do, as they did not look as though they would be continuing.

The following morning Thomas headed up to Abington Street and entered the physician's large house. He was asked to wait on a bench by a servant and after half an hour went in to see Richard Norton. He was an imposing man whose confidence in his own knowledge exuded into his patients putting them at their ease. He rubbed at his long grey beard as he sat behind his table in his crimson robes.

"Ah! Thomas Millson isn't it. I wondered what had happened to you. I did manage to see your father before the battle. How is he? Much the same I would imagine?"

"He is dead sir."

"What! I don't understand; I found no evidence in his blood when I washed it. There was no grease or sediment that would have indicated leprosy. I have written a report for you as you asked, which says, that in my belief he was not a leper."

"The lazar hospital was destroyed by the king along with all its occupants." The physician crossed himself at the news.

"I had not heard that. Please accept my deepest condolences." he got up, and walked over to a chest where he retrieved a large parchment. "Here I have the report though it is probably not much use now." He handed it across to Thomas. "Is there anything else I can do for you?"

"Yes. I have a question?" Thomas explained his concerns.

"Ah, I have heard of such, also came across a case once many years ago when I was in Bristol. Now let me see. If I remember rightly, in that case the lady had been poisoned using Ergot. That is black blight on rye." Thomas nodded his head in understanding.

"And this would cause the symptoms of Leprosy?" the physician nodded.

"If administered regularly enough and with an increase in salt. Could anyone have done that?"

"It is possible I'm not sure. I thank you anyway." Thomas paid the man and left.

Early the following morning Brother Robert escorted Thomas to the hospital gates.

"You will always be welcome here Thomas. This is your home if you need it. Return when all this is over." The monk looked into those deep grey eyes. He saw the agony of hidden memories but also now a spark of excitement and the eagerness of a youth keen to be on his way. They embraced, then shouldering his pack and adjusting the unaccustomed weight of the sword at his hip, he headed down Bridge Street and out of South Gate.

Chapter 14

Summer 1264

Thomas sat by the campfire and rubbed his short sword with a cloth. It was a good sword and he had had the blade sharpened. It shone in the firelight. It was early evening on the twenty-third of May. Kyftyll chatted nervously to him as he sewed on the white cross that all the soldiers were to wear.

Thomas had finally caught up with Simon De Montfort's army six days earlier, having travelled to London to discover that the army had already headed south and were encamped at Fletching, eight miles north of Lewes, where King Henry the third and his army, along with his brother Richard of Almaine and his son Prince Edward, were in residence.

On his arrival Thomas had been assigned to a unit under the command of Nicholas de Seagrave, which contained a large group of Londoners and scholars, a small group of whom Thomas recognised as coming from Northampton. He joined these and discovered Kyftyll.

"I ran away," he said suddenly across the small fire. Thomas looked up from his polishing.

"What do you mean?"

"When we were attacked in Northampton; do you remember we were all on the wall? I panicked and ran off. When the wall collapsed and the great cloud of dust rose up, I thought the devil had truly arrived to carry us off." Kyftyll now had his head down and Thomas had to bend forward to listen as his voice dropped to a whisper. "The South Gate was soon pushed open by the fearful towns' folk. I joined them and hid in a copse outside of the town."

He suddenly looked up his eyes locking onto Thomas. "I felt so ashamed, leaving you all there. It was why I joined the Earl's army." He looked earnestly at Thomas, desperate for support, not rejection. "I have to prove myself or I will not be able to live with what I have done."

"If you had stayed, you would more than likely have ended up dead for no reason. The battle was lost the moment they broke into the town, if it makes you feel better. You probably did the right thing to get away so you can fight another day," Thomas said to try to make him feel better.

"You stayed; so did Heycock and the others."

"We don't know what they did or if they are alive. I stayed because I had to find someone to try to help them."

He fell to polishing the blade of his sword. After a moment he stared at Kyftyll with his piercing moist grey eyes. "I failed too. They died in the flames. They butchered my father too. That is why I must be here." He gave a sad smile. "Together we will meet our destinies and assuage the pain in our hearts. If the Earl and his barons have their way, our time will come on the morrow. Come on we ought to rest. We are moving out at midnight." They settled down around the small fire.

Neither of them found deep sleep and both were thankful for the call to arms. The march south passed through fields of white, as chalk-laden soil reflected in moonlight. The roads were dry and dusty from many thousands of trudging feet. Thomas wrapped a cloth around his nose and mouth, feeling hot even in the cool night air. Ahead of them, growing with every step, was the northern slope of the South Downs, black in the moonlit sky, daunting in the darkness.

Finally they reached its base and halted. Thomas and Kyftyll sat, mopped the sweat and dust from their faces and drank from a water skin. They appeared as an army of ghosts, white with chalk dust. Thomas banged at his tunic.

It was not long before approaching horsemen signalled that it was time to move on. As they waited their turn, Thomas watched the antlike shapes of thousands of pale figures zigzagging up the chalk-land rise.

It was steep but over quickly and as the grey light of dawn approached they came upon the broad grassland down that fell gently towards the town of Lewes. Dropping away steeply on their left was the river valley of the Ouse.

Thomas stared, wide-eyed, across the sun-dried grassland, towards the strong walls of the town, which was dominated by the castle at its centre.

"I hope they come out for we shall never get in.," he mumbled to Kyftyll. Already they could hear the trumpet call and church bells ringing as the town awoke to the approaching danger.

The troop shuffled forward nervously until Seagrave felt they were in position perched at the top of the hill. He raised his hand and called a halt.

As they stood fidgeting with their weapons, up galloped a bishop in his finery surrounded by a retinue of clerics. Seagrave called out across the gathered men.

"Walter De Cantelupe, Bishop of Worcester, wants for us to pray, listen up!"

The bishop called for them to kneel and prostrate themselves before God and then began to pray finishing with "Grant us O Lord, our desire with mighty victory, in honour of your name, Amen." The men slowly began to rise after muttering their own few private messages to God.

Thomas got up and watched the Bishop flying off to the west as other units began to appear over the crest of the hill and take up their positions.

"Eyes forward!" called Seagrave from his charger. Thomas saw a stream of horsemen pouring endlessly from the town gate and heading up the hill onto the Downs. They did not stop but carried on up towards Seagrave's gathered troops.

"Here we go," said Thomas crossing himself.

"It is Prince Edward in the lead," muttered Kyftyll nervously. "May God preserve us."

Thomas, Kyftyll and the few others that had bows or slings made ready. Those armed with lances, spears and halberds lowered their weapons to meet the charge.

Thomas concentrated on the shortening distance, his heart racing and his mouth dry. After the long slow pull up to this spot everything now seemed to be happening so quickly. The riders on their great war-horses were well-spread and difficult targets for falling arrows and slingshots, especially when there was such a paltry number of them. He let loose his arrow, along with the other archers but saw only a few riders fall. By the time he had fired his second arrow the first horsemen had hit the front ranks. Their lances down, they crashed through.

As Seagrave's inexperienced men struggled to regroup, more and more horsemen arrived with lance, sword and mace causing havoc. Seagrave and the other mounted lords rode back and forth shouting orders but the untrained troops began to panic. They were no match for the charging onslaught.

Thomas notched an arrow into his bow and watched the horsemen scatter the ranks in front of him. He blotted out their cries and focused on his revenge. He found himself become inwardly calm. He fired at the horse of the first horseman not ten feet away and watched him topple. Then drawing his sword he charged. Before the man at arms could rise he drove his sword deep into his unprotected side. The shock of the impact travelled up his arm.

He rose up and looked down at the lifeless man at his feet. A nearby cry drew his attention and he turned in time to see Kyftyll take a sword blow full across the neck and drop beneath an oncoming horses hooves. He did not have time to dwell on his own victory as the knight's sword swung at him. He recognised the shield of prince Edward. The blade struck his own small shield knocking him to the ground. His left arm stung with the pain of the blow. The knight rode on.

Thomas staggered to his feet now surrounded by slashing horsed knights and men-at-arms. The ground was littered with the remains of Seagraves unit. He had just gained his feet when a mace blow struck his helm and once again knocked him down. Blood ran down his face and he fainted between the legs of the horse he had slain. It saved him from the hooves of the charging horses and the prying eyes of their riders.

Thomas woke minutes later to see the last of the knights disappearing north, a trail of bloodied moaning bodies in their wake. He pulled himself up, sat on the horse's carcass, and carefully removed his helmet. His head thumped with pain. He knew that the helmet had saved his life. He washed his face and head with some water from his flask and drank the remainder. Looking around him he wondered if the battle was already over. If it was they must have lost. If seemed such a short time ago that they had stood ready a few thousand living breathing men. Now they were scattered, dead and dying.

He looked across to the west along the ridge of the Down and saw to his surprise great units of men. The white crosses on the nearest visible in the sunlight as they marched down the slope towards the town. Thomas recognised the arms of Gilbert de Clare and that of John Fitz-John leading the nearest troops. He saw the 'Red Earl', Gilbert De Clare lift his sword at the head of the men, his distinctive hair hidden beneath his helm. The battle was not lost.

The flash of sunlight on steel drew his attention to the gathered force at the base of the slope a few hundred yards away. Some were horsed, but they were mainly foot soldiers. At their head he saw the arms of King Henry, a great dragon standard. Thomas knew that this was who he must fight to avenge his family. He felt his strength rise with his determination and pumping adrenalin. Picking up a fallen halberd he half ran half staggered down the grassland slope towards the Red Earl's force. Ahead of him he could hear the roar and clash of steel as the two sides met.

He stopped at the rear long enough to take his breath, and wipe away the sweat and blood that was running down his face. He found himself surprised at his calmness as he looked at the bloody chaos ahead of him. With remarkable clarity he heard the call of a skylark above the din and looked up at it rising in the blue sky. Its voice was suddenly lost, as the clatter of battle grew closer; de Clare's army was being forced back around him.

He pushed his way forward towards the dragon standard and saw soldiers falling away from the mounted knights and the king. He forced his way through the retreating men and ducked under the swinging sword thrust of a knight. He felt the tip of the blade bite into his back, but it did not stop his progress, with fixed mind and halberd lowered he charged headlong at the king's horse as it charged towards him.

Thomas quickly dropped the end of the halberd into the earth as the force of the horse drove itself onto the blade. He jumped back as the great destrier skewered itself and fell to its knees. The king, thrown forward, landed with a clatter of armour on the ground before him.

Thomas charged at him, drawing his sword, the fury of battle running in his veins. The king lifted himself to his knees, Thomas made ready to deliver the coup de grace. He stopped and looked into the face of the king.

Hesitating a moment too long, he did not see one of the royal retinue come thundering up to him with a swinging mace. The blow caught him full on the shoulder and threw him to the ground. In stunned amazement he could only watch as the king was helped up and lifted onto another warhorse. King's men-at-arms began to close around him. Thomas staggered to his feet. His body still charged with the battle madness. Swinging his sword with his good right arm he charged amongst them.

They fell back surprised by his suicidal assault. He slashed left and right hitting sword, shield and flesh, but he could not hold them all.

Then suddenly he was not alone. He found himself surrounded by great warhorses crushing his attackers. As the royalists fell back a knight pulled up next to him.

"That was well done soldier," came the echoing voice from his helmet. "I am Hugh de Haversley. Victory will soon be ours, I am sure of that. The Earl has attacked from the west. Richard of Cornwall's forces are fleeing. What is your name?"

"Thomas Millers-son of Buckbie," croaked Thomas, dropping his sword and collapsing to the ground suddenly exhausted. He clutched at his shattered shoulder.

"Find me later," the knight said, holding back his restless horse. Thomas nodded, his body now beginning to shake. The knight released his charger and rode off to rejoin the fray, which had moved further down the hill. Men-at-arms, wearing white crosses, swarmed past him; Henry the Third was in retreat.

He did not know how long he sat there, exhausted. He had watched the fight head down towards the suburbs of Lewes, disappearing eventually from view. Eventually he was disturbed by a grey clad Franciscan who strapped his left arm across his chest and rubbed a sticky herbal paste over the cuts on his head, shoulder and back, then bound them where he could with cloth. Thomas felt vaguely that he ought to be interested in the treatment that the friar had given him but could not think why.

The friar helped him to his feet and carefully dragged him into the cool interior of a church at the edge of the Downs. As he drifted in and out of consciousness, he imagined once again that the great pillars in the Holy Sepulchre at Northampton surrounded him.

After a short time he recovered enough to discover that he was lying on a straw covered earth floor surrounded by moaning or still men, some wearing the white cross; others who were not and were obviously the king's men. A priest came over and gave him water, and then he was left propped up against a mural of the temptations of Christ on an outer wall. He fell back into a fitful sleep.

It was evening when he woke to the smell of smoke filling his nostrils. He levered himself up, using the bloody, chipped sword that he inexplicably still clutched in his hand and staggered over to the door where he came across a priest looking out towards Lewes.

"The town burns. Hell has surely come," muttered the priest. His face was pale and distraught. Thomas looked across at Lewes, which was dominated by two ringed castle mounts, which appeared above the smoke and glow of flames. He leaned against the flint porch, and thought of the suffering going on inside. He remembered Northampton.

"Was it worth it?" the young priest mumbled looking at him.

"I pray that it was the right thing to do." Thomas looked at the piles of corpses around the church entrance, their faces disfigured by death, eyes staring out accusingly at the dark world. "Though at this moment I am unsure." As he turned and stumbled back in, he mumbled. "All I know is that this cause has given me nothing but pain."

The following morning he woke stiff, his head, shoulder and back aching. Going to the altar he knelt and prayed for the souls of the dead, and salvation for the living, then picking up his sword, he left the church of Saint Mary's. Outside he found the broken haft of a spear and used it as a staff. He made his way slowly down the dirt road to the West Gate of Lewes. At the gate, which was open and guarded by men-at-arms wearing white crosses on their tunics, he fell in with a troop of soldiers coming out, who were heading south down a steep road that followed the edge of the town wall.

"The army is around the priory," said one, "the king and Prince Edward have surrendered there. The Earl is to meet with them this morning. Thomas, unable to think, his mind numb with pain and memory, dumbly followed them slowly down the steep hill towards the great walled priory that filled the valley below.

Its majesty was as great if not greater than Saint Peters Burch. He felt he should be overawed by the immensity of the great honey coloured house of God but he felt empty. The death of so many and his part in it left him confused and ashamed, but more overpowering was the sense that he had survived. He knew that part of him had come here to die but it seemed that God had decided otherwise.

A great crowd of soldiers had gathered at the priory gatehouse. Thomas eased himself onto a crowded wall and waited.

It was not long before a large group of horsemen cantered into view, Simon De Montfort's white lion standard at its head. The column rode up to the priory. Thomas recognised other baron leaders in the column. There was the 'Red Earl' Gilbert De Clare the Earl of Gloucester, Simon De Montfort's sons Henry and Guy; he gave a grunt as he saw Henry of Leicester, the priest following in their wake. He had not seen him since the prison and was keen to catch up with him. Following the De Montforts came Sir Henry de Hastings and then he saw the red wolf's head emblazoned on the shield that he had last seen on the battlefield and which belonged to Sir Hugh de Haversley.

It was some time before they re-emerged but none of the gathered men had left. They stood or sat patiently, their white crosses still stitched upon their jerkins. Simon De Montfort, Earl of Leicester pulled out a roll of parchment and began to read.

"'On this day the 15th May 1264 the following Mise of Lewes has been agreed to and signed by the King, Henry the Third. One, the king and Prince Edward will remain in the protection of his barons. Two, peace will be proclaimed throughout the shires. Three, an amnesty is declared for all, who, out of necessity, fought against the king. Four, foreign councillors and castle owners are to be removed forthwith, and five, the Provisions of Oxford are to be made valid once more.'

So men for your country and your king you have secured a great victory." Cheers rang out causing a large flock of doves to take flight from the priory roof. Thomas had no stomach to cheer. His anger was now gone. He slowly retraced his steps back to the small flint church of Saint Mary's.

Thomas stayed a few weeks at the priory to let his body heal. Though it was soon back to its previous state, his mind felt empty. He often wandered aimlessly through the priory buildings and grounds or sat listlessly in the infirmary chapel. His anger was now spent and his love lost. The infirmarer, who, on discovering that Thomas had medical experience, had persuaded him to do the patient rounds with him every day and cajoled him as often as he could in helping him with the medications, as the infirmary was overrun with battle wounded and the monk was struggling to care for them all.

The infirmarer found him sitting before the chapel altar.

"Well Thomas you're about fit enough to move on now what are your plans?" Thomas studied the old grey haired tonsured monk.

"I think I will find Hugh De Haversley; he told me to search him out and I have nothing better to do." Thomas mumbled absently.

"What of your studies? You have no wish to return to your home, Northampton isn't it?" Thomas nodded.

"I cannot study there anymore and have little urgency to search for a cure that I no longer need." The monk looked at him bemused, and Thomas explained to him about the death of his father and his search for a cure to leprosy that had originally sent him to his studies at Northampton.

"No I am not ready to return there yet." He continued. "Where can I find this Hugh De Haversley? Do you know?" the monk thought for a moment his cragged face frowning.

"I think he is one of the Bishop of Worcester's knight's, with estates not too far from the town I believe. I will find out for you." The monk rose and left him. Thomas once again fell to praying quietly, praying for the souls of all those he had killed in the last year and for his own soul; for he felt certain that a man who had killed and killed in anger could not reach heaven.

Sometime later the monk returned with his news. Thomas still knelt before the chapel altar. He coughed slightly to attract his attention. Thomas did not turn; he recognised that only the infirmarer would be so sensitive. He had come to like the ancient monk and had found that he had filled the gulf left by Robert.

"Brother, I need to confess; will you hear me?" The old monk knelt by his side. "Brother I have lived in anger for many weeks; I have killed men here and in Northampton in battle. Is heaven closed to me Brother?"

"To kill is a sin, however the church advocates that to kill in battle is a duty a man owes to his lord."

"I have no lord."

"You have killed in what you believe to be a righteous cause, in battle, where all are on equal terms. This is not murder; many believe God backs your cause. Indeed you all wore the white cross. Even so there must be penance for those who would be Christian men. Your penance has begun because you feel for those lost souls. Remember and pray for them on the anniversary of their deaths." Thomas nodded his head bowed. The monk made the sign of the cross, "in the name of the Father and of the Son and of the Holy Spirit, I absolve you."

"Thank you Brother." Thomas felt relief enter his heart. After they had prayed for a short while, the monk told him that the knight's manor was near a place called Chipping Norton.

A few days later Thomas said his farewells and left the abbey wearing his sword and repaired padded leather tunic. He carried a small bag containing his meagre possessions and food over his shoulder, plus a helm and shield that he had found on the battlefield. He felt sweat run down his back and drip from his forehead as he headed out of Lewes with only a short glance up at the Downs and their fields of death.

Chapter 15

It was mid-June when Thomas finally arrived at the village of Haversley on the edge of the Cotswolds. Entering via a small bridge over a stream, he came across an old wooden church surrounded by houses of various sizes, about twenty in total. To his left was a watermill, which he stopped at for a moment and appraised with a professional eye. The earth road led around the church to a small market square backed by the manor walls, in the centre of which stood a large open oak gateway. Field strips, orchards and open pasture surrounded the small community.

Villagers nodded to him but eyed his attire suspiciously. A man-at-arms guarded the gate. Thomas stood a little way off and studied the manor. It was not large, approximately the size of that at Buckbie but made of stone and tiled, surrounded by a stone wall with ramparts. A square tower stood in one corner. He could make out the thatched roofs of outhouses just above the walls, stables, kitchens and storehouses in the courtyard. It all appeared cosy and in good repair.

The guard sauntered slowly across to him, his spear held across his chest in readiness, wary at the site of the armed man. Thomas called out greetings and told him that he wished to see the lord of the manor, whereupon the guard interrogated him thoroughly. His countenance softened when he learned that Thomas had come from Lewes.

"Sorry about that, it's just you can't be too careful at the present. I was there too you know." He continued proudly. "A good fight that one was. I'll take you to the steward. Sir Hugh is out hunting."

The steward's office was in the small tower. Behind a long trestle table sat a rotund red-faced man; tufts of grey hair protruded from the edges of his capuchon, which was pulled up, even in the summer's heat. Papers lay strewn all across the table.

"Yes!" he bellowed angry at being disturbed. "What can I do for you?" Thomas stood before him and explained his mission.

"We have no need for more soldiers here. I doubt very much whether the master will want to see you. Get yourself some food at the kitchen and then be on your way." The steward looked back down at his papers and began muttering under his breath. Thomas, realising he would get no further, turned and walked out. Standing in the courtyard he wondered what to do. Finally he made his way across to the kitchen and was given some bread and ale, which he carried to the manor wall, where he sat in the shade, ate, and thought about what he should do.

As he was finishing he heard the sound of approaching horses and soon two men rode in, one on a fine charger that Thomas had last seen on the Downs at Lewes. He knew its rider must be Sir Hugh the other carried a peregrine on his arm and Thomas guessed he must be the falconer. Hugh dismounted quickly and handed his reins to a stable boy. Thomas had not seen the man clearly before and now found himself studying a tall broad proud looking man with fine chiselled Norman features and short cut black hair. He strode purposefully towards the manor entrance. A servant ran out of the kitchen causing him to stop as he received a pot of ale.

Thomas jumped up, realizing this was his best opportunity. He moved quickly across to Sir Hugh and waited. The knight looked up from his ale, surprised at seeing a face he did not recognise.

"I do not know you sir. What business have you here?"

"On the battlefield at Lewes you bade me come to see you. I have come." Thomas said simply. The knight looked at him puzzled. "My name is Thomas the Millers son." The knight continued to look puzzled. "The king's horse sir." At this the knight threw his head back and laughed causing all those around to stop and stare. He slapped his thigh.

"Of course now I remember. How could I forget that. You fought like a raging boar." He turned to the servant who had brought him the ale.

"Another pot for our guest," then he turned to Thomas.

"Come in sir and enjoy my hospitality." Thomas hesitated not used to such courtesy from those of higher station than himself. "Come sir, you are equal to any knight after that display on the battlefield." He slapped Thomas on the back and led him up the steps and into the hall.

They entered the dark interior; a well-dressed lady came out of the solar at the far end.

"My wife Thomas, the Lady Maude." Thomas bowed to the lady and waited while the knight greeted his wife. They were very close, Thomas observed, and felt a touch of envy. Maude beckoned them over to the table and bade them sit while she called for ale, cheese and bread. "Sit, drink and eat with us Thomas, while I tell my wife your tale." The bread was good, better than he had tasted in a long time, finer and less gritty than the kitchen bread he had sampled earlier. Thomas listened to Sir Hugh's

231

rendition of the battle and Thomas's part in it. He then finished the story between mouthfuls, explaining how he came to find himself at Sir Hugh's.

"So Thomas you are in need of work?"

"Your steward says you do not need men."

"I have a feeling, sir, that you are more than a hired hand or mercenary. Tell me more about yourself and then we shall see."

"I do have some education sir if that is of any use. I was a student studying the arts and medicine at Northampton before the King took it. I can read and write Latin and English. My French is fair." Thomas remembered the lessons Eleanor had given him when she was young and they played. She had often only spoken to him in French, forcing him to learn. He remembered many of those lessons down by the millpond and its stream. He sighed.

"You have some sad memories, Thomas," said Maude perceptively. Thomas nodded.

"My life has changed much this last year."

"Our steward is in need of some help Hugh. I believe Thomas may be of much use sorting out our books, if he is good at numbers and the written word." The knight's eyes lit up. "I think we may have use of his medical skill as well, for whenever someone is sick we have to send for the physician at the town, who will only travel out at vast expense."

"Yes, a learned man; just what we need. Our steward is a good man but he has no idea of figures. He is a temporary replacement. Unfortunately my last steward was good with a sword and horse so joined me at Lewes where he lost his life."

"He too, was not much of an expert when it came to the figures, God rest his soul," said Maude. "The estate has hardly been turning a profit of recent years." Sir Hugh nodded sombrely.

"Well sir, do you think you could improve matters?"

"I can try, my lord. Though I cannot vouch for my success."

"Then I assume you accept." He turned to his wife, "Though I think we are going to have to find him some clothes more befitting of his new station as clerk to the Lord of the Manor! Finish your meal, then I will introduce you to the steward and our problems."

Thomas settled in quickly to his new role, enjoying the quiet manor life, and his high position within its ranks. He soon mastered the paperwork and accounts and quickly came up with ideas for improving the estates revenue. The steward, after initial hostility, soon began to relax when he realised he was not to be demoted and that his job had been made much easier.

After a couple of weeks, Sir Hugh called him into the solar and told him to pack his bag for they were off to parliament, 'to bask in the pleasures of victory.'

The following morning Sir Hugh, his wife, a young squire, a couple of mounted men-at-arms and Thomas, who was riding rather uncomfortably on a small pony, rode out of the village and on to the rough road that led to London.

A few days later they arrived, saddle sore and weary. The streets were a hive of activity with the approaching parliament increasing the traffic. Jostling their way through the stinking crowded streets they arrived at the small town residence of the Bishop of Worcester, Walter Cantelupe. Thomas remembered the man on the battlefield, leading the prayer and granting absolution for the soldiers' sins before they entered battle. A mighty figure upon his horse, his bishop's robes flowing about him and mitre held aloft.

Sir Hugh had already outlined his connection to the Bishop over ale on the first night of their journey.

"He was my uncle's friend. They studied together in their youth. Anyway Bishop Walter became my godfather and gave me the estate on the death of my father. My older brother took over our family holdings. I owe the Bishop much. He is a good friend of the Earl of Leicester as you know, and has been a strong supporter of the baronial reformers since 1258."

The house consisted of a large hall with chambers above a kitchen and servants quarters to the rear. Thomas was about to take himself off to the kitchens with Sir Hugh's young squire when the main door flew open and the elegantly robed figure that could only be the Bishop stormed in. Seeing the new arrivals, he stopped short, his anger evaporating.

"Sir Hugh, Maude it's wonderful to see you." He gripped them tightly.

"You too sir," replied Hugh, once free from the bishop's grasp. "Are things not well with the council?" Bishop Walter waved his hand exasperatedly in the air.

"Oh it is nothing, you will discover all soon enough. Let us enjoy this night before we are lost in the onslaught of politics." Turning, he saw Thomas and the squire by the kitchen door. Sir Hugh caught the direction of his gaze.

"Let me introduce my brother-in-law and squire, Richard." Richard went forward and kissed the Bishops ring. Thomas, dressed in his leather tunic, wearing his sword and still carrying his kit bag over his shoulder, turned towards the kitchen door in order to make a quiet exit. "And this is Thomas, my new clerk." Thomas turned surprised and unsure at the attention being now focused on him.

"He looks little like a clerk to me," said Bishop Walter with raised eyebrows.

"He is a man of many talents," replied Sir Hugh. Thomas walked forward his heart pumping so loudly he thought they would all hear and kissed the ornate sapphire ring of the Bishop. Standing, he studied the noble features of this powerful middle-aged cleric. With the rise of the Earl of Leicester, he had become one of the most important clerics in the land. Thomas felt the bishop's dark brown eyes appraising him.

"There will be much work for a clerk here I think. It will be certainly useful to have another on the staff, Sir Hugh. You are well trained in letters sir?"

"In Latin and English my Lord and passable in French, which I believe is the main language at the parliament," Thomas said tentatively. The bishop nodded, and turned to his guests.

Thomas made a quick exit to the kitchens where he soon made himself acquainted with the servants via ale and a game of dice.

The following morning they made their way with Bishop Cantelupe and his entourage of flushed looking clerics through the busy streets to the palace at Westminster, which they found to be surrounded by a tent village. With accommodation at a premium many were camping out. They joined a growing number of well-dressed nobles and their staff making their way to the Great Hall. As they entered, Thomas like many of the other attendants, found himself redundant. After some time in desultory chatter, he began to wander the corridors of the great palace.

After the first slow day he soon found himself fully employed, mainly by the Bishop and through the reports and correspondence that he copied, he soon discovered the progress that parliament was making. The Bishop had been elected as one of the nine Councillors that were to run the King's business; all of the Councillors were the Earls men. Four knights were to be elected to represent each shire and new sheriffs were to be appointed by election in each shire. The King's power had finally been controlled.

Although this was what they had fought for, this was not the news being discussed in the servants' quarters and alehouses of the town. The marchers had not come to parliament, nor had the northern lords both of whom were loyal to Henry at Lewes. Henry's wife, the Queen Eleanor had returned to her native France and was said to be raising an invasion force. Many royalist castles had not yet capitulated and disorder ruled in much of the land.

One night the Earl had arrived and had been in long discussion over these very issues. Thomas had been called in to take notes. Sitting in the corner at a small table, he listened intently and made quick notes on the parchment before him. The Earl ranted about the lack of finances to deal with the problems. The king had emptied the coffers on his harebrained schemes such as the mission to capture Sicily, the wars in Gascony and the fact that little money was now coming in from the shires because of the civil war and the disorder.

On the twenty-eighth of June, the signing of the Ordinance and the end of parliament, a grand banquet was to be held at the palace. Sir Hugh and Maude headed out dressed in their finest scarlet and bluet, Maude bedecked in her jewels, her eyes sparkling with excitement. Thomas headed out before them to get up to the palace and watch the arrival of all the nobles. The guards let him through to a good spot before the entrance.

The lords and ladies of De Montfort's England began to arrive. Thomas had never seen so much scarlet cloth and jewellery. At Northampton and Lewes, Thomas had come to know and recognise many of the faces and arms of those lords. He saw Hugh Despenser, Humphrey De Bohun, John Fitz John and Gilbert De Clare. He saw Walter De Cantelupe arrive with Hugh and Maude who gave him a quick wave, then came the Bishop of Lincoln, Richard of Gravesend. He recognised some of the knights who, like Sir John of Buckbie, held lands from De Quincy the Earl of Winchester who was still in Scotland. There was Saer De Harcourt, Peter Le Porter and Thomas Menhill.

His eyes stopped wandering aimlessly through the crowd of dignitaries. He felt pale and faint for walking with Menhill and his wife was their ward, surely a ghost! He gripped the wall with one hand, the other reaching inside his shirt for the brooch that hung upon a leather cord against his chest. He felt the cold jewels in his hand, and watched their slow approach towards his position.

He told himself it could not be real and began to mutter an Ave Maria, closing his eyes. When he opened them she was still there, now before the door. She turned and looked at him stopping in her tracks caught by his gaze. The flow of dignitaries like a river moved around her looking perplexed. Menhill's wife grasped her arm. Thomas Menhill looked on agitated.

"What is it ladies?" Then to his wife, "Is she well?"

"Eleanor!" the word burst from his lips with explosive force, a storm of pent up emotion. He pushed himself toward her. Menhill and his wife turned in surprise. But Eleanor as if released from her trance by his shout flew past them and into his arms, to the raucous cheer from the surrounding crowd.

They clung to each other. He felt her sobs as she abandoned herself. Menhill looked around concerned at the attention.

"Come," he muttered quickly, forcibly pulling them through the entrance and into a passageway out of view of dignitaries and crowd alike. "What is this Eleanor? Explain yourself and quickly." He looked from her to Thomas then back again. She sobbed into Thomas's shoulder. "Speak, for we have little time and already we shall be the talk of the banquet. Who is this man?" He studied Thomas, whose arms enfolded Eleanor protectively, his face creased with joy. He wore the robe of a clerk but looked more like a soldier. He was not tonsured, it had grown out and his dark hair hung to his shoulder. His face was pale but alive and his penetrating moist grey eyes fixed on Menhill with such a piercing stare that he looked away to Eleanor, disturbed by the man's intensity and power.

"Eleanor!" he said. She turned to Menhill's wife and said simply.

"This is the man I spoke of." The lady smiled.

"So he lives and is as handsome as you said, though he could do with a bit of a tidy up and some decent clothes instead of his clerks robe." Eleanor coloured and looked up at Thomas.

"Jeanette what is this?" puffed Menhill, exasperated, "A conspiracy?" His wife ignored him and turned to the couple.

"Hello, Thomas of Buckbie. We have little time, the King awaits." She smiled ironically for all knew that the King was now the Earl of Leicester's puppet. "We are staying at the Dominican Friary. Come and see us at noon tomorrow, until then, I'm afraid, I must part you."

"Thank you," Thomas replied and turned to Eleanor. "I thought you were dead." She smiled up at him, her green eyes glistening like emeralds.

"And I you." Jeanette gently took her hand.

"Until tomorrow," she muttered apologetically. Thomas watched them disappear into the great hall. He stood dazed for many minutes until guards moved him on.

He stumbled away from Westminster, to the first alehouse he found, where he drank until his nerves had calmed. As he sat silent in the corner of the bustling room, rank with the smell of ale and its sweat soaked inhabitants, he studied the brooch now in his hands, the rubies and sapphires glistened in the intermittent light as if they had come alive as he studied the hues of red and blue. He wondered if he had indeed dreamt it all.

He slipped out of the alehouse, which was becoming ever livelier as the town also enjoyed the party atmosphere. He wandered aimlessly through the streets finally ending up at a late hour back at the Bishop's manor. The Bishop had a collection of books in his private solar and to Thomas's surprise he had allowed him to borrow one. He now picked it up and found a quiet corner in the hall where he tried to relax and to read. With a small candle perched on a windowsill, he eventually lost himself in the beauty and intricacies of the illustrated Book of Hours. He turned each page reverently, amazed at the detail and hours of work that had gone into its production.

Presently Hugh, Maude and the Bishop returned. He listened absently to their excited chatter until Hugh and Maude disappeared to the guest room and the Bishop to his solar. Then he settled down in the hall to sleep.

The next morning was spent in nervous anticipation and much pacing before the Dominican Friary, waiting for the noon bell calling the friars within to the service of sext. When it finally came he shot through the gateway and after a moments discussion with the gatekeeper headed for the guesthouse. He found it busy with guests. The Menhill's and Eleanor were sitting on a bench at a trestle table. Thomas noted the pilgrims badge at her breast and smiled to himself, reassured. They beckoned him across and Thomas Menhill handed him a cup of wine. He was grey haired and had a warm wrinkled face and soft voice. Thomas remembered that Eleanor thought highly of him.

"Welcome. Since we last met I have learned much about you. I have to say that I am not totally happy with what I have discovered, although it is nice to see Eleanor smile again, for she has not done so since escaping Northampton. Your stations in society are very different and I'm not sure that Sir John would approve. God rest his soul." As he said this, his eyebrows rose. Thomas looked at them nervously. "Sit Thomas; before we come to any decisions we must first discover all we can. Eleanor's story finished at Northampton. I would know more and I am sure you wish to discover Eleanor's own story." Thomas sat before them and told of his adventures, then looked expectantly at Eleanor. For a moment she sat in silence allowing her mind to travel back to that fateful day, which had become etched into her memory. She hardly knew she was speaking as she relived the events.

Chapter 16

She was back, sitting in her chamber and looking out through the open window. Bearward Street was busy with folks moving hurriedly about their business. Their haste brought her out of her daydream about the previous night with Thomas. Her heart fluttered with remembered passion as tears filled her eyes; for she also felt that it had been the last time. She had always known that their love was to be short lived but now that she felt its end she experienced a sense of emptiness and loss of direction.

Her father had visited that morning in an attempt to coax her into the castle. She had not been able to leave and he had stomped off angrily saying that it probably does not matter as the parley that morning should fix everything. He had left Alfred who sat downstairs armed with a rusty sword and his dagger feeling important as the landlady bustled about him.

Eleanor's maid Clarice tried in vain to draw her from her melancholy but finally gave up and busied herself in tidying the chamber. She unclipped a brooch from the dress that Eleanor had carelessly thrown on the bed, polishing the rubies and sapphires until they sparkled. She placed it lovingly on the sideboard then with a sigh went and folded away the dress.

"They must be at the parley now Miss."

"Mm."

It had begun to rain, heavy drops splashed into the dirt on the street below. Eleanor felt their freshness as they splashed off the windowsill onto her skin.

"Do you wish me to close the shutter miss?"

"No Clarice, I like the feel of it. It is refreshing."

"It is cold though. We'll catch our death." The maid retorted grumpily feeling the chill. She walked out of the room in a huff. Eleanor took no notice.

Suddenly the room seemed to shake and a rumble of falling masonry echoed in through the window. Eleanor, startled, looked out across the rooftops on the other side of the street. A great plume of dust rose up through the rain. The people in the street were shouting and running. She felt their fear, and her own grew.

"What's that? What's going on?" Clarice shouted as she dashed back into the room again, a startled expression on her face.

"I don't know. Something's going on over at the Saint Andrews Priory." Alfred entered sword in hand. "Oh Alfred, will you go over and see if you can discover what's happening?" Alfred touched his forehead and trotted off. Clarice began pacing up and down and looking through the window, which began to unnerve Eleanor.

"Could you get me a drink Clarice, please. I believe there is some good wine downstairs, thank you." Clarice went out quickly pleased to have something to do.

Eleanor sat and watched the plume of dust. Her hands held the pilgrims medallion given to her by Thomas. She traced the contours of the figure of Saint Thomas and prayed that he would be all right. Images of that day, which seemed so long ago, floated through her thoughts.

Soon she could see puffing Alfred returning along the road, damp with sweat and the last of the rain. At the entrance to the house she saw the landlady question him then run out and down the road, a small leather bag on her shoulder.

Steam seeped from the thatched roofs opposite. It reminded Eleanor of smoke; she shuddered. Alfred came running up the stairs and burst in on her contemplation, Clarice hot on his heels.

"They've broken in!" he announced between gulps of air to the two women. "I've seen them, great knights on horseback coming through a breach in the priory wall into the town. I saw young Simon De Montfort come off his horse." Despair crept into his voice. "Your father was there. I think he fell as well."

Eleanor's heart missed a beat. She felt sick and pale, her hand began to shake and she concentrated on holding it still. Though antagonism was strong between them, he was her father and she knew he had loved her above anyone else. He had always given into her wishes, apart from marriage, she reflected. He was also her main protection in a harsh world, though she knew that she could rely on her guardian, Thomas Menhill. She wondered if he too had fallen. As she concentrated on calming herself, Alfred continued. "The students and garrison are fighting them in the streets but they are being forced back towards the Marehold. They are no match for mounted Knights. What shall we do, Lady Eleanor?" She had never heard Alfred say so many words before and saw he too was frightened. "I think they will soon be upon us."

Eleanor stood and looked out of the window, listening to the cries and clash of steel coming from the north. The street below was full of panic. She felt a moment's indecision, realising that the fate of all three of them rested on her shoulders. She wondered what Thomas would say and whether he was fighting in the streets. She fell to her knees, clutched the medallion in her hands and began to pray for guidance. Alfred and Clarice also knelt.

As quickly as she knelt she jumped up feeling an inner strength. She knew she must get out of the town for, whoever won, it would not be safe in the town for a while. If the soldiers were attacking from the north perhaps it was possible to get out via the east or south gates. She turned to the others.

"Come on, pack a few essentials quickly we must leave. Alfred, get food from downstairs, Clarice, warm clothes and blankets."

They were soon ready and stepped out onto the street. It was deserted now. They could hear fighting in the Marehold. "Come on!" she called to the others. They ran down to the Sheepmarket and stopped to catch their breath. Crowds could be seen heading into the square.

"Hang on my lady. I've left something behind." It was Clarice.

"You can't go back now!" shouted Alfred. He tried to grab her arm but he was too late. With a nervous wary look at the two of them Clarice had turned and run back up the street.

"What's she up to foolish girl!" cried Eleanor angrily stamping her foot in frustration. They stood on the corner waiting. "Come on we'll have to go after her before it's too late." They began to move up the street back towards the house but suddenly ahead of them the clash of steel grew louder and they could see the fighting and the top of the road. Armed students, townsfolk and garrison soldiers were retreating towards them.

The street in front of the house was soon full of fighting men. An exhausted scholar with a gash on his head came staggering past them.

"Get out of here lady. We cannot hold them!" he shouted, not bothering to stop. Eleanor stood spellbound watching the battle ahead. Alfred grabbed her arm. The roar of fighting filled her ears.

"Come on!" he shouted. She looked at him dazed. He stood, sword in hand before her. Taking her hand in his they ran back down to Sheepmarket. There she gained control of her emotions and again took charge.

"Come on Alfred this way up to the Holy Sepulchre. We'll go round the top of the town, along the inside of the wall to East Gate."

"But…" Alfred held back.

"The king's men have headed towards the centre and the castle. They have not gone that way; come on." Her heart in her mouth she prayed that she was right. They headed north, past the church to the wall. There were few people about, as most had already run south. Eleanor's intuition had been right. There were no soldiers in sight.

At the East Gate they came upon a huge crowd. The gate had been pushed wide open and the gathered mass of people was siphoning themselves through. Holding on tightly to each other they slipped in amongst the crowd. It took a while to reach the gate but once through the congestion eased.

"Where to?" said Alfred stopping and wiping his brow at the Saint Edmunds crossroads. The church stood before them, doors open. It was full of people who, unsure of where to go had entered and were praying for salvation. Eleanor took some deep breaths. She felt exhausted but knew she could not stop yet. They were not safe until they were well away from the town. Even then the road would be dangerous. Taking her silence for indecision Alfred continued. "We could head for Buckbie?" Eleanor shook her head.

"No, my half-brother." She coloured slightly remembering his lustful comments of the past. "He would not behave honourably towards me." Alfred nodded, accepting her decision without comment. "We will go north to Hemington. The Lady Menhill will be there. We will be safe in her care. We must take care on the way. The journey will be fraught with danger. We will stay off the road as much as possible." Alfred listened and nodded. Eleanor thought of the attack that Thomas had related to her as she headed up the road that led via Ecton to Wellingborough and from thence to Peterborough.

Chapter 17

After a moment's quiet in which they all digested her story, Thomas reached inside his shirt, undoing a leather thong tied round his neck, he pulled free a brooch and held it out to her.

"This was in the hand of your maid, Clarice." Eleanor nodded. "We buried her thinking it was you."

"Yes I know, we returned to Northampton on the way here and I spoke with Brother Robert at the hospital, where I discovered you had left to join the Earl's army." Eleanor folded Thomas's fingers across the brooch, "You keep it. I already have a replacement." She touched the plain pilgrim's badge. Her hand remained on his.

"So," said Thomas Menhill, "what is to be done now." They all fell silent. Thomas looked from Eleanor to the table and nervously waited. Finally Jeanette grabbed her husband's hand.

"We will let you two discuss amongst yourselves. We will be in the garden," she said tactfully and rose, pulling her unwilling husband with her.

"Well what is to become of us Thomas? We have found each other and once again I can see no way forward. My father is dead. I cannot return to the protection of your half-brother."

"He is yours also!"

"Yes, true, but I do not trust him and neither do you." Thomas nodded solemnly. "Losing you was painful and has made me aware that I do not want it to happen again." She looked down at her hands sadly.

"The Menhills', how do they feel about all this?"

"They have treated me as a daughter ever since the loss of their son. They want the best for me. But they have also said that if Nicholas orders me to return, they have no jurisdiction to stop him, as he will be my legal guardian until I am wed. They fear that you can offer me no security and only lower my status." This time Thomas looked away. Geoffrey's words echoed around his skull. 'Control yourself laddie… you may be a freeman but that's little different to a villein to our John'

"What about you? Is that how you see me, only just above a villein!" he snapped angrily.

"You, no, that is not so!" her lip quivered in indignation. "Come let us not fight. We must find a solution." She took his hand and he squeezed hers gently.

"I am sorry, it's just I see no way forward for us."

Later that evening Jeanette Menhill and Eleanor were in their room at a small table; the remains of their small meal scattered upon it. Thomas Menhill paced backwards and forwards across the creaking wooden floorboards.

"So you wish to marry him!" he finally said. "Is this not folly?" He turned to his wife for reassurance but she looked away. "Correct me if I'm wrong. You are a Norman, the daughter of a knight. He is a Saxon commoner the son of a mill owner who became a leper!" Eleanor jumped up.

"He was no leper! Thomas has the proof!"

"Well that's one good thing, but the gulf between you is still vast!" Menhill stopped.

"Not so vast. We grew up together. We share a half-brother. We both have little money, and the only way I can escape my half-brother is to marry."

"He will not approve of such a match. He will certainly refuse the dowry your father willed. You need his permission." Menhill said wearily turning to look out of the window. He did not want hostility with another landholder in his shire.

"You know his feelings about me. Would you have me return there?"

"So what will you gain by this marriage and where will you live?"

"Thomas is a clerk for Sir Hugh," Eleanor said lamely and sat down.

After some pacing Menhill concluded, "We must speak with this, Sir Hugh; I presume he knows nothing of all this?" Eleanor shook her head.

They stepped out of the friary and walked through the London dusk to the house of the Bishop of Worcester.

When Walter Cantelupe returned to his house that evening with the Earl of Leicester he found the Menhills' and Haverleys' in discussion at a table in the main hall.

"Ah Menhill," shouted the Earl. "A surprise indeed. The company rose bowing to the Earl and Bishop. Thomas and Jeanette then knelt to kiss the Bishops hand.

"Forgive our intrusion. We came on a matter of business with Sir Hugh."

"It is no matter," said the Bishop, turning to look at the Earl, who smiled and shook his head.

"No, the more the merrier. The company will now be greater and the conversation much improved by your presence." Simon De Montfort smiled at the Bishop.

"So what is this matter then, if I'm not prying perhaps we can be of help," the Bishop looked at the Earl enquiringly.

The Earl nodded, "Carry on sir, it will be a welcome break from the tedium of parliament."

The bishop turned to an approaching servant. "Wine."

"It concerns our ward, the Lady Eleanor daughter of John of Buckbie." The wine was passed around in elegantly forged glasses that made Jeanette and Maude envious.

"Sir John, the name… ah yes, he fell at Northampton, a bad business that."

"The very same my lord. She wishes to marry a man in the employ of Sir Hugh." The Bishop and Earl looked at him in surprise.

"He is but a clerk sir, though he can fight better than many a knight," said Sir Hugh, "He was at Lewes." He finished by way of explanation.

"That can only be Thomas," the Bishop grinned. "No ordinary clerk, though Sir Hugh, from what you have told me of him, a scholar, skilled in letters, with some medical knowledge, fluent in English, Latin and French, a warrior veteran of Northampton and Lewes. I have mentioned him to you already Simon; the one that unhorsed the king."

"Did what!" Thomas Menhill stepped back in surprise. "He did not tell us that!"

"And wisely so, the less who know the better," replied the Earl. Jeanette's face was pale with fright. "I do remember you mentioning him, an interesting man for sure. I would like to meet him. Where is he, Sir Hugh?" The knight pointed out to the garden, Sir Hugh went over and called through the open doorway.

Eleanor and Thomas walked in together and both stopped, surprised by the company.

"Thomas Millson of Buckbie, Lady Eleanor, meet Simon de Montfort, Earl of Leicester," said Sir Hugh, with a wry smile at the young man's awkwardness. He bowed and Eleanor dropped into a curtsey. "And this is the

Bishop of Worcester, my lady." He continued turning to Eleanor.

"Well I certainly see what he sees in you, young lady!" said the Earl in way of greeting. "So Thomas, I have been keen to meet the man who unhorsed the King." Eleanor's jaw dropped and she looked at Thomas. "Ah, you do not know everything about this young man I see." The Earl was enjoying himself. A servant came out and whispered to the Bishop.

"Food is prepared. Let us sit and eat. Thomas join us."

"Yes, I wish to hear more of your Lewes exploits," chipped in the Earl. They sat at the table. Thomas sat at the far end opposite Eleanor. He was nervous in their company and with having to converse in French, which made him even more worried that he was going to say or do the wrong thing.

He looked up the table and thought how strange it was that he should sit here now dining with two of the most important men in England, having such a short time ago walked from his home carrying all his possessions. Fate is a strange bedfellow. He studied the Earl dressed in bluet and burnet with no sign of extravagance; he could have passed for a shire knight except for his poise and expression. His thin tanned and cragged features exerted power. He wore a well-shaped beard, which like his hair was cut in the short style; both were flecked with grey. Thomas guessed he was in his fifties.

The Earl was controlling the conversation, as he liked to control all things. Thomas felt mesmerised by the strong voice that filled them with confidence and assured them that the Earl's way was the way forward.

Thomas tasted sweetmeats and foods he had never seen before except from his accustomed seat in the kitchen, as they were prepared. He drank of the heavy luxurious wine and began to feel light-headed. As he listened to the voices, he began to convince himself that perhaps it was righteousness and not revenge that had driven him to battle. His gaze rested on Eleanor dressed in blue velvet.

"So Walter, what is to become of our two lovers?" Thomas was jolted out of his dream by the Earl's comment. He looked up the table to see all eyes focused their way. De Montfort smiled good-naturedly, enjoying the moment. "Good at languages and letters, a warrior, an apprentice physician, good with accounts and an understanding of how to farm and run a mill. The man would make a good tenant don't you think, especially if he swears an oath of fealty. What say you Walter?" Thomas felt that he was toying with them. The Bishop nodded, unsure what direction the Earl was moving in. The success of the parliament had left him in a jovial mood, which is what the Bishop had tried to take advantage of by bringing him to the manor, but at present he did not feel in control.

"The various lands you have been after Walter." The Bishop held his breath. "I have a mind to give them to you." He paused and drank, a twinkle in his eye as he held their attention. "In fact I will," he said this looking at Thomas. The Bishop let out an audible sigh. "There is a small estate amongst them, Ashton Magna. I believe it borders on your estate at Blockley." The Bishop nodded again. " …Of about eight pounds per annum I think, a reasonable revenue though I hear it's a bit run down. Still that would suit an up and coming young gentleman and be just the reward for his campaigning and for the loss of his wife's father."

The Bishop nodded and smiled his assent. Just like Simon to hand out rewards that did not financially affect him, the lands having recently been held by one of Henry the Third's half-brothers, William Lusignan. He looked down the table at Thomas whose jaw had dropped. He would get the property and a good tenant. So he too felt satisfied.

"I believe there can be no impediment to that marriage now," he said.

"I do not think we will hear any complaints from your half- brother either," said Jeanette Menhill, squeezing Eleanor's hand.

"Let us drink to the couple, their future success and to the Bishop's new acquisitions." The Earl raised his goblet. Thomas was unable to speak, amazed at his change of circumstance.

As the Earl and his retinue were about to leave, Thomas went over and thanked him.

"Right place at the right time," he replied with a smile, as he left. "Mind it will be useful to have you swear fealty and be ready to fight again, if necessary, for the Council may yet have need of dependable warriors." The Earls face was grave as he walked out.

Two days later they were married in a side chapel at Westminster Abbey by the Bishop. Thomas was dressed in a new burnet coloured tunic and cloak, Eleanor in a richly embroidered expensive scarlet gown. There followed a small wedding feast at the Bishop's residence, at the end of which the Bishop took them to one side.

"Soon you will make for your bridal chamber with your beautiful wife, but before you go up I have these papers for you. The first is your right to tenancy of the land the second is a mise from Henry of Leicester regarding your father." Thomas looked up in surprise. "Eleanor has told me what you believe has happened and she showed me the reports you have from various medical men. I took it upon myself to see the priest, Henry. I hope you do not mind. He was most happy to write a report rescinding his previous decision and I also have ratified it with my seal. The third is a mise carrying the seal of the crown requesting that you be returned the mill as your rightful inheritance. Compared to the manor that you are to move in to it is a small thing but I understand it is important to you; so accept it as my wedding gift." Thomas was speechless. His countenance brought a smile to the Bishop's face.

"Thank you sir, this means a lot to me. I hope one day I will be able to repay you."

"All I ask is that you run that estate to my satisfaction." Thomas nodded still feeling dazed as he was whisked off to dance.

Chapter 18

Winter 1264/65

Aston Magna manor was an old hall; its timbers were strong and dark with age but the roof thatch was covered in a heavy coat of green moss. The old wooden ramparts were in a state of disrepair; the remains of a moat surrounded the structure and seemed more in keeping as a fishpond. The small estate was just three miles from Blockley, the site of the Bishops residence, which was the reason he had been so interested in obtaining it. The manor stood atop a small rise; the cluster of cottages that made up the village sat to its west; on the north and east the ground dropped away to two tributaries of the river Stour. The view from the battered ramparts was breath-taking, especially at dawn and dusk when Thomas liked to watch the sun's rays rise and fall across the rolling Cotswold Hills, and woodlands.

Inside, the hall had a cosy warmth, there were few drafts and smoke from the central hearth seemed to dissipate well. At one end was a raised dais above the earth floor behind which a flight of wooden steps led up to a small solar into which Thomas and his pregnant wife Eleanor quickly settled. The earth floor was soon covered in new rushes sprinkled with Meadowsweet and the hall once again felt lived in after a long and empty silence during which successive owners had left it to fend for itself.

The villagers appeared pleased to finally have the hall reoccupied and to know who was master of the estate and seemed to accept them. Although young in the eyes of the villagers, Thomas was firm, understanding and competent. It helped that the harvest was good that year although other news was disturbing.

Thomas had not been in residence long when he received a letter from London which one evening he read to the assembled villagers in his hall.

"A horde of aliens is preparing to invade the land from France. They will spare no one and are thirsting for English blood. At this time of crisis no one should plead harvest or some other everyday business as an excuse not to turn out, signed Simon De Montfort, Earl of Leicester, Steward of England."

The following day Thomas rode out wearing a new gambeson underneath his new chain mail shirt his sword at his hip and ten villagers armed as foot soldiers with a hostile spear and a pugio- close quarters dagger, each. They headed for Barnham Down near Canterbury to join the largest army England had seen for two hundred years.

The threatened invasion by Queen Eleanor, the French wife of Henry the Third did not materialize and after a month Thomas returned to the manor but not before finally getting a chance to visit and pray before the tomb of Thomas Beckett at the towering cathedral of Canterbury.

As the weather turned cold and the trees became skeletal in the grey skies of November, Thomas once again got the call to join the feudal army, gathering this time at Oxford and once again he rode out with his ten armed villagers, this time huddled in his warm woollen cloak. The gathered army turned and marched west against the rebelling marchers from Wales who had been released after their capture at Lewes but had now sacked Hereford, Gloucester, Bridgenorth and Marlborough and were in fact getting remarkably close to Thomas's new home.

The army did not meet the marchers on the campaign as they fell back quickly across the Severn and finding themselves caught between a Welsh force under Llewelyn coming out of Wales and the Earl's approaching army, they quickly surrendered at Worcester.

Thomas and his men returned as soon as they were able to their village. Now seasoned campaigners, the ten villagers enjoyed telling their tales of travel and adventure in the local ale house though as yet none had faced the madness of battle.

That winter was a time of calm and quiet at the manor as the country did its best to settle down and wait out the winter months, ever looking forward to the coming spring with optimism and the hope that there will be no more civil unrest and war.

Thomas enjoyed his evenings sitting by the fire in his solar with his wife. The Steward of England was now in control of most of the country and headed to Kenilworth castle along with a kingly entourage of one hundred and forty knights for the Christmas festivities.

At the beginning of April in 1265 Sir Hugh De Haversley and his wife Maude arrived along with Bishop Cantelupe and Thomas and Jeanette Menhill for the christening of Thomas and Eleanor's new boy. Thomas was also pleased to see Henry and Brother Robert who rode down from Northampton and on the evening of their arrival he filled them in with the story of his adventures and his meeting up once again with Eleanor.

The ceremony took place in the packed small chapel in the village. The parish priest named the boy Walter after his grandfather and his new godfather the Bishop. After the ceremony they headed to the manor with most of the village. Thomas felt proud and excited as he sat on the dais at the top table of his first banquet with his main guests and watched the hall below fill up.

As they fell to eating, Thomas remembered the delicacies of the Bishop's table and was pleased to see that he gave a contented nod at what Eleanor had caused to be laid before them. Thomas squeezed her hand, for she had worked hard for this day. They started with swan, heron and sturgeon in a pike sauce; then came sucking pig, rabbit and chicken in egg and saffron, finally quail, perch and sweetmeats. The guests emptied and filled their trenchers, and the hounds, scavenging around and below the tables, had a veritable feast. Wine flowed freely at the top table, ale at the others where the meal had been less elegant but still a feast to be had at the close of winter.

As musicians played, the chief cook finally came out, followed by two men bearing a Soltetee made of sugar and pastry. It was a model of the hall; the guests roared and clapped as it was broken up and eaten.

As the villagers danced amongst the flotsam of the meal on the rushes of the floor, the men of the top table gathered together, the women left for the solar. The polite chatter of the meal now turned to politics and the news from court.

Top of the agenda was the recent Hilary parliament where discussion had revolved around the release of Prince Edward and the other hostages and the dispatch of justices to the shires. Sir Hugh was excited by the whole process having been elected to represent his shire at the parliament.

"Indeed what a step forward a true government of the land, elected knights and burgesses representing each shire and involved in decision making."

"Representing their shires, yes, but not totally involved in the decision actually made," chipped in the

Bishop. "Let us not forget that the Earl is the power in this land at present."

"So it is not as democratic as you would have it?" asked Menhill astutely.

"The cause has come a long way but there is much still to be done and much that concerns me."

"Aye, there is too much rivalry and feuding. Edward has been released, I am unsure as to whether that is right or wrong. I certainly think that the Earl should not have ordered the arrest of Robert De Ferrers," responded Sir Hugh. The Bishop's forehead had furrowed and his grey bushy eyebrow rose. He slowly nodded his head.

"What!" exclaimed Thomas Menhill. "The Earl of Derby, on what grounds? For that will surely set the cat amongst the pigeons."

"Lord Robert had taken Chester," stated the Bishop. Thomas listened intently.

"So where is the Simon De Montfort now?" he said. Sir Hugh laughed.

"Gone to Odiham with a retinue of one hundred and sixty knights!" turning to the Bishop he continued, "He must have a care; many knights are losing faith as they watch the Earl's personal growth in wealth and the promotion of his own sons above others."

"I fear Gilbert de Clare, Earl of Gloucester is taking it all badly," said the Bishop, frowning worriedly. "I have expressed my fears to Earl Simon already. Clare had gone to Wales to protect his lands against Llywellyn. Earl Simon is not helping either, for he has written to De Clare to surrender Bamburgh, which is to be controlled by the Council under the terms of Edwards' release. Faction is dividing the court and De Montfort is not helping his cause

I fear." He paused for breath. " I will be returning to court directly. Tomorrow, if the weather is good."

"What of Prince Edward, where is he?" Thomas asked.

"Oh, released from prison but…" the Bishop chuckled. "He is now escorted everywhere by Simon's knights."

As his guests departed over the next few days Thomas pondered the news but the quiet secure countryside around Ashton Magna gave him a sense of security that he could not imagine being broken. He realised he had not been so happy since before the day his mother died. He enveloped himself with his new family and the running of the estate, cutting timber, planting new saplings, caring for the calving cows and farrowing sows, supervising the dairy maids as well as the last of the ploughing, the harrowing and the seeding of vegetables and corn.

Chapter 19

Summer 1265

The tranquillity of Ashton Magna was disturbed in early May by the arrival of Sir Hugh and his men-at-arms. They swamped the hall and churned the small outer yard to mud. Their busy comings and goings filled the hall with life and that evening a lively feast was held. But their coming was not purely on social grounds as Sir Hugh explained whilst they sipped wine at the top-table, watching the cavorting and laughter in the hall.

"Simon De Montfort is at Gloucester with the King and Prince Edward, plus an army. Six of the nine Councillors are with him."

"Bishop Cantelupe?" asked Thomas.

"No, Peter De Montfort, Giles De Argentein, Roger Saint John, Humphrey de Bohun, Hugh Despenser and John Fitz John."

"What's the problem, Sir Hugh?"

"He has gone to negotiate with Clare. You remember how he was vexed at the Earl?" Thomas nodded. "Well I do not know yet whether De Montfort will sort the issues out but I travel with a messenger who has brought news that John De Warren and William Valence have landed at Bamburgh with an army."

"Those were two knights that escaped from Lewes and took ship to France?"

"Yes that's right. The thing is Bamburgh was still in the hands of De Clare. So I wonder whether he has already chosen which side he now supports. I am going to join the Earl's troops. I fear civil war looms ahead again Thomas."

Thomas sipped at his wine digesting this information. He looked across at Eleanor who had been quietly listening to their conversation. As he listened to the laughter and chatter of merriment around him he realised he had missed the excitement, fear and comradeship that a campaign brought. He felt tempted to ride out with Sir Hugh. Eleanor caught his eye. She was watching the emotions play across his face with concern. She had seen his grey eyes light up with the idea. He saw the worry in hers as they moistened with tears that she tried hard to suppress. Her green eyes sparkled like pools in the firelight. They settled him and made him take stock of his situation.

"I will take council from the Bishop," he said finally. Eleanor let out a sigh. Sir Hugh nodded.

The next morning Sir Hugh rode off with his men and the quiet tranquillity once again closed in on the small village at the edge of the wooded vale. Thomas found it hard to believe that he had been keen to ride off and leave this idyll. He knew he must stay informed of the situation and wait for the bishop to return so he made regular trips on his grey mare up onto the hill south of the village from whence he sometimes turned northwest for news at the village of Broadway or sometimes east to Morton in Marsh. Both villages were on the main highway. His other port of call was the bishop's palace at Blockley, where he learnt that the Earl had moved to Hereford.

Often times he would just sit upon his horse on the hill looking west as the sun set then back down the quiet valley at the smoke rising from the small cottages and the manor.

"No news is good news," said Eleanor trying to settle him one evening.

A month after Sir Hugh had ridden away to join the Earl a messenger arrived from Blockley with news that Bishop Walter De Cantelupe had arrived and was in residence at the palace. Thomas immediately had his horse saddled and rode back with the messenger the short distance to Blockley.

The Bishops residence sat on the edge of a steep slope which dropped down into a small river; at its base behind the manor could be seen the tower of the church which was set at its rear. They rode quickly up to the gatehouse and Thomas left his horse with a groom and was soon ushered in for an audience with Bishop Walter. The bishop looked tired and strained. He drained a cup of wine then refilled it along with another, which he passed across to Thomas, as they stood before the open window of the bishop's private solar.

"The news is not good Thomas." He fell silent for a moment gathering his troubled thoughts. Thomas looked out of the window, across the valley. The sky was summer blue, birds sang in the woodland on the opposite side of the valley. He watched a lark climbing higher as it warbled. In the sudden silence he could also hear the sound of the small river that meandered through the valley bottom sparkling like a pearl necklace in the summer sunshine. Swallows swooped down upon it and then returned to their nests in the eaves of the palace buildings. He waited patiently for the Bishop and concentrated on calming his nerves. He took a deep breath filling his lungs with the scented meadow air that drifted up the valley. The Bishop coughed, Thomas turned to face him.

"Prince Edward is free. He has joined with De Warrene and De Valence. De Clare and Mortimer have also taken sides with him. Shrewsbury, Ludlow,

Gloucester and Worcester are all taken. The Earl and his army are trapped in Hereford." Thomas gave a sigh. His thoughts turned to Sir Hugh and he wondered how he fared. He looked back out of the window. The view now seemed somehow different. If De Montfort fell, all that he had gained would be lost.

"What will he do?" Thomas muttered taking a large gulp of his wine. The Bishop went and sat by the fireplace; leaning forward he rested his arms on his knees and studied the ashes in the grate with intent.

"He must cross the River Severn and meet up with his son Simon who has forces in the east."

"And if he cannot cross?" the Bishop stood up but could not look at Thomas for he also felt the pain of dreams coming to an end.

"All is lost." He walked back to the window and stood beside Thomas looking out. "I have sent friars west to monitor and report back here. They tend to be quite successful at passing through the regions unnoticed."

Thomas returned to Ashton Magna and sombrely passed on the news to his wife. He began to train his village troops.

Time went by slowly with little noticeable change apart from the comings and goings of the Bishop's messengers at Blockley. Thomas rode over every other day to catch up on news and talk with the Bishop. The Earl was still at Hereford having made an unsuccessful attempt to cross the Severn at Monmouth.

The mood in the village and at his manor was becoming sombre. Thomas and his sergeant, Edgar, continued to train the men and the estate busied itself with the work of the summer season.

On the second of August a fine, warm, Sunday, Thomas took his family over to Blockley. The Bishop had also asked that he bring his men and be ready to march out with him that afternoon.

After the service that morning, they went into the Bishops solar for lunch.

"Eat well Thomas for we have a bit of a journey before us," the bishop said, tearing off a leg of chicken. Eleanor looked at him worriedly but dared not speak. Thomas tucked into the plentiful food before them. "Montfort has left Hereford and is crossing the Severn just south of Worcester. He intends to meet with his son," he continued between mouthfuls. "I want to head out this afternoon to join them at Evesham." He smiled at Eleanor trying to alleviate some of her concern. When they had finished he called Thomas to come with him and they entered his small private chapel and knelt before the altar. After a moments silence the Bishop turned to Thomas. "Pray Thomas for there will be a battle again and I fear that this time Prince Edward has the upper hand. I must get to Evesham to see if I can negotiate between the King and the Earl. The Prince is closing in and I would abate the terrible slaughter if I can. The fields at Lewes were not a pretty sight." Now Thomas saw the concern in the Bishop's face that he had kept hidden all morning.

"I hoped that after Lewes…" the Bishop nodded sombrely, patted his shoulder and turned to pray. Thomas listened, his eyes closed to the mumbled Latin words, hoping that the power of the Lord would fill him with strength. He tried hard to still his raging heartbeat.

He left his family wondering if he would ever see them again but knowing he must go, for victory for the Prince would be his ruination. He hugged his wife and child then climbed upon his small grey mare. His wife passed up his shield, her green eyes brimming with tears.

His men formed up behind him and they joined the retinue of the Bishop as it marched from the palace on the twelve-mile journey to Evesham. They rode out in silence through the cool woods up the escarpment and onto the main road, which in truth was no more than a dirt track often impassable in the winter. They travelled light with just a few mules carrying their gear.

After some five miles, they stopped for a rest at the edge of the steep escarpment that dropped away into the Vale of Evesham. Every time Thomas came this way he stopped at this spot to take in the view before him. The abbey tower and Evesham stood small in the distance. The vale was speckled with furrowed land, now laden with crops, pastured areas where small dots of animals grazed, lush green woods broke up the regular village patterns, each small community identified by small columns of rising smoke from cooking fires. The vista was capped by a blue summer sky, scattered with puffy white nimbus clouds leisurely making their way east.

It was dusk when they finally arrived, exhausted, sweaty and dusty on the edge of Evesham. The great abbey stood upon its small hill surrounded by the glittering river Avon, the sun slowly sank behind it, the huge tower became silhouetted in light, many of the small party sank to their knees and mumbled a prayer, Thomas crossed himself feeling a sudden strength.

"All will be well," he muttered to no one in particular.

They rode across the bridge and up into the small town surrounding the abbey walls. As they approached the top of the rise they turned into a gateway that led into the abbey precinct past two parish churches set side by side. Thomas looked on in surprise.

"One for the pilgrims, one for the parish," exclaimed the Bishop. Passing through a small gateway they came into a vast courtyard in front of the abbey, where they were met by grooms and lay brothers who took the horses, and organised the men and priests in their party.

The Bishops retinue was greeted by a Benedictine monk who introduced himself as the prior and took them into the abbot's lodgings which he explained were at the Bishop's disposal for the duration of his visit, there being no abbot appointed since the death of the last one in 1263.

They entered the large hall on the west side of the cloisters and the prior filled them in with what news he had as they sipped at some wine. The Earl and his army were expected to enter the town at any time within the next few days. He had no news as to the whereabouts of the Earl's son or where Prince Edward and his allies were.

Soon a great mass of food was placed before them, and the prior excused himself to see to his duties and check that all the guests had been catered for.

"A wealthy abbey this one," muttered the Bishop between mouthfuls of duck. "Old Abbot Henry was only in office for a few years but he turned round their financial situations. A good man he was very astute when it came to numbers, much like yourself, I feel." Thomas smiled at the compliment. "I hope the monks are not forgetting their vocation." After their meal, they entered the abbey church to pray before retiring. It was equal in splendour to that of Lewes and Peterborough. At the altar, they knelt.

"On this spot the Virgin herself appeared before the lucky Bishop Egwin, that holy saint was a Bishop of Worcester, a predecessor of mine. Let us pray perhaps

Mary will hear our prayers on this holy spot." Thomas remembered the sunset behind the tower of the church and was sure that God would help him and the cause. He chanted an Ave Maria. Moonlight filled the choir in a pure white glow.

The following morning a message arrived for the Bishop from his manor at Kempsey. It was from the Earl and stated that he was there with his army, which was crossing the river. They would be resting there for the day and would head for Evesham that evening. Thomas spent the rest of that day in anticipative agitation. He checked on his men, then wandered through the small market town and along the river back to the abbey, finally saddling his horse he rode up the hill to the north of the town to see if he could see anything of the Earl's or the Prince's armies. He felt certain that both armies were close and it made his spine tingle and the hairs on his neck stand up. After a few hours riding he returned to the abbey where he prayed and prowled the grounds until it was time to turn in.

As the monks prayed at the service of Lauds, on the morning of Tuesday the fourth of August, Thomas was woken by a tremendous clatter of hooves and shouts of men within the great courtyard. Rising he grabbed his sword and looked quickly through the unshuttered window. His blood calmed as he recognised the rampant white lion banner of Simon De Montfort. Dressing quickly he rushed down into the hall to find it filling with mail-clad knights. Thomas looked about him soon recognising the Earl and the King. Bishop Cantelupe was already in conversation with them. The knights looked weary as they sat at the tables and divested themselves of their armour. Lay monks rushed round with food and ale. Thomas approached the Earl to see what he could find out.

Standing a little way off he leant against the wall and grabbed an ale from a passing monk.

"... Simon, my son, was attacked at Kenilworth but he still has some forces we believe. I was hoping he would be here already." The Earl was saying. "Edward is, I guess, somewhere between there and here perhaps in Worcester though I believe he is heading this way in an attempt to cut us off. Let us hope that Simon arrives first." The Bishop then led the King and the Earl away to try his hand at negotiating some sort of settlement before it became too late.

"Hello Thomas." He turned to see Sir Hugh, a chicken leg in one hand and an ale in the other. Thomas's face lit up, and he grasped his friend.

"It's good to see you Hugh. I'm glad you're well."

"Oh yes, though I can't say our campaigning has been much to write home about. If I could write that is." He chuckled. They turned at the sound of the Earl's voice.

"Knights, eat up for then we will enter the church and hear mass with Bishop Cantelupe. Then we will rest. We must head for Kenilworth as soon as possible." With that they all headed out into the dawn and the chapel of Saint Lawrence for the mass.

As mass came to a close a messenger arrived with news that an army approached and it was flying the banners of his son. The knights let out a cheer and headed back to the abbots hall.

"Make the army ready!" called out the Earl. "We will join my son!" Hugh gave Thomas a weary smile.

"At last with the Earl's son's troops we will be a force worth reckoning with." He walked off to assemble his men and ready his horse. Thomas hung back until the

Bishop emerged dressed in his gold and white robes. He stopped at Thomas's side.

"How did the negotiations go sir?" he enquired.

"They did not Thomas; the King refused unless he was released. The Earl refused that, saying once he had met up with his son, Prince Edward would want to negotiate a settlement anyway." He sighed, "I hope he is right. Will you ride out with them or stay as part of my retinue."

"I must go sir. It is my duty." Walter Cantelupe nodded and they walked slowly across to the great courtyard where Thomas found Edgar assembling the men and readying his grey mare.

"What's happening sir?" he asked as he held the horse's reins. Thomas explained the news and saw the relief on the faces of the men. He then went into the abbot's hall with the intention of packing up his things. As he made his way to the stairway, Nicholas, the Earl's barber, came rushing in.

"Where's the Earl?" he called out.

"Why?" returned Thomas suspiciously.

"I've been in the tower, the abbey tower, sir. Those banners, the Earls' sons; well they've gone. The only banners I can see are those of Prince Edward and his men and the Marchers." Thomas looked at him in surprise.

"Are you sure?"

"Yes sir, I know heraldry sir." After a moment's hesitation, Thomas retraced his steps and banged on the Bishop's door. He heard a shout and entered to see the King eating. The Bishop and Earl also sat at the table but had not touched their food. They all looked up. The Earl's brows came together annoyed at the intrusion.

"Yes!" he shouted

"The army sir, your man here says it is that of the Prince and the Marchers." The Earl suddenly noticed Nicholas.

"Is it by God? Nicholas?" he looked questioningly. The man at Thomas's side bobbed his head. The Earl's brow furrowed even more and his eyes blazed. The King smiled between mouthfuls of food. Thomas studied him, seeing the man behind the title for the first time. He wore a small coronet, down each side of his face poured silken brown hair, which curled at its ends. His face was thin, with high cheekbones, his pronounced jaw covered by a short beard. His eyes glared with Norman pride but his forehead was lined by the sense of injustice he felt he suffered. The twitch at the corner of his thin mouth betrayed the sense that his situation had just improved and that possible victory could be ahead.

"You are trapped Simon," he said with relish. "If you advance your pitiful force will be destroyed; you must yield now." Simon ignored him. Hearing the news, Henry, one of the Earl's sons, Hugh Despenser and Ralph Bassett arrived. They stood behind Thomas and Nicholas listening.

"Where is this force now Nicholas?"

"On the hill to the north across the road sir." Nicholas looked afraid.

"You could retreat across the river and thence to Kenilworth," said Walter Cantelupe. The Earl shook his head.

"No, they would attack us as we attempted it. No, we cannot run nor do I wish to. What about you sirs?" He looked across at the knights and Thomas. The knights looked at each other and shook their heads.

"We stay." Hugh Despenser said simply. The Earl nodded

"Then we must prepare." He stood up.

"First confession and absolution," said the Bishop standing. Thomas noticed how his shoulders were stooped with the strain, his face looked grey. "I will be at the chapel." He made his way out past Thomas. The knights followed, Thomas in their wake.

At the chapel of Saint Lawrence, Thomas waited his turn. Monks, friars and priests were already moving amongst the men listening to their confessions. Thomas wanted to see the Bishop.

He reached him and looked upon his face, now older than his years.

"You do not have to fight Thomas. You came as part of my retinue."

"And yet I was to go on with the Earl. No sir, I cannot walk away now." The Bishop nodded in understanding. He made the sign of the cross.

"I absolve you in the name of the Father, the Son and the Holy Ghost. May God go with you and the Lady of Evesham protect you." Thomas stood up.

"My lord, will you… it's my family…" the Bishop touched his arm.

"I will care for them as best I am able if… well." He gave a wan smile. "They will see you soon, I'm sure." With mixed emotions, Thomas turned and went back to his lodging and donned his padded gambeson and mail shirt. He buckled on his sword belt and picked up his helm and shield then went out into the courtyard to his men.

He found them gathered together round his mare. He saw fear in their faces. They gripped their weapons nervously. The news had spread through all the ranks.

"Well Edgar," Thomas said trying hard to stay and sound calm. "Are the men ready? Has everyone eaten and said confession?" he looked around at them and they nodded.

"Yes sir." Edgar replied for them. "But sir what news have you? We have been told to prepare for battle little more." Thomas noticed some other men moving closer to hear his reply.

"Prince Edward and the Marchers are just north of the town on the hill. The Earl intends to attack." Edgar nodded. Thomas did not tell them that they were seriously outnumbered and that he thought they had little chance, but he was trying hard not to think about that fact himself. He looked at the small grey mare; it had no armour and was not a warhorse.

"Put the horse in the stables. She will do no good in battle. I will walk and fight with you and pick her up when this is all over." He tried hard to make his voice sound positive. The soldiers began to move off passing under the great archway of the main gate. They turned right and began to head north up the town's main street. The town was full of troops preparing for battle and making ready to move out.

As they began their slow march up the main street, with each unit juggling and pushing to get into position, the blue morning sky began to cloud over with dark fast moving clouds which came in from the northwest, the direction of the enemy. Thomas looked up worriedly, feeling dread reach in like a cold hand. He saw gloom and fear about him in every face. Suddenly with fierce force rain lashed down, pinging and clanging off metal and stinging exposed flesh, lightening flashed across the hill and a clap of thunder echoed overhead. Horses rose up and shied all around them. Men dropped to their knees into the mud, Thomas with them. They crossed themselves and prayed. He wondered what it could mean, but it did not feel like a good omen.

Shouts from mounted knights riding down the verge roused them and they stood and moved slowly forward through the beating rain, the road soon a thick brown stream. The army was saturated and mud splattered. Thomas felt the rubbing of his drenched clothes and wiped the water from his nose and forehead.

Having left the town the army began to spread out on the pastures that flanked the road, as the men moved themselves into position, glad to be off the road and in the damp grass. The rain ceased and the black clouds slid away leaving grey skies.

Sir Hugh spotted Thomas and his men and rode over.

"Good luck!" he called out raising his sword in salute. Thomas held up his hand and called over.

"What is our intention Hugh? What does the Earl plan?" Hugh trotted over and Thomas patted his great beast, who snorted with pleasure.

"To drive through their line and make our escape I believe. We are well outnumbered," he whispered not wanting the men around to hear. Thomas nodded, and put out his hand. Hugh gripped it tightly and for a moment all seemed still as they drew strength from one another. Then in an instant Sir Hugh let go, wheeled around, and galloped off.

The slow forward march had brought them onto the level plain of pasture on the brow of the hill and the vast army ahead of them came into view. To the left and right the plain dropped away to the Avon, which curved snake like around Evesham.

Thomas drew his sword and pulled his shield into position. To his right he could see Humphrey De Bohun, who was commanding the welsh foot soldiers, racing off to try to lead his men around the enemy's left flank. Ahead of him the royalist horseman began to charge. Thomas felt the ground grumble from the wall of charging armour. The sight amazed him, yet he felt his muscles constrict with terror. Men all along his front stopped rigid with fear. The wall of charging steel crashed into the Montfortian knights like a surging bore wave and the air was rent with screams and the ringing of metal, many of the horsemen came right on through and headed for the foot soldiers. De Bohun's men were being cut down as they ran. A shout from along his own line woke him and he suddenly saw the field before him with clarity as the adrenalin within took charge.

"Stand fast men! Wedge your spears." The line of remaining men-at-arms, including his own, stood behind their spears, wedging the hilts into the ground and raising the points.

The tide of horsemen crashed into them. A horse in front of Thomas, reared and he drove his sword into its neck. The line was breaking. He raised his shield to protect himself from a sword blow then drove his sword into the rider's leg. Blood splashed across his arm he was fighting men on all sides now as soldiers moved to encircle them. He was fighting for survival.

"The white lion has fallen!" One of his villagers was shouting near him; his voice tremored with panic. "The Earl's banner is gone. All is lost." The man shrieked as a mace crushed his skull. Thomas turned to see another of his men pinioned on a spear. He struck out at the assailant severing the hand that held the spear. They would soon be surrounded. He knew he must break out before they were totally cut off, for there would be no quarter given on this field.

"Follow me!" he shouted above the din of battle. Raising his sword he charged madly into the royalists on his right where he judged them to be fewer. As he crashed into the men-at-arms visions of his homeless family and lost father filled him with battle-crazed momentum. Soldiers jumped back at his ferocity. He felt the surge of men behind him being urged on by the wild shouts of Edgar. They were quickly through and the men began to charge across the pasture following the fleeing Welshmen. The army was in total rout. Thomas ran too not looking back, the battle madness seeping out, to be replaced by despair. They crossed the road and ran down through the meadows towards the river.

Thomas stopped and turned to see the royalist troops swing round after them. Over their heads he saw the knights fighting for their lives aboard their great destriers. He saw Ralph Bassett collapse from his saddle and Piers De Montfort. They were falling every second. He caught a glimpse of Sir Hugh his sword flashing to the left and right and then his horse collapsed beneath him and he was gone.

"Hugh!" he screamed and began to move back toward the battle but found himself held. He turned raising his sword ready to strike his grey eyes flashing wildly.

"No!" shouted Edgar, holding up his hands. "It's too late sir. Don't throw your life away. He is captured or dead and there is nothing you could do to change that. The Earl is unhorsed too. We must flee now or perish." Edgar turned his gaze to the approaching foot soldiers. "Come on!" he pulled Thomas towards a road that ran down to the river. Thomas stumbled blindly behind.

The grassland was strewn with bodies and stained with blood. Everywhere Royalist horsemen and soldiers chased, harried and hacked down, the fleeing men. They dodged round groups of horsemen and struck out at any that stood in their way, Edgar remorselessly leading them on. Finally Thomas dropped to the ground at a large standing stone by the road side placing his back against it he looked down to the river across the meadow.

"Come on sir! We must cross the river. It's our only hope now!" Edgar cried urgently. Thomas shook his head, his chest heaving with the effort.

"I can't' go on. This mail…" he pointed to his shirt his voice almost a whisper. Edgar grabbed Thomas's shield and drove it into the face of an approaching man-at-arms, then threw it to the ground. He quickly dropped down beside Thomas as a group of jubilant royalists charged past. The six-foot monolith gave them enough cover. Thomas crossed himself.

"Our Lady protects us," he croaked.

"Then let us do what we can." Edgar crossed himself, then wrenched off Thomas's helm and mail coat, dropping them at the base of the great stone. They looked down at the river, only a few hundred yards away across a battle-strewn meadow. Montfortians fought desperately on its bank.

"Can you swim?" Thomas asked Edgar, now feeling stronger without his mail; Edgar nodded. Thomas pointed down to a section of the bank. "Over there, they are intent on attacking the welsh men. We can surprise them from behind and perhaps get through to our own troops, then get down to the river." Edgar nodded again. It was a long shot, they had by now been cut off and royalists were running down to join the massacre all around them, seemingly oblivious to their presence next to the great stone. Thomas took a deep breath. "Ready?" Edgar held out his sword and dagger then with a roar they both charged across the meadow hacking and slashing at passing royalists as they went.

Surprise was on their side and they were soon amongst the pack of straining terrified Welshmen who were slowly being slaughtered. The river was thick with dead and dying its brown mirk tinged with red.

Thomas turned and fended off a sword blow driving his hilt into the soldiers face. He lost Edgar in the confusion. He drove his sword deep into the belly of another attacker feeling his arm jar at the shoulder. Letting go of his sword he pushed back through the last few men on the bank and leaped into the river.

He felt the undercurrent pull him down. The water closed over his head; the noise of the battle became dull and distant. Welsh bodies floated over him. The sky was red with blood. He felt his feet sink into the silt and realised he had no more strength. His arms seemed to flay uselessly against the water. His clothes became heavy. He felt the air escaping from his lungs and watched the bubbles shining silver and red rise up and burst upon the surface. He knew he could do no more.

Chapter 20

One of the bodies above suddenly dived down towards him and grabbed his arm. He felt himself rise slowly from the mud. His face burst through the surface into the glare of the sun and the sounds of battle still raging on the bank. He gasped, his lungs automatically sucking in air with a sudden rush. Edgar pulled him to the bank.

With a death rattle in his throat a man fell backwards over their heads into the water, blood gushing from his chest and abdomen. Edgar helped Thomas get free of his sodden gambeson, ignoring the cries around him.

"We must swim down river and find a place to get out on the far bank." Thomas nodded still breathing deeply and unable to speak but feeling considerably lighter without his quilted jacket. He thought of Eleanor and his son Walter and with sudden determination pushed off from the bank. Edgar followed him closely.

They swam across the river pushing bodies out of the way as they went. The current carried them south. They reached the far shore at the entrance of a large stream that flowed into the Avon. Panting and heaving with effort they staggered and swam up it until they reached a small bridge. Pulling themselves underneath it they collapsed exhausted.

It was at about midday that they were disturbed by horsemen crossing the bridge, laughing and chattering as they went.

"Hunting royalists," whispered Thomas with a grim smile to Edgar. The foresters thin tanned pock marked face looked weary, but Thomas knew they would need his skills to escape. As the sound of the horsemen disappeared they once again relaxed. "Why did you save me Edgar?" he asked. "You could have got away much more easily without me," Edgar smiled at him.

"Beats me sir; I've only ever looked after myself. Still perhaps I am; for though I can survive in the forest it's not much fun being an outlaw." Thomas got the impression he was speaking from experience. "With you well…" he looked away. "You stands a better chance of making a deal so to speak and getting us back into the world, if you get my meaning."

"And there was me thinking you loved me." They laughed, "Still I owe you. I would not have got this far without you and I think I'm going to need you to get us out of here to. Can you get us back to Ashton Magna without us being detected?" Edgar smiled.

"I'll give it a try. Let's follow the stream first." he stood up instantly ready to go; then looked hesitantly at Thomas, not used to being the leader.

"Yes, now's as good a time as any." They followed the brook's course southeast past a small village. After about two miles it became a shallow stream passing into woodland; where they felt much safer.

They eventually left it and tracked carefully through woods and fields keeping away from all roads, running quickly across them where necessary.

By late afternoon they had arrived at the foot of the downs that rose up out of the Vale of Evesham. Broadway lay to their south and they could see horsemen on the main route up the hill.

They climbed slowly, exhausted, hungry, thirsty and fearful of discovery, for they knew that would mean death. Finally they reached the ridge at the top and ducked quickly into a deciduous wood at the sound of horsemen patrolling along the ridge. Crawling into a mass of thick bramble, neither of them noticing the pain, they collapsed, falling quickly into a fitful sleep.

It was dark when they decided to move on and from the position of the stars bright in the summer night sky Thomas estimated it to be near midnight. Slowly they trekked the last few miles eventually arriving at Blockley at dawn.

They hid in the valley below the manor along the small riverbank and watched the buildings. There was little movement but they could see no sign of Prince Edwards's men, Thomas finally decided that they had not realised that the Bishop had been present and that he would have returned to his manor. It would not be long before they found out and arrived though. He was sure they would turn up at some point that day.

He felt strange skulking about like a criminal when only a couple of days earlier he had rode in before his men full of pride. Dirty and dishevelled they staggered into the manor; where they were met warily at first, as both were unrecognisable from the men that had ridden out with the Bishop on route to Evesham.

After a short explanation a message was sent to Walter Cantelupe and to the Lady Eleanor, who came running into the large hall and into his arms. She said nothing but sobbed into his shoulder. Thomas let out a sigh of relief, pulling her in close to him and burying his head in her soft fragrant hair, scented with herbs. He felt his legs shake as the stress of combat and hardship began to evaporate.

A servant returned asking that Thomas attend the Bishop immediately. Thomas entered his solar with

Eleanor and sat down at the table exhausted. A servant place bread cheese and a goblet of wine before him, but he hardly noticed.

The Bishop had returned the day before but to Thomas he too seemed different. The once proud man had visibly shrunk, his grey hair was lank about his tonsure, and his face was pale and wrinkled with lines of stress, his back hunched with tension. He had not stood up to receive Thomas but sat at the table as if he had not moved in an eon.

Thomas related his story from the moment he had marched out from the abbey. The Bishop hardly uttered a word and to Thomas sometimes seemed lost in a trance but every time he stopped Walter De Cantelupe beckoned him to continue. When finally he had finished he sat back and picked up his wine drinking deeply. He looked at Eleanor. She was pale, her cheeks stained with tears, her green eyes tinged with despair. The Bishop finally spoke and Thomas had to lean forward to catch his quiet words.

"You live but so many are lost. The cause is finished. Sir Hugh…"

"May yet live," interjected Thomas.

"You saw the Earl fall, you say?" Thomas nodded.

"It was a massacre."

"I rue this day. What have we done?" the Bishop mumbled. He turned in his chair and stared out of the window across the valley, forgetting Thomas's presence. Thomas realised his hunger and turned to the food before him.

"What is to happen to us, Thomas?" Eleanor took his hand. He had totally forgotten about his own dire situation in his desperate bid to escape from the battlefield and as it once again dawned on him he did not know how to answer. He looked at her and his red-rimmed grey eyes told her what she needed to know.

"We will lose the manor?" he nodded.

"I guess so, they will want retribution. The land will surely be forfeit." He shrugged a little uncertain, his body aching, his brain sluggish with exhaustion. Events seemed to have run away with themselves. He no longer knew what to think. "The Bishop may be able to help," he whispered.

"Will we return to Ashton?"

"It may not be safe. I think perhaps we should stay here for now."

She nodded, then, after he had finished they excused themselves, though the Bishop appeared not to notice, and she led him to their chamber. He stroked his baby son in the cot and then collapsed into a fitful sleep. Eleanor sat beside him, studying his strained features and wondered at their future.

Later that evening a friar arrived with news that the Earl was dead, his body mutilated. All that had remained to be buried before the abbey altar was his torso. Other lords known to have lost their lives were the councillors Hugh Despenser, Peter De Montfort and Roger Saint John. The Earl's son Henry De Montfort was also dead as was Ralph Bassett but the name that meant the most amongst the list of the dead was that of Hugh De Haversley. His body had been taken to the abbey by the monks and buried in the Abbey graveyard. Over thirty knights all told had lost their lives along with most of the army, nearly seven thousand men.

Thomas, Eleanor and Walter De Cantelupe listened in silence to the friar's report. The King had lived and had returned to Worcester with the army. Evesham was now left alone with just the dead for company. Thomas felt the words shatter his new world like a hammer blow. After just one year it was all over, like a beautiful dream from which he had just awoken.

The next morning, Thomas planned to ride out to the Haversley estate but a priest, who told him the Bishop wished to see him, stopped him. He returned to the Solar. Walter Cantelupe looked up at him from his desk.

"Eleanor has told me of your intention to ride out to Haversley; it is too risky." Thomas tried to reply but the Bishop held up his hand. "You have risked yourself enough; your family need you now. I will send a friar. The King's troops will not touch a man of the cloth." The Bishop waved him away before he could reply. So Thomas resignedly left and feeling angry with his wife he went to find her. She was sitting in the enclosed garden on a small bench singing quietly to their son. His anger eroded as he watched them and he went and sat beside her. She smiled sadly at him. He saw the tears in her eyes.

"I'm sorry. I could not bear to lose you again so quickly."

"I would have rather told Maude myself."

"It is not safe Thomas," he nodded, accepting and understanding.

"What will become of her? Will they take her lands to?"

"I'm sure they will eventually."

"Where will she go?"

"Her parents stayed neutral. They will take her in."

"We must pray for them."

"And the Menhills," after a moment silence he continued, "If I am not to go to Haversley. I will ride out to Ashton." He held his hand up to stop her protesting. "I have a duty to the people there, besides I cannot just sit still." She nodded and looked away down the valley.

After a lunch of bread cheese and wine, he rode out to Ashton Magna, against the Bishop's advice, with Edgar on the back of his grey mare, which the Bishop had brought back from Evesham. With the knowledge that the King's army had headed north he was sure that the small journey would be safe and he felt he had a duty to inform the people there of what had happened and tell them of the loss of his men for he knew of none that had made it.

That night he sat alone in his solar. He had had a fire made up although it was a warm August night. He stared into the flames swirling his wine absently. He thought of the men he had led to their deaths and of the anger in the villager's faces at his return with just Edgar for company. All in the fief felt the loss and blamed him. Tears fell down his cheeks as he realised that all he had brought to the village was pain; and such a short time ago he had arrived with such high hopes. He drank deeply and drank again finally falling into a fitful sleep on the bench, where he fought his demons and none could hear his shouts and see the sweat of his nightmare.

The following morning he awoke early his head pounding. He drank more wine, shunning food; then ordered the servants to pack up his family's belongings. By lunchtime the manor was stripped bare. The tapestries removed beds packed up and a train of mules and the village's ox cart carried it all to Blockley. Thomas sat watching the proceedings a jug of wine close at hand.

That night as he sat before the fire he thought of the hate he had had for the King when he had lost Eleanor and discovered his father was dead. He knew that the people around him must feel the same hate for him for taking their loved ones.

He realised he had not spared a thought for his men or the impact that their loss would have on this small community. He had been lost in the worldliness of his position as 'Lord of the manor'. They had just been commodities. He had enjoyed riding ahead of them like other great knights. It was only now as he sat alone on the verge of losing everything that the roots of his past gripped him and wrenched his emotions apart, that he realised with horror what he had done. He laid his sword upon his lap fingering it nervously. Finally, he once again fell into his demon filled sleep alone in his empty hall.

When he awoke he discovered how alone he really was, for on calling out to the servants he found that no one answered. He hastened around the manor grounds to discover that they had all gone, taking with them whatever they could carry. He stood at a loss in the dawn mist in front of the manor in the courtyard.

Edgar found him still standing forlornly in the yard. It was not until he tapped him on the shoulder that Thomas realised he was no longer alone.

"Oh hello Edgar," he mumbled, "Everyone seems to have gone." Edgar nodded knowing what had happened already.

"I guess you're not flavour of the month right now. Besides they know you're finished here. Come." He led Thomas into the hall and fetched some wine. "Drink;" Thomas obliged, and Edgar refilled his empty goblet, "And again;" When Thomas had done so he sat down. "It's over here sir." He continued. "We need to move on before anything happens." Thomas looked at him puzzled. "Once people realise you're alone and with no protection."

Thomas nodded at the danger of his situation dawned on him.

"You said we?"

"I'll be coming with you if that's alright sir."

"But this is your home Edgar."

"Was sir; like you I'm an outcast here now. I have no family to speak of and the village are finding it hard to come to terms with my survival. They never liked me much anyhow and would probably turn me over to the King's men for a penny. Besides when I pulled you up from the river, if you remember..."

"I shall not forget that in a hurry," Thomas butted in. Edgar smiled and nodded.

"Yes, well if you remember, I said then that I reckoned I fancied my chances better with you so I'm sticking to that; if you'll have me, that is?" Thomas nodded.

"Of course, I only hope that you are making the right decision and I can honour such trust and repay the debt I owe you for my life. I'm afraid I have little to offer once this is gone. I have no noble blood and even fewer useful connections."

"We'll do fine, sir."

"Thomas, call me Thomas now."

"Yes sir," they smiled. "Best be getting on I'll ready the horse." Thomas nodded.

"Yes, let's get back to Blockley."

It was mid-October when they learned that the manor of Ashton Magna had been occupied by a knight loyal to the crown. Thomas stood at the Bishop's solar window, feeling the autumn breeze rush over him as he listened to the Bishop. Walter De Cantelupe sat hunched in his chair before a roaring fire. He looked a shell of the fine man of a year before. He had given up. His shoulders were hunched. His hair now totally grey hung limply around his tonsure. When he had finished imparting the news he stared emptily into the flames. The defeat at Evesham had set him on the road to collapse but when the papal legate Ottobuono suspended him from office, he seemed to have lost the will to live.

For a while, the room stood quiet, but for the two men's breathing. Finally the Bishop spoke.

"When I'm gone Thomas there will be little for you here, you know that?" Thomas nodded. "You must move on." The Bishop's weak hand pushed a leather purse towards him. "Here this may help you." Thomas thanked him and picked up the heavy purse. "It will help in the upkeep of my godson." The Bishop gave a rare smile as he thought of the small child. "Do you have any plans?" Thomas shook his head, at a loss as to what to do. "I'm sorry I can do no more, but Ottobuono ties my hands." He shrugged and seemed to drift away again as he turned back to the fire. Thomas left with the purse and returned to his guest quarters, where he found Eleanor nursing their infant son.

"Well?" she looked up. He showed her the money.

"A gift from Bishop Walter," She continued to watch him knowing there was more. "He thinks we should leave soon. He says that when he dies there will be no protection here for us."

"He will not die yet," said Eleanor crossing herself, but they both knew that he was willing away his life. "What will we do?"

"This makes us wealthy. As to where we should go…" he shrugged his shoulders. "I could return to my studies, perhaps at Oxford. We could live well enough there." He shrugged again. "I have no other suggestions."

"We could find the Menhills and join them." Thomas shook his head.

"We have had no news of their circumstances and I fear they can be little better off than us, after all your ward was a friend and staunch supporter of the Earl of Leicester." After some hesitation Eleanor reached into a leather bag hanging from her chair and produced several pieces of parchment. Thomas recognised the documents.

"The mill?"

"It is yours by right. Our half- brother will not argue with this. It bears the Kings seal, and the King and his men will not be interested if he tries to have us thrown out, plus you have your fathers will." She watched the emotion spread across his face. "It is not the living of a lord but we would be independent. At least it would give us a start and with the Bishops money we would be reasonably, comfortably off. We could build a new house and live as well as our half-brother in the manor."

Chapter 21

Winter 1265/66

They rode quietly through the village and down to the mill. It was dark; the small cottages that lined their route were quiet. All that could be heard was the snuffle of animals and the crunch of their ponies' hooves in the snow.

The small cottage at the mill was cold and damp. Thomas got down and helped his wife and son from their mounts and led them into the small dwelling. Edgar took care of the animals. The interior had been stripped of furniture. They stood in the doorway surveying their barren uninviting new home. Eleanor squeezed Thomas's hand. Neither felt saddened by their surroundings.

"I'll get a fire going." He leaned out of the door. "Edgar, get the animals in the byre there." He pointed along the side of the cottage to another door, which led into the animals' section of the building. Edgar huddled in his cloak, nodded and pulled the animals along, their hot breath leaving clouds of water vapour in the cold air.

Thomas soon had a fire going in the central hearth and had also found some stools and a trestle table in the mill. Placing a sheepskin rug on the floor he took Walter from Eleanor's lap and lay him down by the fire.

They ate and drank, all three staring quietly into the flames, lost in their own thoughts. Though it all seemed desperate, Thomas felt strangely elated and he knew Eleanor too was experiencing similar feelings, after the impotency of sitting at Blockley under the protection of the Bishop, watching him slowly fade away until he had finally died on the twelfth of February in the new year of 1266.

Though the Bishop had wanted him to leave and find safety abroad, like many of the rebels, Thomas, who did not want to go abroad and was unsure where else to go, had found himself unable to drag himself away from De Cantelupe and the last vestige of what had been. Thomas had slowly become more morose and short tempered with those around him; shunning his wife and taking to praying at the church behind the manor or riding up to the road and out to the downs edge where he would sit and stare out toward Evesham.

The Bishop's death finally spurred him into action, knowing that the terms of surrender were not being offered to De Montfort's supporters and that the King still hunted them and was fighting them in several places, notably at the De Montfort's main stronghold, Kenilworth Castle.

When knowledge of the Bishop's final demise reached London, King's men would soon arrive to claim Blockley and deal with any rebels that were there. The King had up until then turned a blind eye to Blockley, content with the fact that De Cantelupe had left Evesham before the battle and had only been there initially to try to coordinate some sort of peace settlement. The Bishop had also declared that he had been wrong to support Earl Simon and had received absolution from the papal legate.

On the fourteenth of February Thomas rode out of Blockley for the last time along with his wife, son and Edgar. They turned northeast and headed for the small village of Buckbie from which Thomas had walked over two and a half years earlier. They hoped that in that small village that had been their home, they would be able to hide inconspicuously as millers for none there knew of their adventures since the battle of Northampton.

Thomas pulled his wife to him and she felt the new vibrancy within him. She sighed, contentedly. It did not look much now but in a year they would have a new house and the comforts of a good home amongst the people that they had known most of their lives. As she thought of her neighbours, trepidation at their coming meeting with their half-brother Nicholas crept in, making her shiver even in the heat of the fire.

"Don't worry. He cannot and will not touch us. We are safe here. Nobody here knows that I fought for the Earl at Evesham or that we have come from Blockley. As long as we keep them in the dark we will be alright. It is not quite what we have been used to for the last few years but we will soon make it home."

The following morning saw the arrival of Alfred and Elias who entered armed with sticks in preparation to remove squatters. Their surprise at discovering both Thomas and Eleanor, when he had assumed both were dead, brought tears to his eyes. Elias was soon scampering off to fetch the priest, Geoffrey and food for a welcome home breakfast. He returned with half the village eager to see them and hear their news. Geoffrey clasped Thomas to his ample chest and would not release him. On that cold fresh clear morning a party was soon in full swing; the villagers only too keen to delve into the dwindling stocks of food and ale in order to break the monotony of a relentless winter.

At around midday, when the villagers had left to get back to work and Alfred had taken Edgar off to show him the mill, Thomas, Eleanor and Geoffrey sat down around the fire.

"You know, for all the pain and death and struggle, nothing changes. Even De Montfort's original values were lost in greed. For two years the country has wrestled with itself and for what? It is right back where it started. Was it all for nothing? I might as well have just stayed here." Thomas said as he sipped at his ale.

"The world may not have changed and yes, people have died but you have returned with a wife and son and the rights to your own home, plus money at your belt." Geoffrey replied.

"What of the friends I have lost? The men I have led into battle? I see their faces in my dreams."

"Do not forget them. Learn from what you have done, from your experiences. Let them make you a better person, then what happened will not have been wasted." They all fell silent at sound of a horse's hooves. Eleanor gripped Thomas's hand. He squeezed it once, got up and went over to the door; he recognised the shape of Nicholas, the Lord of the manor, on his large brown palfrey. Thomas stepped out from the shadow of the doorway and the horse stopped in the yard.

"So, you have returned Thomas." Thomas looked up into his cold brown eyes and noticed the annoyance there. "Ran out of money did you and decided to come back. Well unfortunately, I don't need you anymore. The mill has been run quite adequately without you." The sides of Nicholas's mouth curled in a smile. "You may rent the cottage though if you can afford it."

"So! Nicholas, some greeting for your brother," Thomas turned as Eleanor came out to the cottage, "and sister." Thomas took her hand and smiled up at the surprised Nicholas.

"Eleanor," Nicholas stuttered, "I had not realised you were here also. You should have come up to the manor."

"I thank you brother, but I will stay with my husband." She looked at Thomas. Nicholas looked on askance at what he was discovering.

"There is much you do not know Nicholas," Thomas carried on, not wishing his brother to have time to recover. "For instance, my father was found not to have leprosy after all. But perhaps you knew that anyway?" Thomas noticed the sudden fear in Nicholas; his cheeks lost their colour. It confirmed his suspicions that his father had indeed been poisoned.

"I don't know what you mean!" blurted out Nicholas.

"I believe he was poisoned Nicholas; by someone here in the village."

"Be careful what you say Thomas, I am lord here!"

"Mm, that maybe so brother but you are no longer owner of this mill and its land. My father completed a new will. The mill and the lands are mine by right. Eleanor pulled the papers from a leather satchel at her hip and unrolled the parchments, holding them up for Nicholas to see. So it looks as if we are to be neighbours Nicholas." Nicholas looked at the two of them and scowled. He was lost for words.

"How is Lucy?" Eleanor said disarmingly.

"With child," he mumbled.

"I will come and see her as soon as we are settled. I hope that will be alright." She smiled up at him. He nodded now totally confused. Unsure what to say, he looked down at them awkwardly; then with a huff he pulled his horse round and trotted up the lane.

"Well that showed him." Eleanor said as she watched him disappear. She brushed her hands down the side of her dress and looked smugly at Thomas, who frowned uncertainly back. She took his hand. "It'll be fine, you wait and see."

"I have a feeling that it is not over between us. I cannot believe our brother will sit back meekly and let us live contentedly at his side."

"Come let us rejoice in your return for now;" said Geoffrey walking across to them. "He is the only one in this village not pleased to see you both!"

Chapter 22

Summer 1266

Eleanor and Thomas quickly settled in to their new life with vigour, enjoying the freedom and the lack of politics. Thomas lost himself in hard work, deliberately shutting out much of the painful memories of the past. He worked with Edgar at on the mill lands which had lain fallow since he had left, preparing them for planting. They purchased some animals, a cow, pig and chickens and began work on extending the small cottage.

As winter gave way to the summer of 1266, there had been little contact between the manor and the mill, Eleanor found herself unable to get past the reeve to see Lucy who had remained confined to the manor precincts since their arrival. Often as she walked in the village or worked in the yard at the mill she had felt eyes upon her and turned to see Nicolas watching her from the manor wall or from his horse in the lane by the mill. It always sent a shiver down her spine.

One June evening as the sun was setting; Thomas, Eleanor, Geoffrey and Edgar sat around a trestle table set up in the yard watching the sun come down and the swallows darting around the mill along the brook. Eleanor ladled some pottage onto their trenchers, keeping one eye on young Walter who crawled across the dusty yard following a beetle.

"So…" said Geoffrey looking across at Thomas; "what do you think of the news that Guy has escaped from Dover across to France?" Thomas gave Geoffrey a hard look.

"I hadn't heard that."

"You don't come up the village much. I was hoping to see more of you up at Margery's since you came back."

"Mm, I'm not ready for gossip yet." Thomas mulled over the news that the last of the De Montfort's had left the country. Edgar answered Geoffrey for Thomas.

"Let's hope we can have a bit o'peace with them all gone now."

"Here's to that," agreed Geoffrey, picking up his ale and taking a large gulp. He looked across at the three of them, "so your adventures are over for good then."

"Definitely," said Eleanor.

"Well I'm pleased about that although I am still keen to hear about the adventures you have had. I still know nothing of what you have been up to and it's cost me a small fortune in ale trying to get any information out of Edgar up at Margery's." Edgar smiled; Thomas and Eleanor both turned on him and he reddened, holding up his hands.

"Never said a thing!"

"I'll back him up there, very loyal," Geoffrey chuckled.

"When the time is right Geoffrey we will tell but do not pry and protect us from rumours." Eleanor's green eyes flashed at him holding his gaze until he nodded and reached across the table, touching her hand.

"I would protect you with my life; you are the only family I have." Eleanor squeezed his hand. "There are plenty of rumours going about the village that's for sure, but I admit defeat and will pry no more." He took another large gulp of ale and slurped down some pottage. "Ah this is good Eleanor."

"Thank you Geoffrey."

"I have one last thing to say on the subject." They all stopped and looked at him. "Have a care with that brother of yours. He has sent a message to London. He has some contacts there. He wants to know more of your movements. He is digging for information to use against you." They sank into silence, drinking and eating as they mulled over this.

After Eleanor had cleared away with the help of Edgar and the sun had finally set Geoffrey got up to leave but Eleanor grabbed his hands.

"Before you go I must ask what news of Lucy?"

"She misses you and desperately wants to see you. I have told her that you have not been allowed in. Her pregnancy does not go well. If it had not been for her feeling so unwell I think she would have rebelled and come down to see you.

"She has about two months to go?" Geoffrey nodded. "If only I could see her. He is a cruel man!" Tears formed in the corners of her eyes.

"I will go and see her tomorrow and give her your love and wishes."

"Thank you Geoffrey," she said taking his hand and squeezing it.

Later that evening as Thomas and Eleanor climbed into bed. She turned and laid her arms across him, looking into his eyes with concern.

"I have been thinking on Geoffrey's words."

"So have I."

"Do you think we are in danger?" He shook his head unsure.

"I don't know. There may be some at court who remember us, clerks, priests, and such like; others that may remember our marriage and our receiving Blockley.

Certainly they will know that we are connected with Bishop Walter and as such the rebellion."

"He received absolution from the papal legate." Eleanor said hopefully.

"I did not think Nicholas would go too such lengths. At least rebels are not being treated so badly now and if he turned us in, the King would get the mill so that would not help him. He is more likely to use what he finds for some sort of blackmail."

They woke in the middle of the night to the sound of banging on the door. Thomas jumped up shouting,

"Hold on; patience, I'll be there in a minute!" He looked at Eleanor. His heart was racing she looked back wide eyed. Walter began to cry. Eleanor reached over and picked him up, clutching him to her breast in a bid to silence him. Light was filtering in through the cracks in the walls and the roof, from the morning sun. The banging continued. The door rattled on its hinges. "I'm coming! Who is it that wakes us so rudely?" He picked up his sword and knife, their blades glinting in the half light.

"Have they come for us?" whispered Eleanor hoarsely, the words struggling from her dry throat.
"It cannot be," Thomas replied, but raised his sword as he faced the door. "Answer!" he shouted, "Who is it?" His voice shook from fear and adrenalin.

"The reeve!" Eleanor drew in a breath.

"He has brought the King's men." They glanced at each other.

"What do you want?"

"Open up! I have a message for you!" Eleanor moved across to Thomas, clutching Walter tightly.

"At this hour?" replied Thomas.

"Open the damn door will you! It's the Lady Lucy!" Eleanor grabbed Thomas' hand. Thomas stood uncertainly. Then another voice piped up.

"It's okay Master Thomas; It's just the reeve and I have a sword at his back."

"Edgar, okay Edgar, thank you." Thomas moved forward and opened the door carefully, his sword before him. They were confronted by a flustered looking reeve with Edgar behind him.

Thomas lowered his sword allowing the reeve to enter. Edgar followed him in.

"Tell him to put his sword down," the reeve said looking nervously at Edgar. For a moment Thomas enjoyed seeing the edginess in the reeve; but then beckoned Edgar to lower his blade.

"Well reeve, to what do we owe this pleasure?" He said sarcastically. With Edgar now less of a threat the reeve gained his old confidence. He looked around the room and leered at Eleanor. Thomas stepped in front of her and began to raise his sword.

"Out with it!" Thomas was becoming annoyed.

"Your sister- in- law requests that your wife attend her immediately. Nicholas is away at present; gathering information." He looked pointedly at Thomas and gave a cruel smile. "I'm not sure he would agree to this," the reeve now became serious, "but anyhow, them at the manor made me come. They think she may be miscarrying." Eleanor gasped and grabbed Thomas' arm.

"We must go!" He nodded not taking his eyes away from the reeve.

"We will come immediately; run back and tell them we are on our way."

"Don't you be giving me orders lad," he said but moved towards the door as two swords were raised. After a moment's hesitation he turned and ambled off determined to take his time.

"I'll get the horse."

He returned quickly and helped Eleanor up, passing her Walter. Then he led them up the quiet road. In an hour or so all would be active he thought. They walked in through the outer gates of the old castle wall. Thomas looked around; he had not been here for two years and it had been untidy and uncared for then under Sir John but he felt it looked worse now.

They moved on quickly to the inner bailey and to the manor door, a boy ran out and took the horse. Inside the hall was dark and gloomy. The manor staff who had been disturbed from their slumber in the great hall sat disconsolately around the hearth yawning and occasionally glancing up at the solar. They took little notice of the new arrivals.

A cry rent the air. Eleanor gripped her dress and ran up the steps at the far end of the hall and disappeared behind the curtain and into the solar. Thomas put Walter down on the floor and moved across to the table where he picked up a jug and poured some ale into a leather cup.

Some of the servants now watched him. He moved across and sat on a bench by the cold central hearth.

"Who's up there?" he questioned the nearest servant.

"Margery's come. Her maid's up there too; doesn't sound so good though."

"How long?"

"Since midnight;" The man who Thomas did not recognise began to relax. "Maid came out a while ago shaking her head and asking for the Lady Eleanor." He looked around and lowered his voice, "reeve started going on but she said it probably wouldn't matter anyhow as things did not look too good." The whole group was now watching him, gauging his reaction. Thomas nodded to a few faces that he recognised from the village.

More cries echoed through the hall, reverberating across the high beamed ceiling, blackened by years of smoke. The cries slowly dropped in intensity finally becoming a constant moan. Thomas paced across the dirty reed covered floor, unnerved by the sound.

As dawn gave way to morning he suddenly realised that the sounds of the upper room had been replaced by the hustle and bustle of the village and outer bailey. He focused, trying to hear anything from the solar. He realised that the halls other inhabitants had also stopped chattering or moving around and were staring towards the upper door. For the briefest moment there was an intense silence within the hall, undisturbed by the crackle of the newly lit hearth, the snuffling of the dogs as they rooted amongst the floor reeds or the noise of the waking village. The depth of the silence seemed to suck away the noise, nobody moved.

The moment was broken by a sudden cry, Thomas recognised the voice as did Walter who pulled himself up into a wobbling standing position and pointed towards the door.

"Mama" he looked across at his father. Thomas ran up the steps to the solar door and stopped unsure, not wanting to progress further. Just as he made his mind up to enter the door burst open and Lucy's maid ran into him with a surprised cry. He looked across her shoulder at Eleanor and Margery who knelt by the bed. Eleanor looked up at him tears in her eyes, unable to speak.

"Thomas we need the priest," said Margery calmly, "be as quick as you can please, I don't think we have long." Eleanor let out another sob. Thomas quickly turned and ran down the steps, passed a confused young Walter and out the door. He grabbed the horse and galloped through the outer bailey scattering villagers and animals alike. Angry curses and shouts followed him as he continued through the village to the church. He slid from the horse shouting for Geoffrey, who appeared from the back of the church dropping his habit down across his ample thighs.

"Oh, hello Thomas, I was just watering the vegetable patch," he said smiling and rubbing his dirty hands down his sides. His smile faded when he saw Thomas' serious expression. "What is it?"

"It's Lucy." Thomas breathed deeply struggling to speak. "Margery says she is in need of a priest." Geoffrey bobbed his head in understanding.

"The baby?" he queried, Thomas nodded realising he was unsure of the full situation. "Right come on then." Geoffrey made to stride forward. Thomas grabbed his arm.

"Quicker on the horse."

"Me no, no," Geoffrey shook his head but then seeing the concern in Thomas' eyes he finally just nodded an assent. Thomas cupped his hands and boosted the large unhappy priest onto the palfreys back. As Geoffrey bounced along up through the village, Thomas jogged at his side. This time they were greeted with laughter instead of angry shouts as they moved through the village and the manor precincts. He helped Geoffrey down from the horse and puffing, they both entered the hall. Lucy's maid had come down and met them in the hall she was holding Walter.

"She's gone sir,"

"The baby," said Thomas. She shook her head.

"The mistress, we could not stop the bleeding after she miscarried," Thomas stared at her uncomprehending. There seemed little sadness just pity in her voice. Lucy had been a difficult mistress. Geoffrey trundled passed them and up the stairs. Automatically Thomas followed in his wake.

By the time he arrived, Geoffrey was by the bed giving the last rights. Thomas stood at the door mesmerised by the appalling scene. Eleanor sat on the bed holding Lucy's pale hand; bloody sheets covered the lower bed and the floor. Stepping forward, he saw Lucy's white face and empty eyes. The murmur of Latin suffused the air.

"Oh God!" the sound seemed to burst from his lips. Eleanor looked up at him through tear stained eyes. He moved to her side and took her hand. Kneeling he closed his eyes, listening to Geoffrey his mind began to drift.

He felt the warm breeze across his face as he ran laughing as a child across the water meadows by the mill, a young Lucy and Eleanor in hot pursuit.

He heard a cough and felt movement as Margery rose, Geoffrey had gone silent. The image of his past evaporated.

"I must go," said Margery, shuffling towards the door. Geoffrey gave her an annoyed stare. She ignored him. "Besides don't want to be here when his lordship returns. You two ought to be out of here before then as well" she continued, looking at Thomas and Eleanor. "Leave the priest to deal with him." She turned to the maid who had put Walter down and followed them up the stairs. "Once you've sorted the corpse, made her look good, you come and stay with me. A storm will be brewing in the manor and you'd best be out the way for a while." the maid nodded.

"She's right," said Geoffrey as Margery's head disappeared down the steps. "Nicholas is due back today. The reeve sent a messenger to meet him. He could be here any time.

"But," Eleanor began. Geoffrey held up his hand.

"No Eleanor, say your good-byes to Lucy and leave. You have done all you can. I will watch over her." Thomas went forward and kissed Lucy's forehead. It was already cold to his touch. Eleanor grabbed Lucy's hand and did the same; he watched as a tear fell slipped down Eleanor's face and splashed upon Lucy's cheek. Taking Eleanor's hand, he gently pulled her away.

Chapter 23

Thomas leaned on his hoe and took a large swallow of the weak cool ale in the leather flask then handed it to Edgar.

"Thank you Geoffrey kind of you to bring it over. It's hot work today."

"Yes, saw you working from the church yard, thought I'd come down." He plonked himself down in the dirt trying not to crush the growing vegetables. "to be honest I didn't want to be on my own, not after yesterday."

"I felt the same," said Thomas. Edgar looked on quietly. "How was Nicholas?"

"He arrived late in the afternoon. Went into a rage; smashed up the solar, hit the reeve."

"Well can't say I'm sad about that. He deserves it." Geoffrey gave him a side long glance. "The reeve I mean."

"Mm, well we are all God's children."

"When is the burial?"

"Tomorrow." Edgar passed the flask down to Geoffrey who took a large gulp then mopped his sweating brow with the sleeve of his habit. They listened to the sound of nature in silence thinking on this news. A lark sang as it rose in the sky nearby, the flute of warblers drifted across to them from the willows along the stream, bees buzzed in the hot air amongst the growing crops, behind it all was the steady whirl of the mill wheel and grating noise of the grinding stones turning.

Their meditations were disturbed by a sudden shout and then a scream from the cottage yard.

"Eleanor," murmured Geoffrey. Thomas and Edgar were already running. Thomas arrived in the yard to find a flour covered Alfred laid out on the ground and Nicholas kicking Eleanor who was bunched up at his feet.

"Stop!" he shouted lifting his hoe and swinging it at Nicholas, hitting him across the arm. He fell backwards over Eleanor, who dragged herself awkwardly over to Thomas.

"Bastard!" shouted Nicholas. "You killed her both of you didn't you; Soon as I turned my back. Killed her so she…" he pointed at Eleanor; "so that she would inherit the lands." He pulled out a flask and drank; the ale running down his chin. He staggered drunkenly to his feet and pulled out his sword. "Come on then, brother!" he slurred sarcastically. "I know what you are now… traitor!" This last word he spat out with menace which made Thomas wince. He knew now they were no longer safe. He helped Eleanor across to a bench and carefully wiped the blood and dirt from her face. She groaned squeezing his hand.

"Look at me bastard!" Thomas turned, angry now.

"I think it is you that is the bastard, don't you dear brother! I at least was born in wedlock." Nicholas gave a loud angry cry and dashed the flask of ale at Thomas then came at him with his sword. Thomas reacting quickly jumped up blocking the blow with his hoe which broke apart. He staggered, trying to dodge the swinging sword. Falling backwards he hit the ground; the hard earth reverberated up his spine painfully. He looked up at Nicholas, who with a wild madness in his eyes raised the sword above his head. Thomas raised his arm to try to ward off the coming blow.

"Time to die, traitor!" Nicholas shouted, spittle running down his unshaven chin. His face broke into a crazed grin as he prepared to swing. Suddenly there was a crash of metal on metal, a grinding shriek as two sword ran down each other as Edgar came flying over Thomas, parrying Nicholas' sword then driving his own deep into Nicholas' chest.

Nicholas fell back dropping his sword, pulling himself from the blade, his expression changing to one of shock as he looked at the blood seeping quickly through his tunic. He looked up at Edgar in dismay and then across at Thomas. For a moment silence filled the air and no one moved, then Nicholas toppled onto his side his eyes empty and staring, blood trickling from his mouth.

Geoffrey moved first rushing over to Nicholas and quickly began to give the last rites, ignoring the others around him.

Edgar looked at the bloody sword in his hand. He threw it to the ground and turned to Thomas; his face now anxious.

"Thank you Edgar, you saved my life." He nodded back.

"I have killed him, I'll hang for this," he mumbled.

"You saved my life Edgar. That will not happen." He pulled himself up. Eleanor staggered to her feet and came over to Thomas tears streaming down her blood caked face. Having hugged Thomas she reached over and kissed Edgar on the cheek.

"We are all in this together," she said through swollen lips. Geoffrey, who had now stopped muttering in Latin looked across at the three of them.

"It was self-defence, I was witness to this and will swear to it if need be. There may be a trial. I will write to the bishop and the prior at St Andrews. I will also write down our statements of what has happened. For now though we must get the reeve and Margery to deal with the body. It seems that there will be more than one funeral tomorrow."

The reeve arrived with a bevy of Nicholas' men armed with cudgels and swords. He looked down at the covered body of Nicholas then across at them. Alfred had by now been carried in to the cottage.

"So which one of you did for him then? I'm thinkin' you." He pointed his sword at Thomas, "you two never cared for each other."

"It was not him reeve." said Geoffrey. The reeve gave him a disdainful look. "He was killed in a defensive act for he intended to kill Thomas."

"Was it you then priest?"

"No" stammered Geoffrey. "It was…" he could not bring himself to say.

"I killed him in defence of my master Thomas." Edgar stepped forward looking defiant he had his sword in his hand. Thomas also had his and stepped forward next to him.

"We will have to lock him up and contact the king's justices. They will want to deal with this," said the reeve sneering at them. "Perhaps we should lock you both up." Thomas raised his sword. There was an uneasy stand-off.

At that moment Eleanor came out of the cottage where she had been caring for Alfred and little Walter. She had listened quietly to the conversation outside.

"It seems to me reeve that you need to take instruction from your new master don't you."

"New master, what do you mean?" the reeve looked confused as did the men behind him.

"I mean the heir to Buckbie."

"Who?" slowly his face changed as it dawned on him. Eleanor approached him and stood between him and

Thomas and Edgar. "What..?" she waited folding her arms, enjoying his discomfort. Then slowly he bowed his head "What will you have us do mistress?" she heard shuffling behind her.

"Thank you reeve. It seems you are quicker than my husband." She turned and said, "As the last living member of my family, daughter to Sir John, and half-sister to Nicholas, I am sole heir. As my husband, you are now master of Buckbie, Thomas, as I am mistress." She smiled at Thomas' confusion, Geoffrey chuckled. "Edgar will stay in our custody and I will contact the appropriate authorities. He will not be locked up if he swears to stay within the parish boundaries." She looked at him. He nodded.

"I do mistress."

"But you can't trust…" Eleanor held up her hand stopping the reeve.

"I do trust him reeve, so do not question my decision. Now get you men to carry Nicholas to the church. He will be buried tomorrow with his wife."

Chapter 24

Summer 1267

After the Assize in Northampton Thomas, Edgar and Geoffrey all felt weary and drained. Nicholas had no friends there and it was remembered that his father had been part of the revolt so Edgar had been cleared but not without a few nervous and tense moments. Luckily Thomas had not been recognised and he had not visited Brother Robert so after the trial they wandered slowly from the castle down to St John's Hospital.

There were few signs of that terrible and desperate fight now just a few remaining plots containing the remains of burnt timbers now overgrown with weeds. The buildings on Bearward Street where Eleanor had lodged had been rebuilt but Thomas had steered well clear of them during his short stay. The memories of seeing them burn still too strong and stressful in his mind.

Brother Robert had been just as pleased to see his old friend Geoffrey and they had sat talking most of the previous night whilst Edgar and Thomas had wandered up Bridge Street to the inn which had been his old haunt and sank a few ales.

There were no students there now. Thomas felt the echo of their voices as he sat quietly sipping his ale with Edgar. Neither felt like speaking much. Edgar was lost in quiet relief and Thomas felt the loss of so much over the last few years; the echoes and ghosts floated about him as he sat in the now quiet inn.

The next day their moods rose as they walked past the castle and across the bridge out of Northampton. It felt like final closure of all the past events as the headed back to Buckbie. Brother Robert was to come to Buckbie in a few months as he had asked the Abbot at St Andrews for dispensation to travel there for St Gregory's Fair. He was keen to see Eleanor, young Walter as well as Eleanor and Thomas's new child born in April 1267 just before they had come to Northampton, a baby girl. She was to be named Jeanette after Eleanor's ward's wife Jeanette Menhill who they still had not heard from although news received from Robert suggested that they may be abroad in Europe.

A little saddle sore, especially poor Geoffrey, they finally arrived at Buckbie in the late afternoon. They made their way across the green and through the outer bailey to the manor hall. Servants quickly took their horses and more arrived with flagons of ale.

"There is food inside," said Eleanor standing at the door. "I am glad that you are all back." She looked purposefully at Edgar, moving across to him she gave him a hug. "I have been worried but I can see that all has gone well"

"Yes mistress." She moved to Thomas giving him a kiss.

"You still look pale and weary" she nodded. Young Walter came charging out grabbing Thomas' leg. Thomas patted him on his head. A wail from inside reminded them of their new daughter, who appeared at the door in the arms of the maid recently returned from Margery's to care for Eleanor.

Thomas and Eleanor had moved into the manor soon after Nicholas and Lucy's funeral, not wanting to leave the place empty and create a feeling of indecision. On the whole the village had been keen to accept them and they worked hard to dissipate the tensions that had built up in the small community over the last few years.

"Don't think I'll ever be able to sit down again," said Geoffrey, waddling uncomfortably passed them into the hall, "where's that food and more ale please."

The harvest that year had been good and soon preparations were underway for St Gregory's fair. The usual excitement buzzed through the village as they made costumes for their play and prepared the stage, especially as the village community grew with the arrival of salesmen, tinkers, performers and singers.

The day before St Gregory's festival a large carriage with men-at-arms at front and rear, arrived in the green and made its way slowly across to the outer bailey. Thomas had stood on the wall watching its approach, feeling slightly nervous at the arrival of obvious wealth and power.

As he looked down he recognised a figure sitting on the front of the carriage.

"Brother Robert!" he called excitedly. Robert waved up at him. Thomas ran down the steps and out the gates of the inner Bailey, clasping hold of Robert.

"It's good to see you, friend"

"You too young Thomas," Robert said standing back and looking up into his tanned face and grey eyes. "Perhaps not so young but I see a certain contentment that was always missing in the past." Thomas smiled and nodded, then looked up at the carriage.

"What company do you keep Brother? That is a fine carriage." Robert followed his gaze.

"Yes I have come with some other friends of yours. I hope you will be able to make them welcome. She was most keen to come and see you." The door was being opened by another figure that he realised he knew.

"Henry!" Thomas blurted out. Henry lifted his hand and smiled but continued with his task. Thomas held his breath as out stepped Matilda Gobion; she turned and helped down a small boy, slightly older than Walter.

"He is two and a half," whispered Robert, "born nine months after you left." He continued with some meaning. "His name is Thomas." Thomas breathed in deeply, feeling a little faint.

"Matilda's husband and old Master Gobion?"

"Both dead, she runs the lands and business now." Matilda walked towards them. She took his hands and then kissed him quickly on the lips. They turned at the sound of calling from the gate as Eleanor approached.

"Brother Robert, Matilda, what a wonderful surprise."